SKYLANDERS™

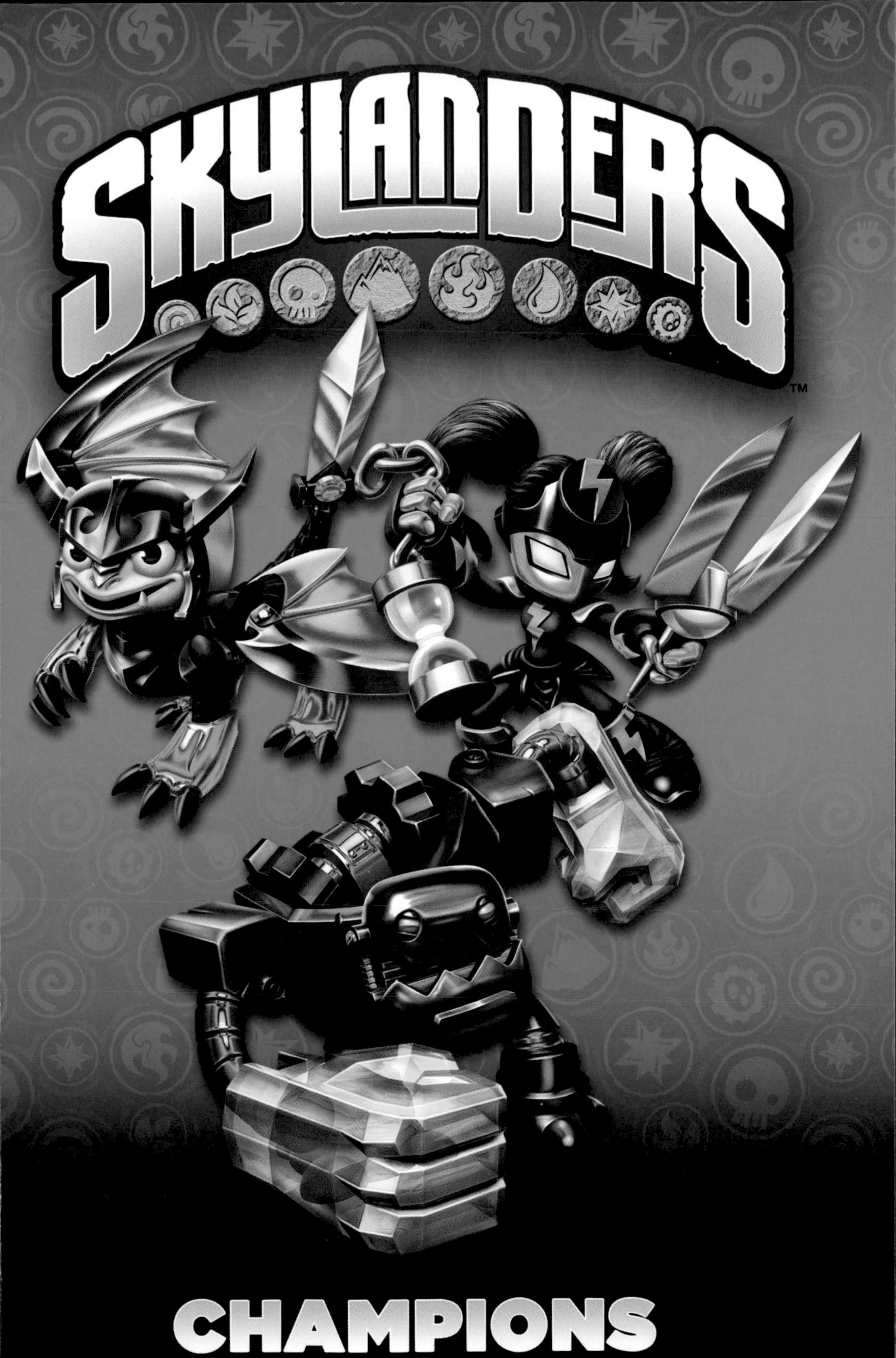

CHAMPIONS

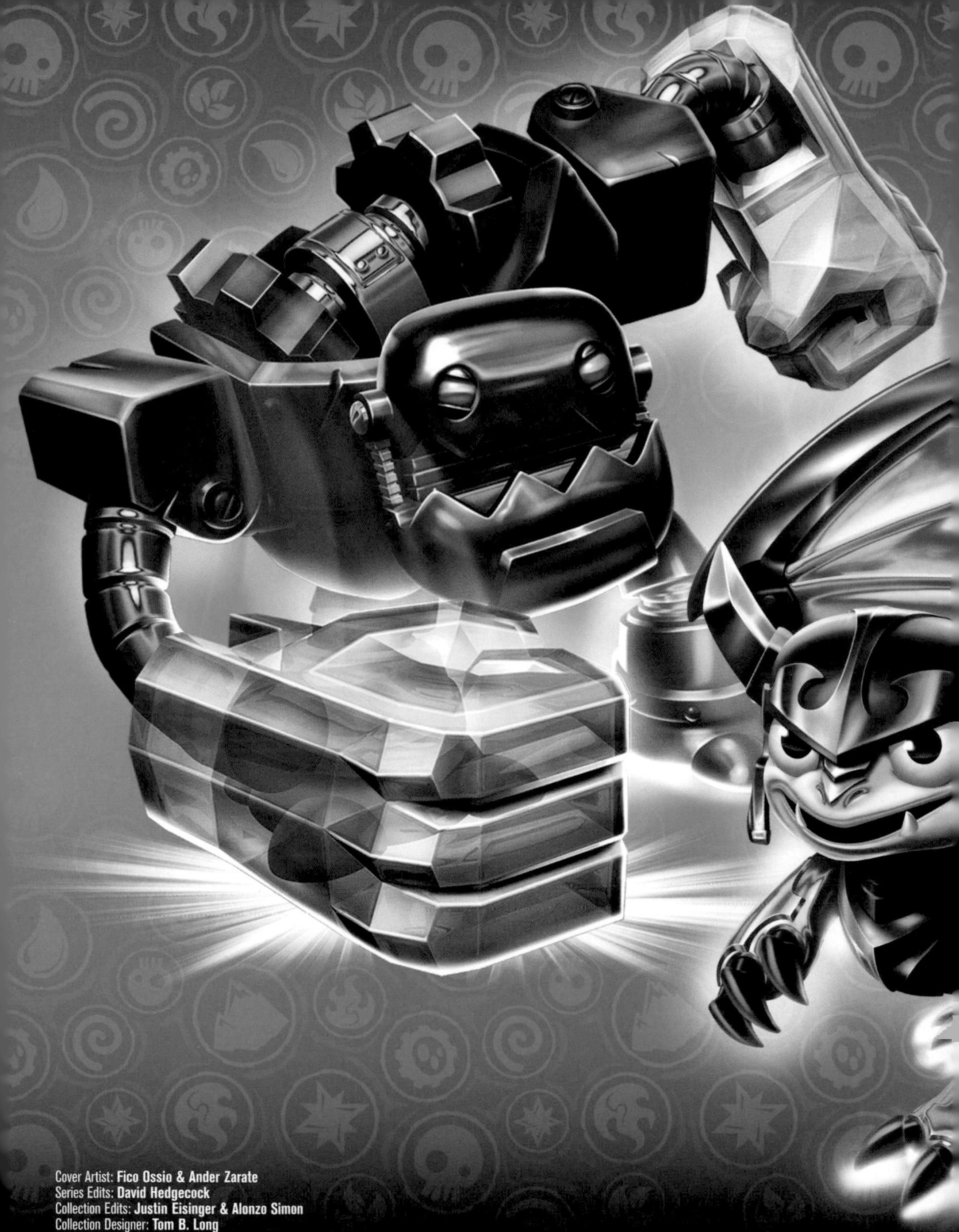

Cover Artist: **Fico Ossio & Ander Zarate**
Series Edits: **David Hedgecock**
Collection Edits: **Justin Eisinger & Alonzo Simon**
Collection Designer: **Tom B. Long**
Bio designs by: **Sam Barlin**

ISBN: 978-1-63140-229-6

18 17 16 15 1 2 3

IDW
www.IDWPUBLISHING.com
ACTIVISION®

Ted Adams, CEO & Publisher
Greg Goldstein, President & COO
Robbie Robbins, EVP/Sr. Graphic Artist
Chris Ryall, Chief Creative Officer/Editor-in-Chief
Matthew Ruzicka, CPA, Chief Financial Officer
Alan Payne, VP of Sales
Dirk Wood, VP of Marketing
Lorelei Bunjes, VP of Digital Services
Jeff Webber, VP of Digital Publishing & Business Development

Facebook: **facebook.com/idwpublishing**
Twitter: **@idwpublishing**
YouTube: **youtube.com/idwpublishing**
Instagram: **instagram.com/idwpublishing**
deviantART: **idwpublishing.deviantart.com**
Pinterest: **pinterest.com/idwpublishing/idw-staff-fave**

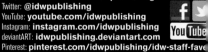

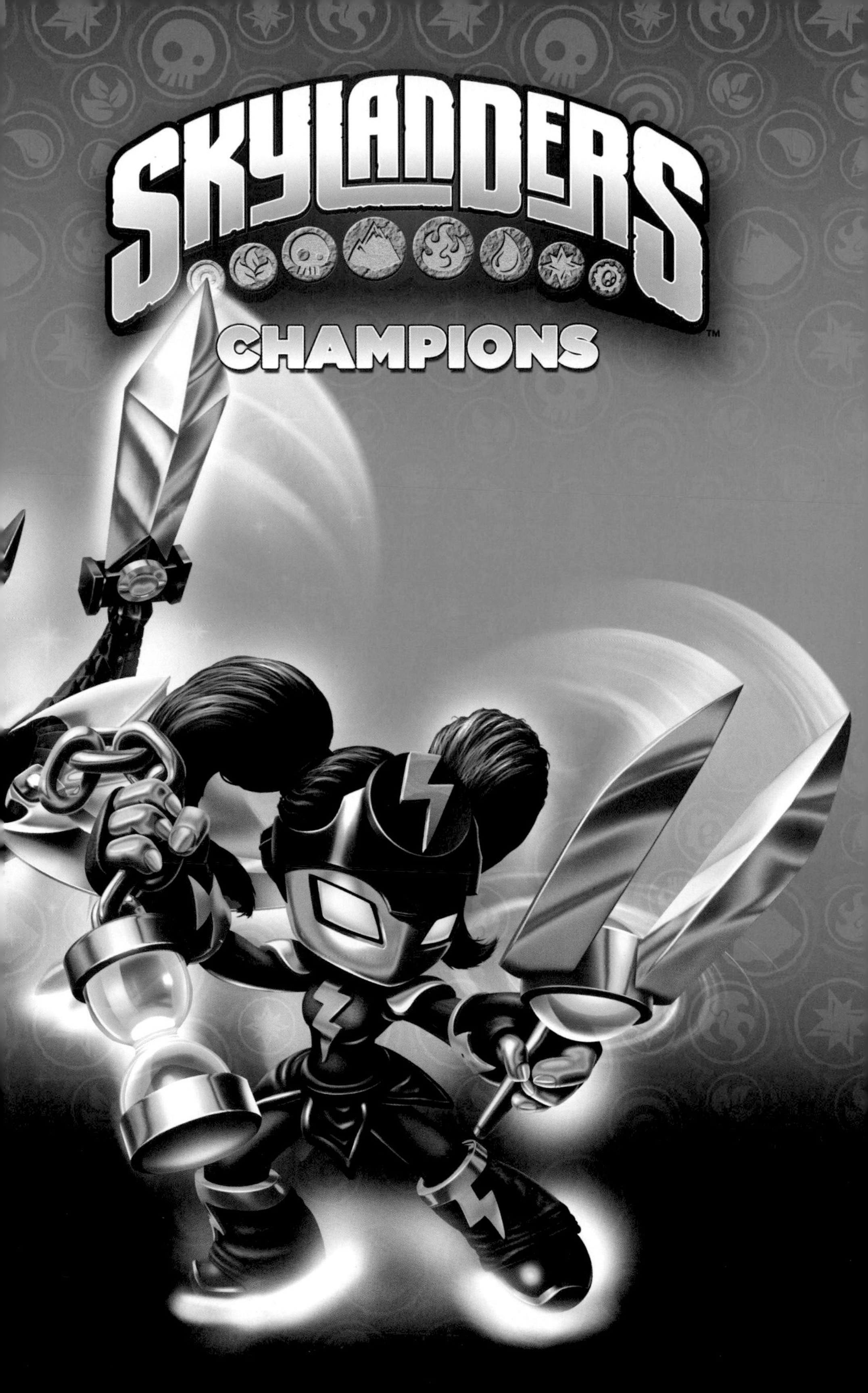
SKYLANDERS™
CHAMPIONS

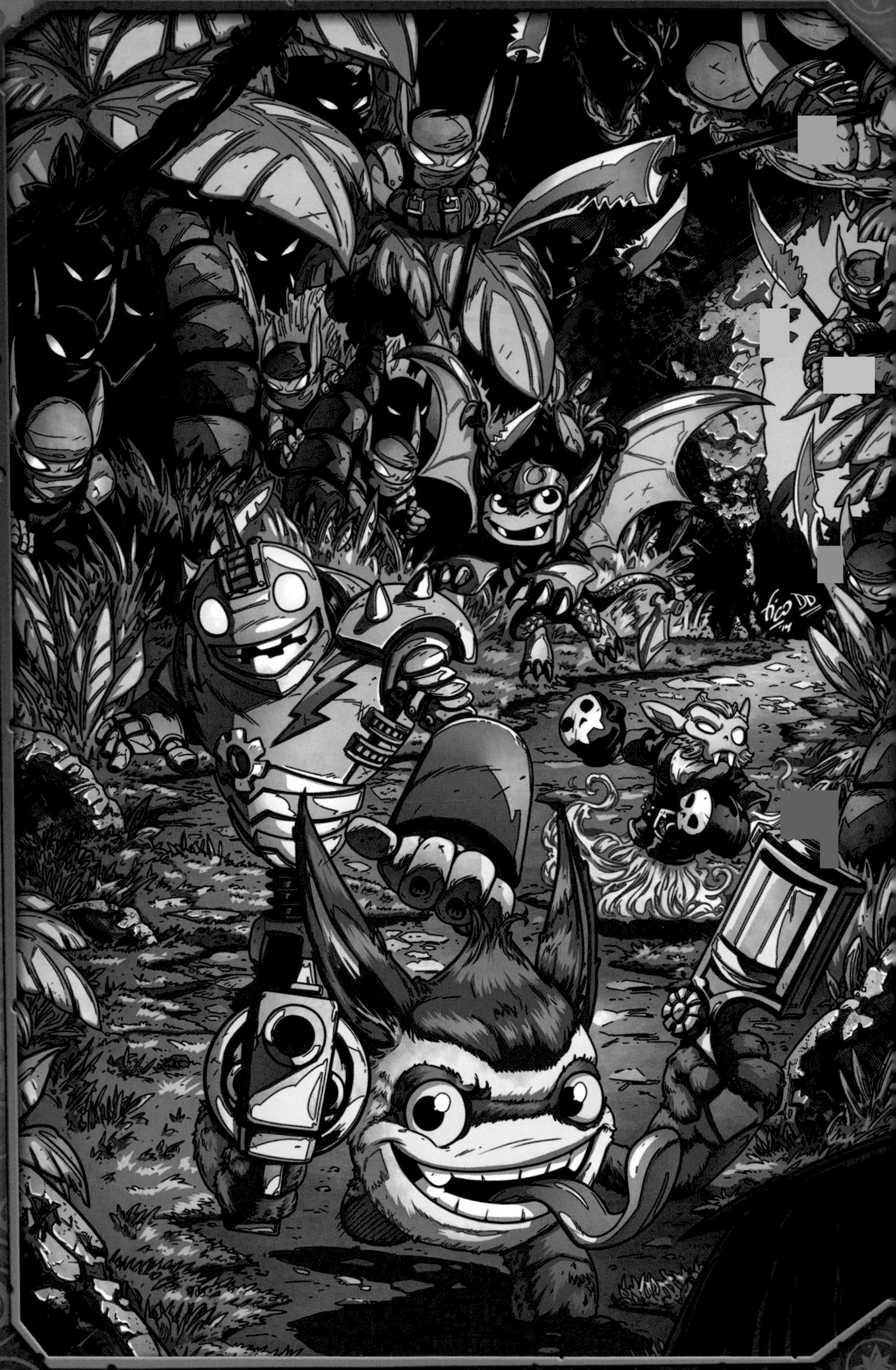

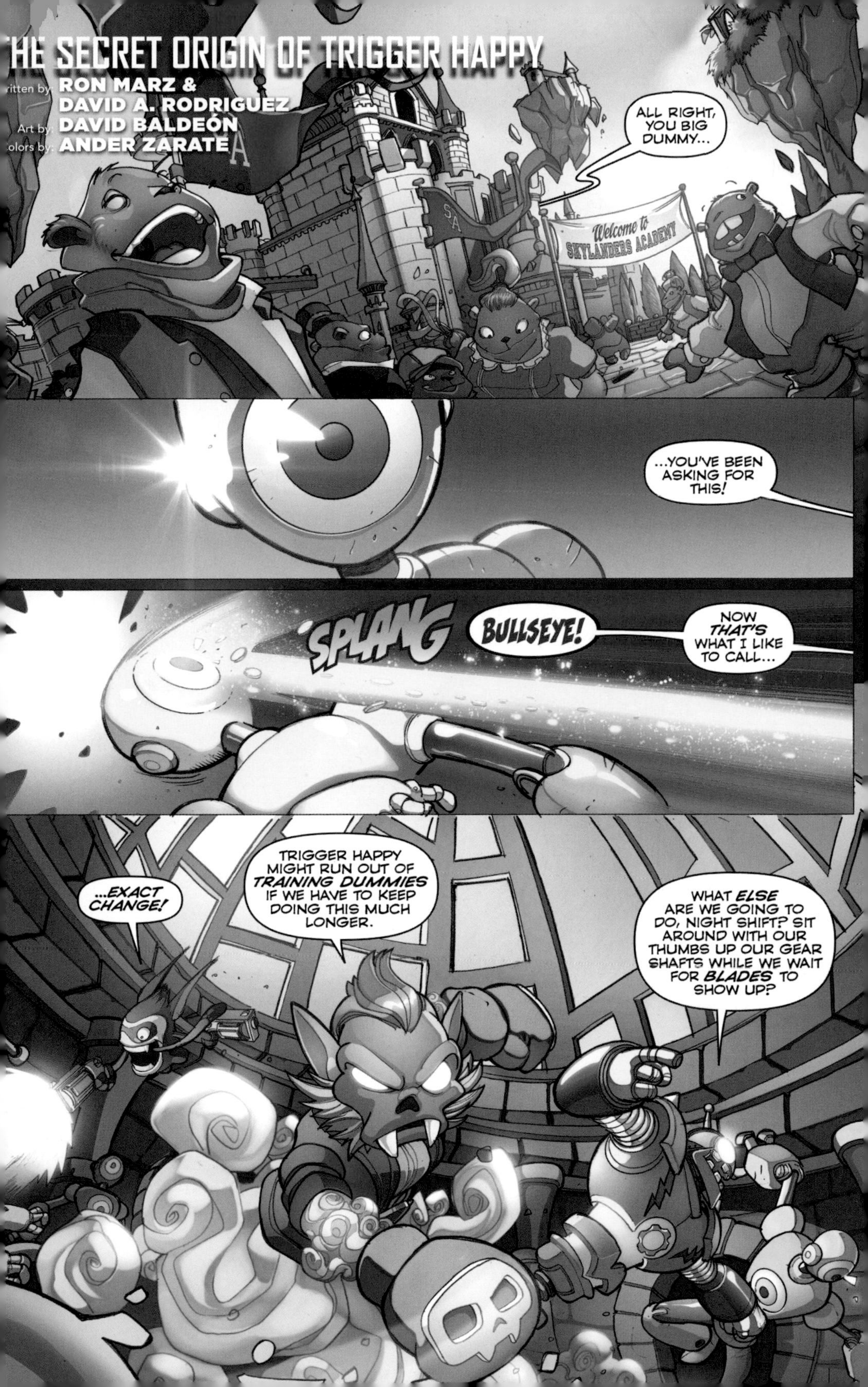
HE SECRET ORIGIN OF TRIGGER HAPPY
ritten by: RON MARZ &
DAVID A. RODRIGUEZ
Art by: DAVID BALDEÓN
olors by: ANDER ZARATE
ALL RIGHT, YOU BIG DUMMY...
Welcome to SKYLANDERS ACADEMY
...YOU'VE BEEN ASKING FOR THIS!
SPLANG
BULLSEYE!
NOW *THAT'S* WHAT I LIKE TO CALL...
...*EXACT CHANGE!*
TRIGGER HAPPY MIGHT RUN OUT OF *TRAINING DUMMIES* IF WE HAVE TO KEEP DOING THIS MUCH LONGER.
WHAT *ELSE* ARE WE GOING TO DO, NIGHT SHIFT? SIT AROUND WITH OUR THUMBS UP OUR GEAR SHAFTS WHILE WE WAIT FOR *BLADES* TO SHOW UP?

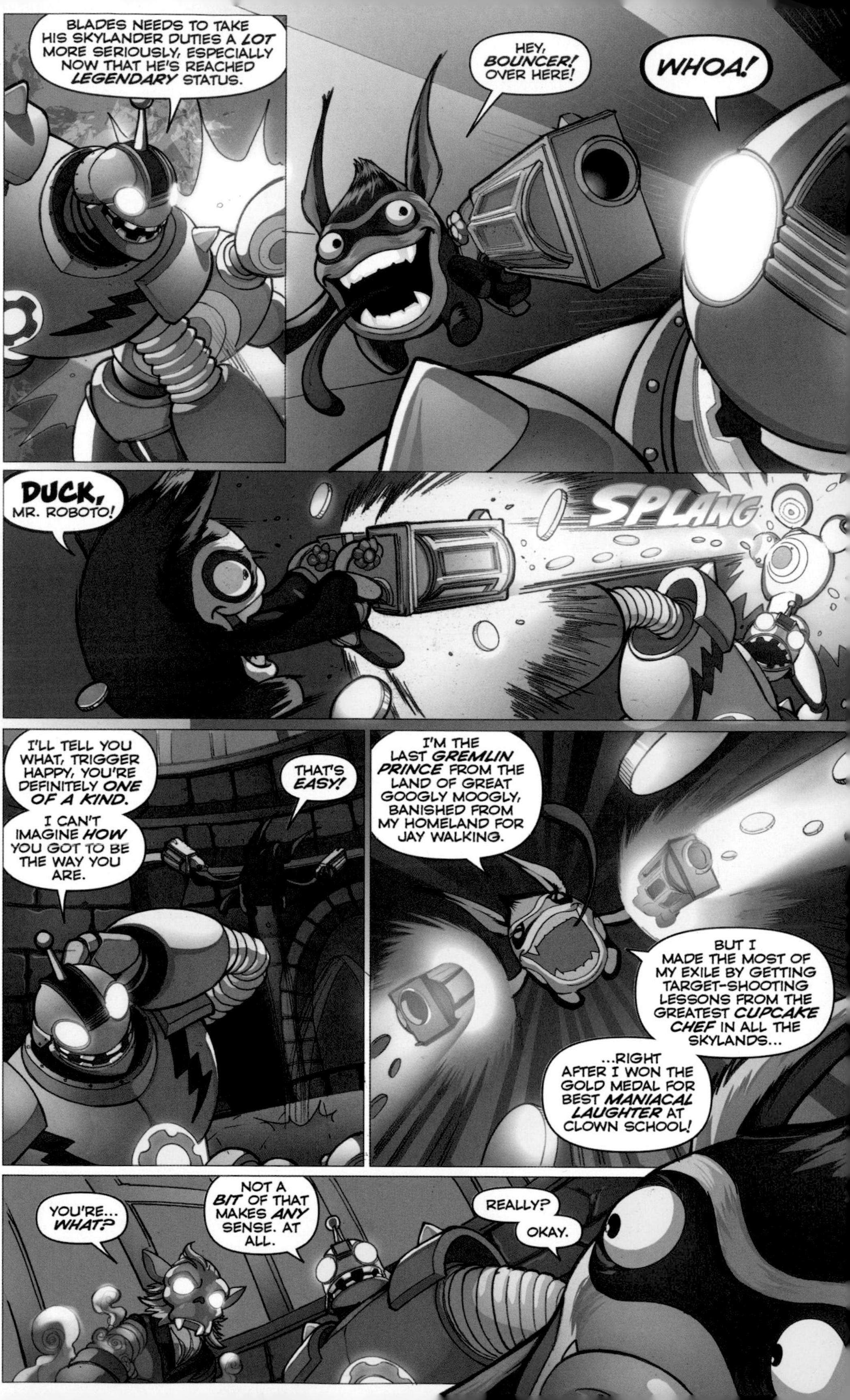
BLADES NEEDS TO TAKE HIS SKYLANDER DUTIES A LOT MORE SERIOUSLY, ESPECIALLY NOW THAT HE'S REACHED LEGENDARY STATUS.
HEY, BOUNCER! OVER HERE!
WHOA!
DUCK, MR. ROBOTO!
SPLANG
I'LL TELL YOU WHAT, TRIGGER HAPPY, YOU'RE DEFINITELY ONE OF A KIND.
I CAN'T IMAGINE HOW YOU GOT TO BE THE WAY YOU ARE.
THAT'S EASY!
I'M THE LAST GREMLIN PRINCE FROM THE LAND OF GREAT GOOGLY MOOGLY, BANISHED FROM MY HOMELAND FOR JAY WALKING.
BUT I MADE THE MOST OF MY EXILE BY GETTING TARGET-SHOOTING LESSONS FROM THE GREATEST CUPCAKE CHEF IN ALL THE SKYLANDS...
...RIGHT AFTER I WON THE GOLD MEDAL FOR BEST MANIACAL LAUGHTER AT CLOWN SCHOOL!
YOU'RE... WHAT?
NOT A BIT OF THAT MAKES ANY SENSE. AT ALL.
REALLY?
OKAY.

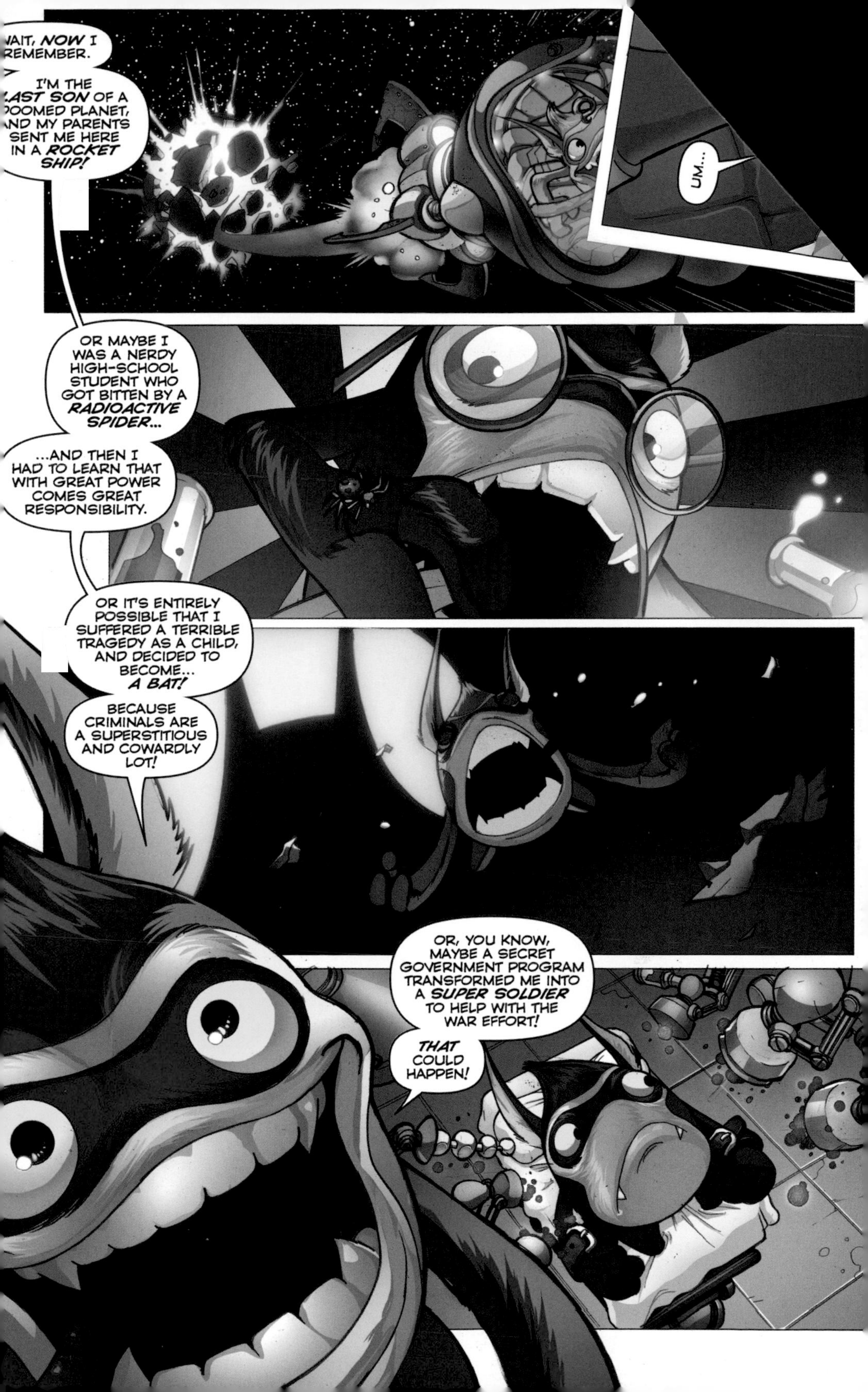
WAIT, *NOW* I REMEMBER.
I'M THE *LAST SON* OF A DOOMED PLANET, AND MY PARENTS SENT ME HERE IN A *ROCKET SHIP!*
UM...
OR MAYBE I WAS A NERDY HIGH-SCHOOL STUDENT WHO GOT BITTEN BY A *RADIOACTIVE SPIDER*...
...AND THEN I HAD TO LEARN THAT WITH GREAT POWER COMES GREAT RESPONSIBILITY.
OR IT'S ENTIRELY POSSIBLE THAT I SUFFERED A TERRIBLE TRAGEDY AS A CHILD, AND DECIDED TO BECOME... *A BAT!*
BECAUSE CRIMINALS ARE A SUPERSTITIOUS AND COWARDLY LOT!
OR, YOU KNOW, MAYBE A SECRET GOVERNMENT PROGRAM TRANSFORMED ME INTO A *SUPER SOLDIER* TO HELP WITH THE WAR EFFORT!
THAT COULD HAPPEN!

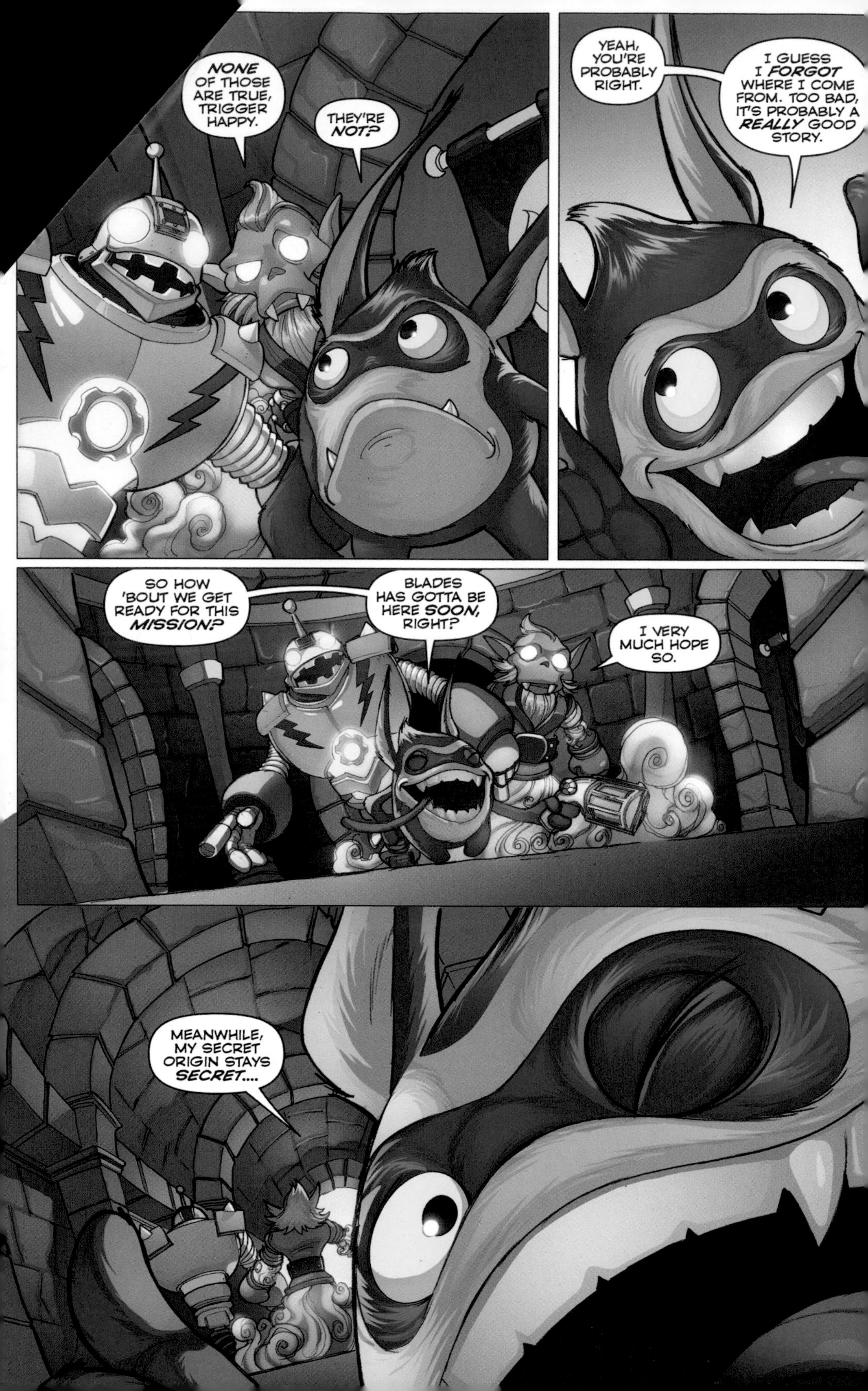
NONE OF THOSE ARE TRUE, TRIGGER HAPPY.
THEY'RE NOT?
YEAH, YOU'RE PROBABLY RIGHT.
I GUESS I FORGOT WHERE I COME FROM. TOO BAD, IT'S PROBABLY A REALLY GOOD STORY.
SO HOW 'BOUT WE GET READY FOR THIS MISSION?
BLADES HAS GOTTA BE HERE SOON, RIGHT?
I VERY MUCH HOPE SO.
MEANWHILE, MY SECRET ORIGIN STAYS SECRET....

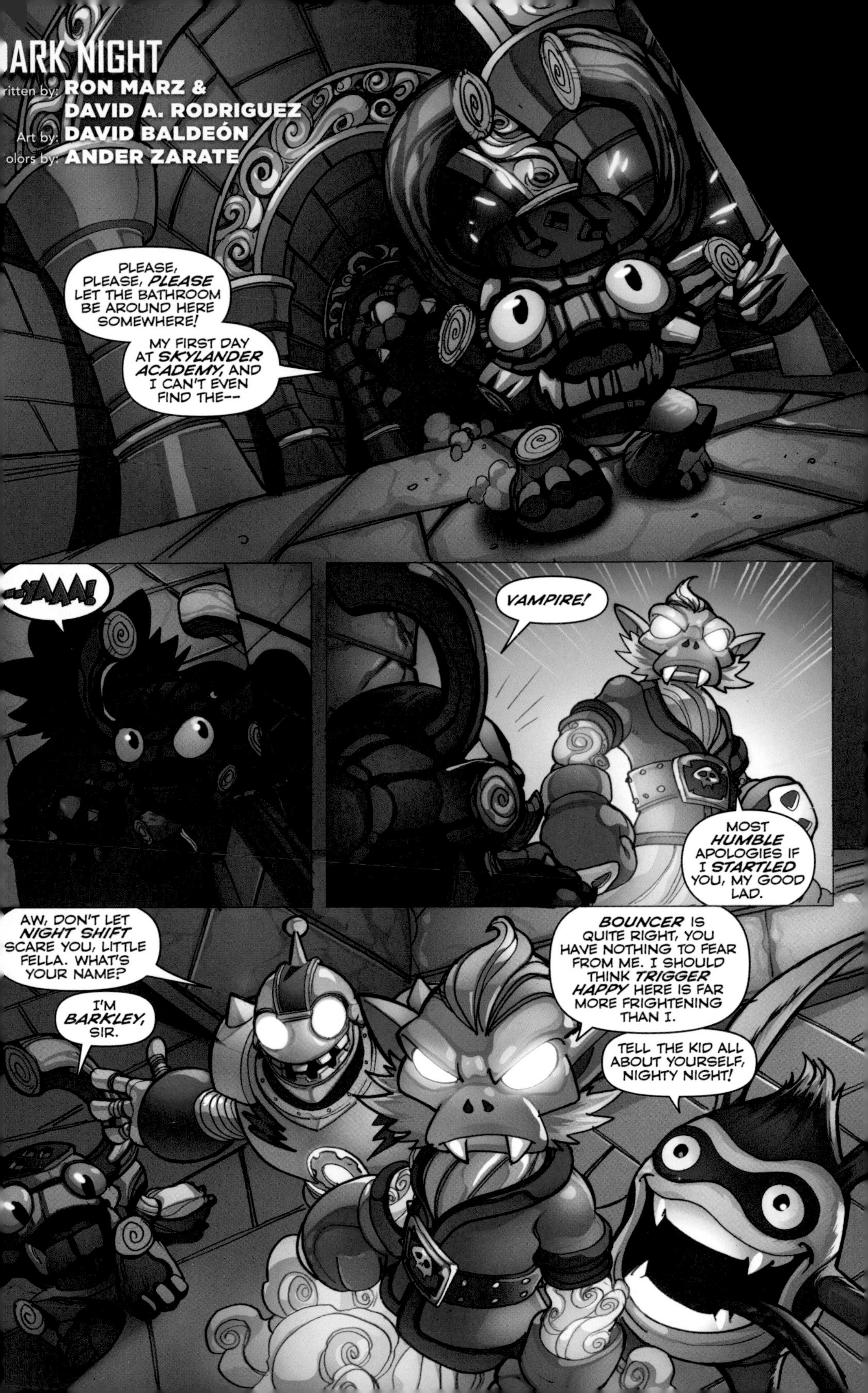

ARK NIGHT
ritten by: RON MARZ & DAVID A. RODRIGUEZ
Art by: DAVID BALDEÓN
olors by: ANDER ZARATE
PLEASE, PLEASE, PLEASE LET THE BATHROOM BE AROUND HERE SOMEWHERE!
MY FIRST DAY AT SKYLANDER ACADEMY, AND I CAN'T EVEN FIND THE--
--YAAAA!
VAMPIRE!
MOST HUMBLE APOLOGIES IF I STARTLED YOU, MY GOOD LAD.
AW, DON'T LET NIGHT SHIFT SCARE YOU, LITTLE FELLA. WHAT'S YOUR NAME?
I'M BARKLEY, SIR.
BOUNCER IS QUITE RIGHT, YOU HAVE NOTHING TO FEAR FROM ME. I SHOULD THINK TRIGGER HAPPY HERE IS FAR MORE FRIGHTENING THAN I.
TELL THE KID ALL ABOUT YOURSELF, NIGHTY NIGHT!

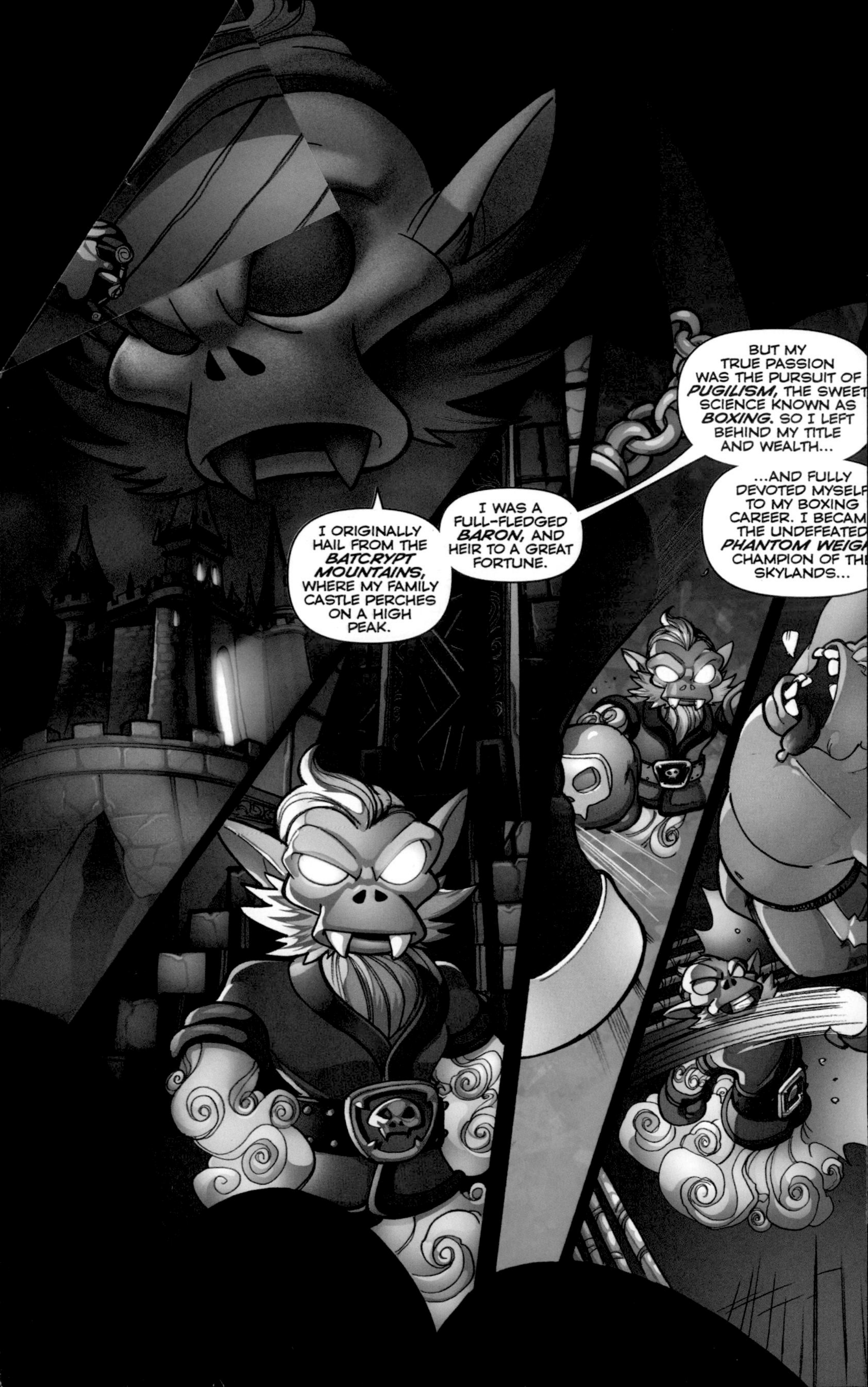
I ORIGINALLY HAIL FROM THE ***BATCRYPT MOUNTAINS,*** WHERE MY FAMILY CASTLE PERCHES ON A HIGH PEAK.
I WAS A FULL-FLEDGED ***BARON,*** AND HEIR TO A GREAT FORTUNE.
BUT MY TRUE PASSION WAS THE PURSUIT OF ***PUGILISM,*** THE SWEET SCIENCE KNOWN AS ***BOXING.*** SO I LEFT BEHIND MY TITLE AND WEALTH...
...AND FULLY DEVOTED MYSELF TO MY BOXING CAREER. I BECAM THE UNDEFEATED ***PHANTOM WEIG*** CHAMPION OF TH SKYLANDS...

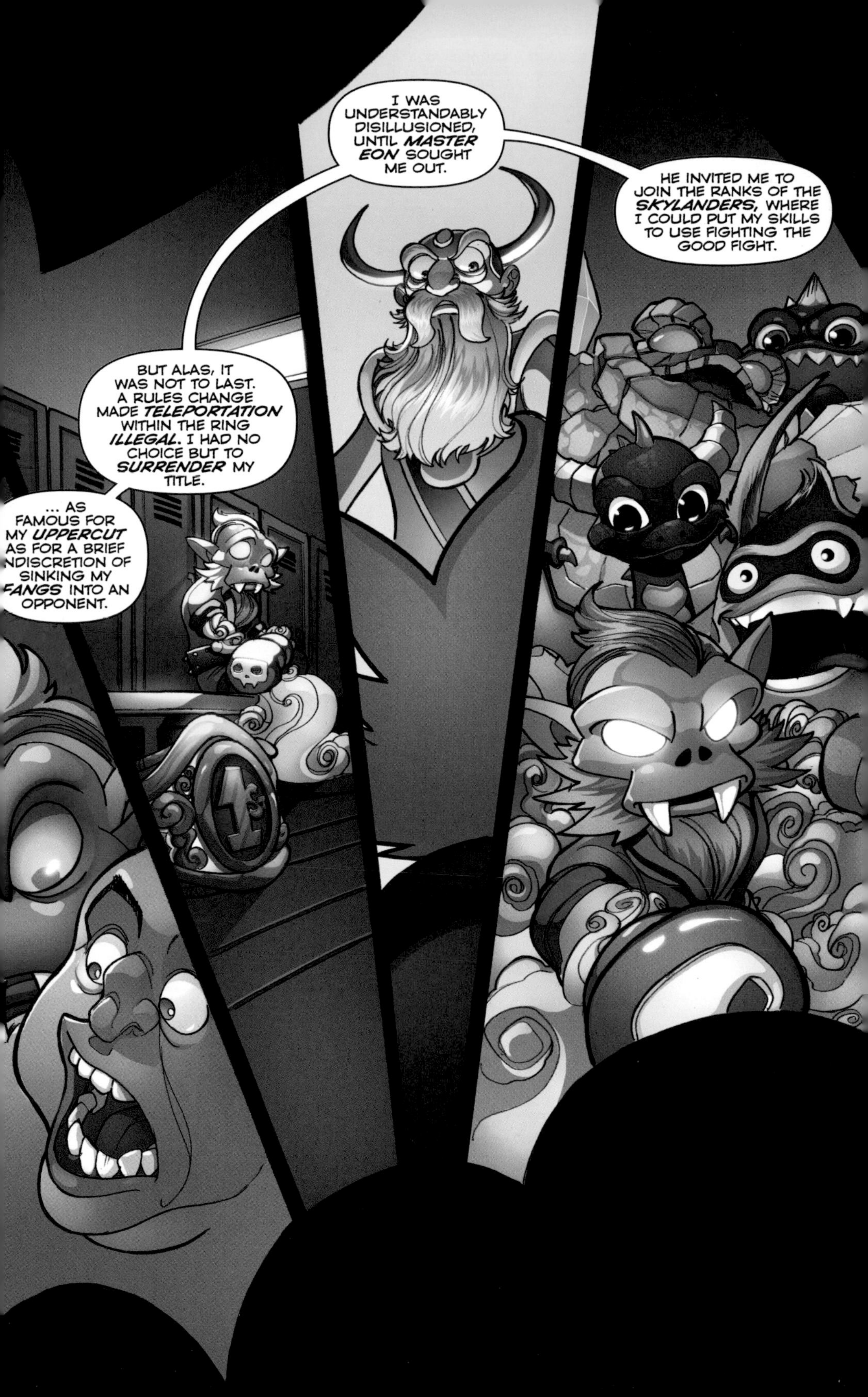
... AS FAMOUS FOR MY UPPERCUT AS FOR A BRIEF INDISCRETION OF SINKING MY FANGS INTO AN OPPONENT.
BUT ALAS, IT WAS NOT TO LAST. A RULES CHANGE MADE TELEPORTATION WITHIN THE RING ILLEGAL. I HAD NO CHOICE BUT TO SURRENDER MY TITLE.
I WAS UNDERSTANDABLY DISILLUSIONED, UNTIL MASTER EON SOUGHT ME OUT.
HE INVITED ME TO JOIN THE RANKS OF THE SKYLANDERS, WHERE I COULD PUT MY SKILLS TO USE FIGHTING THE GOOD FIGHT.

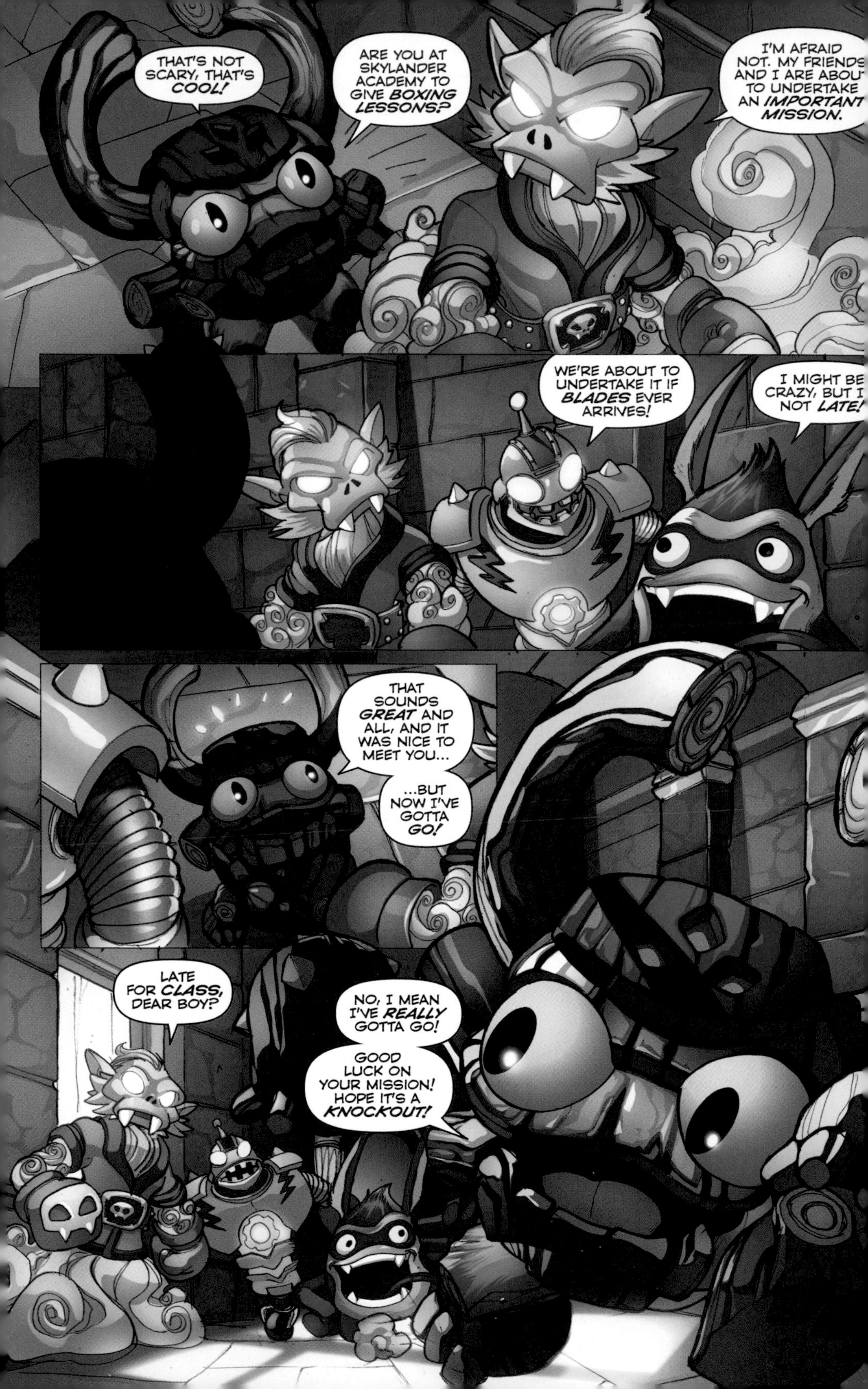
THAT'S NOT SCARY, THAT'S *COOL!*
ARE YOU AT SKYLANDER ACADEMY TO GIVE *BOXING LESSONS?*
I'M AFRAID NOT. MY FRIENDS AND I ARE ABOUT TO UNDERTAKE AN *IMPORTANT MISSION.*
WE'RE ABOUT TO UNDERTAKE IT IF *BLADES* EVER ARRIVES!
I MIGHT BE CRAZY, BUT I NOT *LATE!*
THAT SOUNDS *GREAT* AND ALL, AND IT WAS NICE TO MEET YOU...
...BUT NOW I'VE GOTTA *GO!*
LATE FOR *CLASS,* DEAR BOY?
NO, I MEAN I'VE *REALLY* GOTTA GO!
GOOD LUCK ON YOUR MISSION! HOPE IT'S A *KNOCKOUT!*

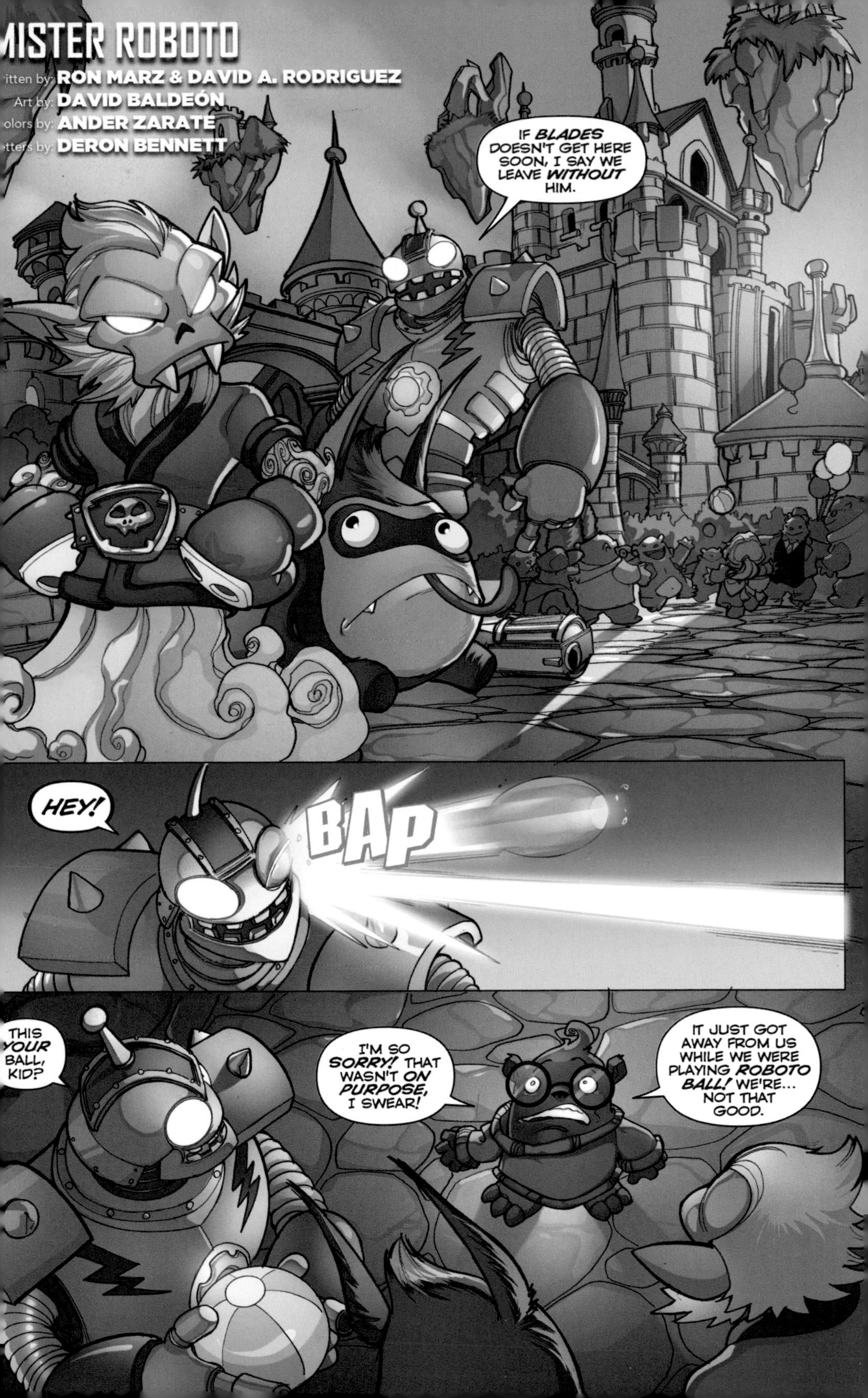
MISTER ROBOTO
itten by: RON MARZ & DAVID A. RODRIGUEZ
Art by: DAVID BALDEÓN
olors by: ANDER ZARATE
tters by: DERON BENNETT
IF BLADES DOESN'T GET HERE SOON, I SAY WE LEAVE WITHOUT HIM.
HEY!
BAP
THIS YOUR BALL, KID?
I'M SO SORRY! THAT WASN'T ON PURPOSE, I SWEAR!
IT JUST GOT AWAY FROM US WHILE WE WERE PLAYING ROBOTO BALL! WE'RE... NOT THAT GOOD.

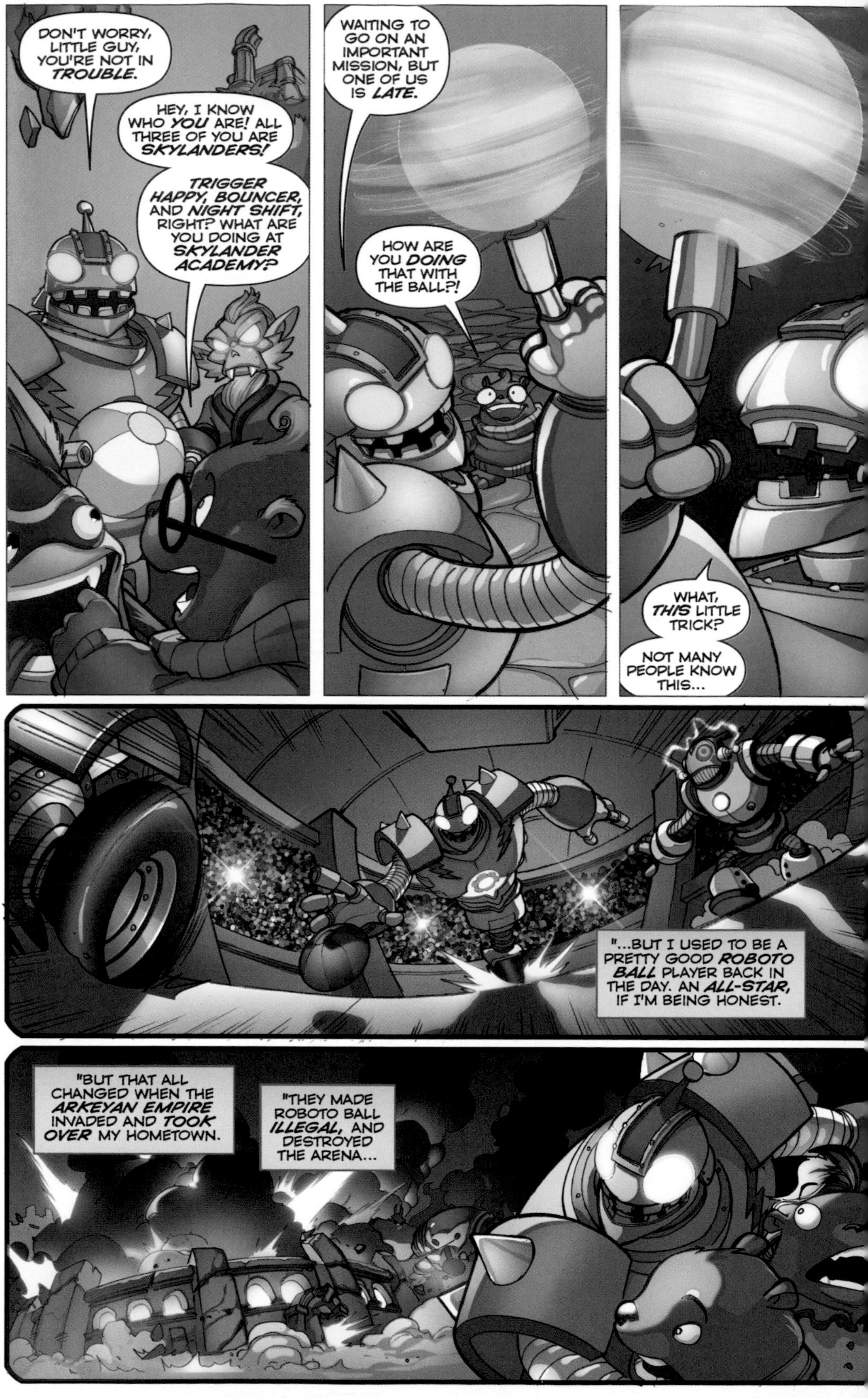
DON'T WORRY, LITTLE GUY, YOU'RE NOT IN TROUBLE.
HEY, I KNOW WHO YOU ARE! ALL THREE OF YOU ARE SKYLANDERS!
TRIGGER HAPPY, BOUNCER, AND NIGHT SHIFT, RIGHT? WHAT ARE YOU DOING AT SKYLANDER ACADEMY?
WAITING TO GO ON AN IMPORTANT MISSION, BUT ONE OF US IS LATE.
HOW ARE YOU DOING THAT WITH THE BALL?!
WHAT, THIS LITTLE TRICK?
NOT MANY PEOPLE KNOW THIS...
"...BUT I USED TO BE A PRETTY GOOD ROBOTO BALL PLAYER BACK IN THE DAY. AN ALL-STAR, IF I'M BEING HONEST.
"BUT THAT ALL CHANGED WHEN THE ARKEYAN EMPIRE INVADED AND TOOK OVER MY HOMETOWN.
"THEY MADE ROBOTO BALL ILLEGAL, AND DESTROYED THE ARENA...

"...AND CONVERTED ME INTO A *SECURITY-BOT* IN THE MINES. I DON'T MIND TELLING YOU, IT WAS *TERRIBLE.*

"BUT THEN SOMEONE *RECOGNIZED* ME. IT TURNED OUT THAT ALL THE MABU WHO WERE BEING FORCED TO WORK IN THE MINES *REMEMBERED* ME FROM MY PLAYING DAYS.

"THEY CONSIDERED ME A *HERO!*

"IT GOT ME THINKING THAT IF *THEY* BELIEVED I WAS A HERO, MAYBE I REALLY *COULD* BE.

"I LED THE MABU IN THE *MINERS OVER MATTER* REBELLION, AND WE *OVERTHREW* THE EVIL ARKEYANS!"

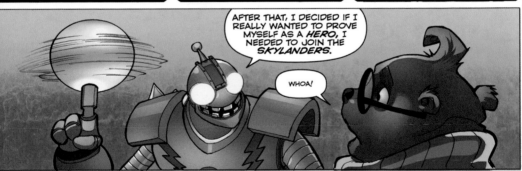

AFTER THAT, I DECIDED IF I REALLY WANTED TO PROVE MYSELF AS A *HERO,* I NEEDED TO JOIN THE *SKYLANDERS.*

WHOA!

HERE YOU GO, KID. MAYBE *YOU'LL* BE A SKYLANDER SOMEDAY!

YOU REALLY *THINK* SO?! THAT'S TOTALLY WHAT I WANNA DO!

YOU GUYS, I MET SOME *SKYLANDERS!* I MEAN, *FOR-REAL* SKYLANDERS!

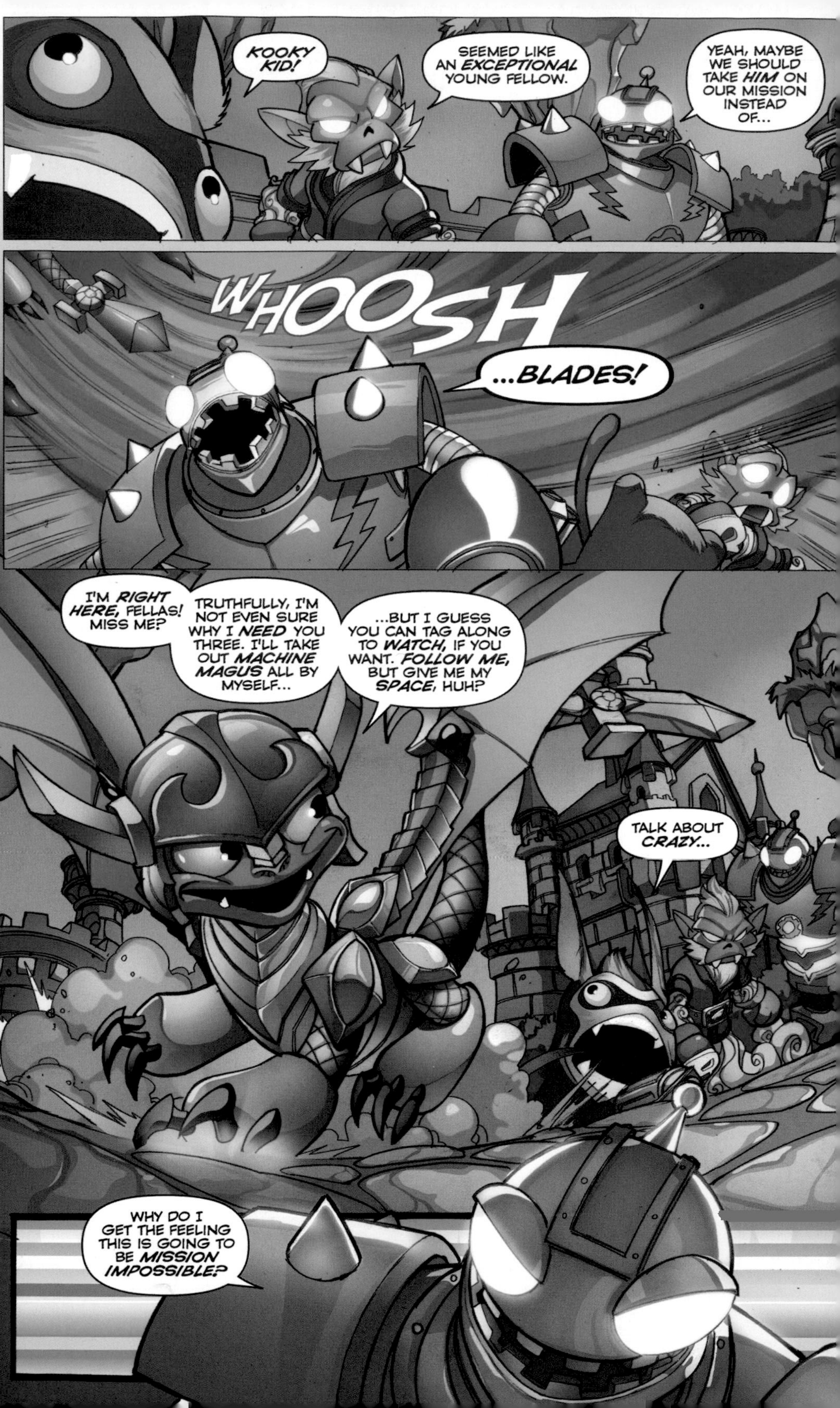

KOOKY KID!
SEEMED LIKE AN EXCEPTIONAL YOUNG FELLOW.
YEAH, MAYBE WE SHOULD TAKE HIM ON OUR MISSION INSTEAD OF...
WHOOSH
...BLADES!
I'M RIGHT HERE, FELLAS! MISS ME?
TRUTHFULLY, I'M NOT EVEN SURE WHY I NEED YOU THREE. I'LL TAKE OUT MACHINE MAGUS ALL BY MYSELF...
...BUT I GUESS YOU CAN TAG ALONG TO WATCH, IF YOU WANT. FOLLOW ME, BUT GIVE ME MY SPACE, HUH?
TALK ABOUT CRAZY...
WHY DO I GET THE FEELING THIS IS GOING TO BE MISSION IMPOSSIBLE?

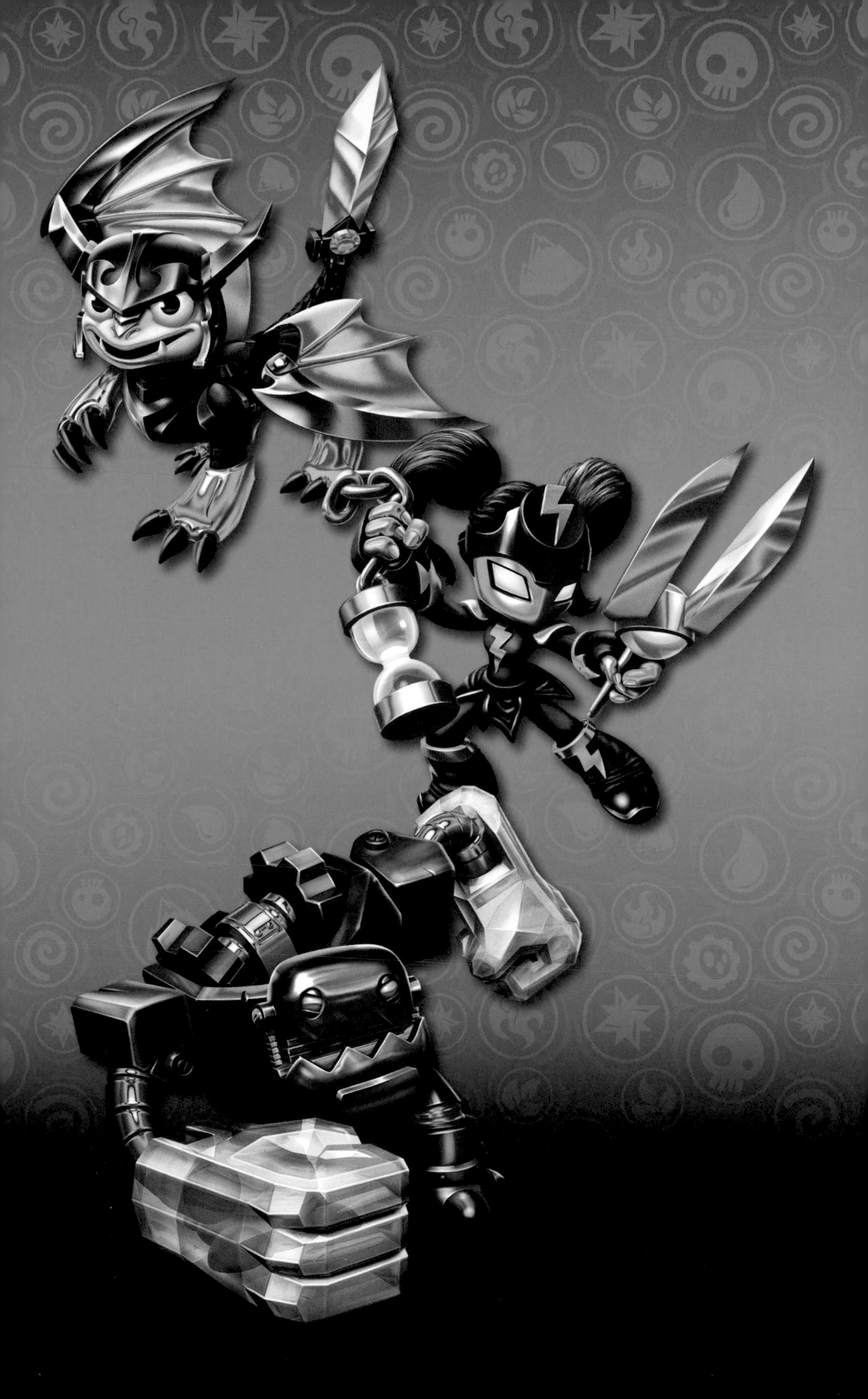

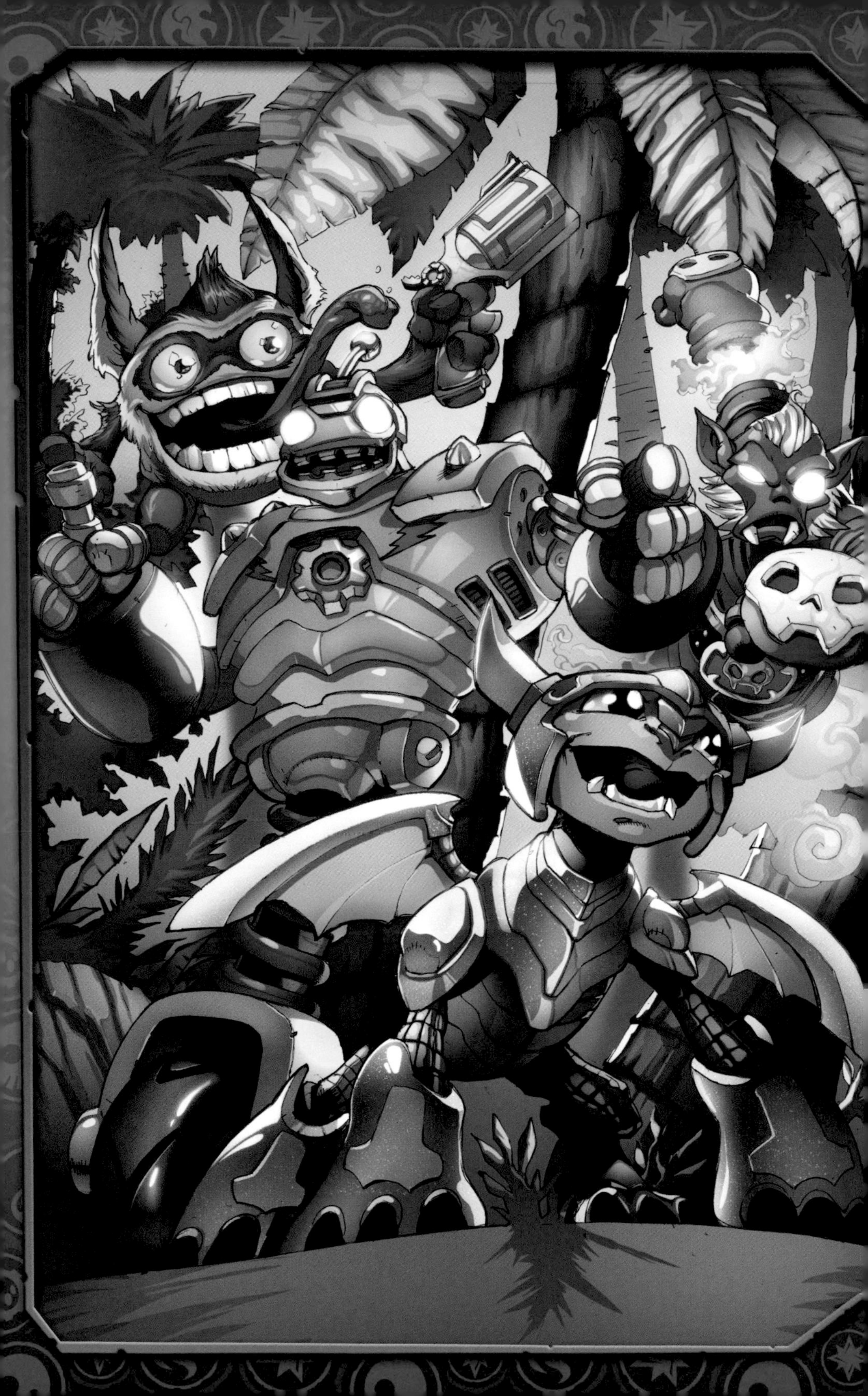

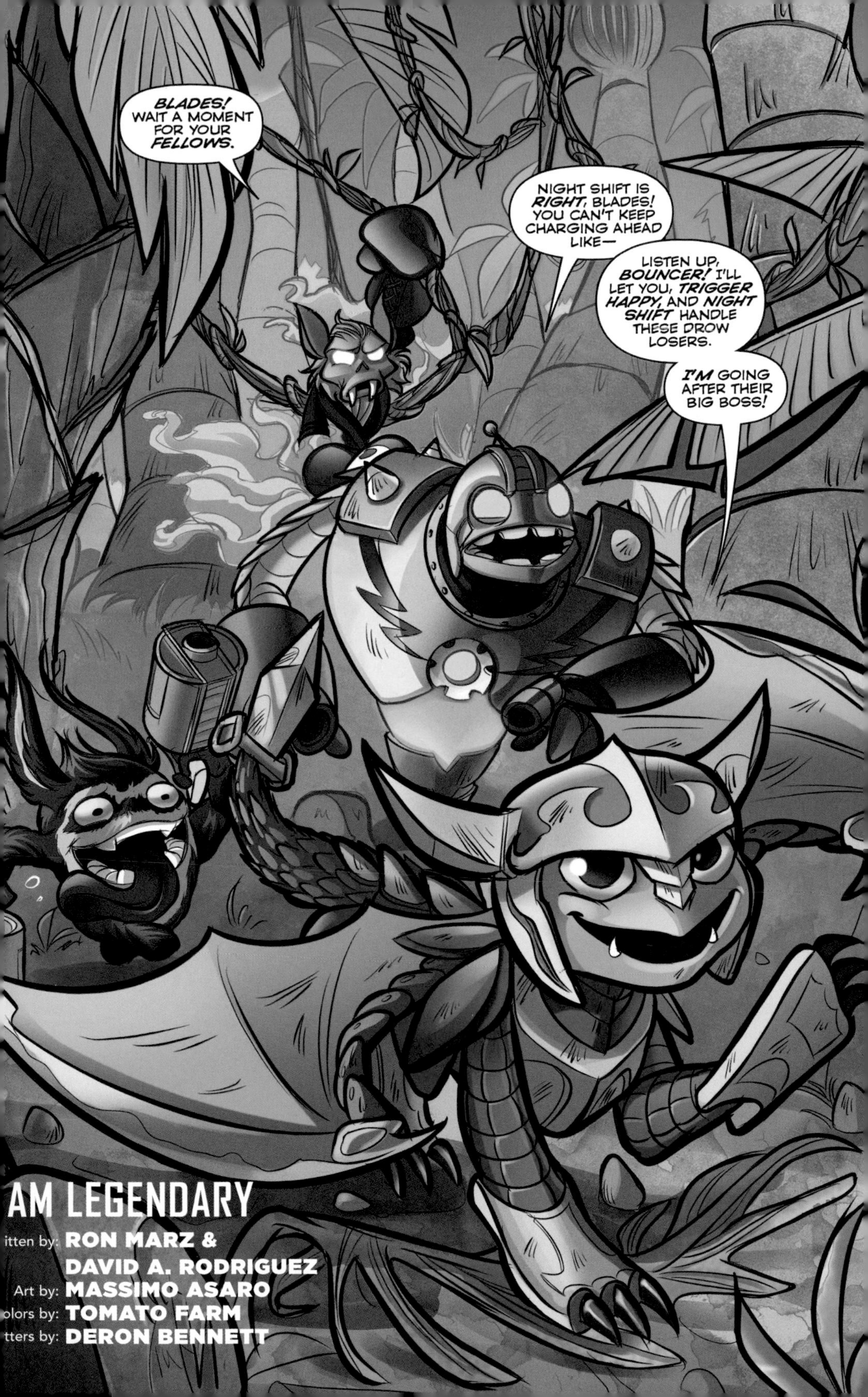
BLADES! WAIT A MOMENT FOR YOUR FELLOWS.
NIGHT SHIFT IS RIGHT, BLADES! YOU CAN'T KEEP CHARGING AHEAD LIKE—
LISTEN UP, BOUNCER! I'LL LET YOU, TRIGGER HAPPY, AND NIGHT SHIFT HANDLE THESE DROW LOSERS.
I'M GOING AFTER THEIR BIG BOSS!
AM LEGENDARY
itten by: RON MARZ & DAVID A. RODRIGUEZ
Art by: MASSIMO ASARO
olors by: TOMATO FARM
tters by: DERON BENNETT

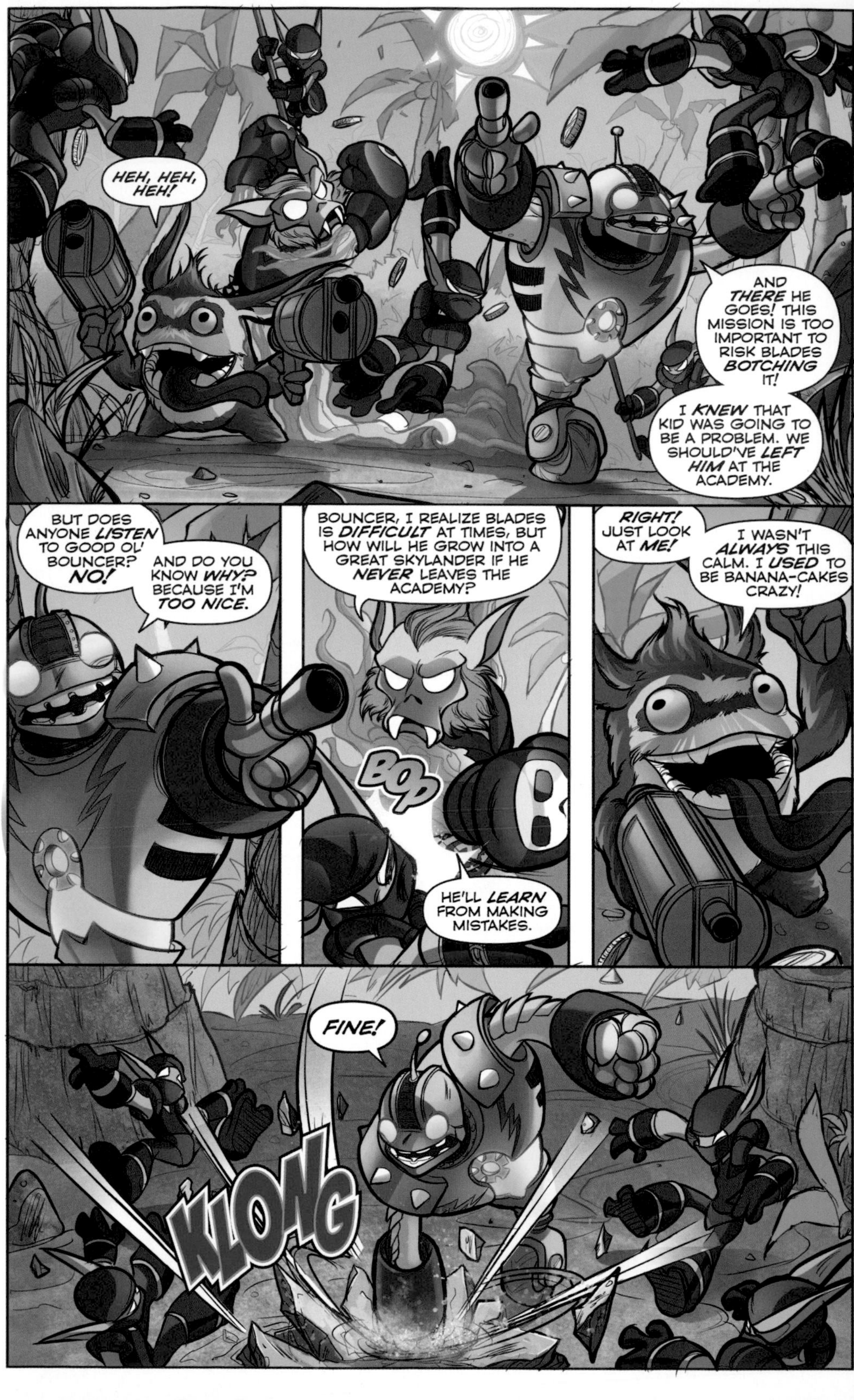

HEH, HEH, HEH!
AND THERE HE GOES! THIS MISSION IS TOO IMPORTANT TO RISK BLADES BOTCHING IT!
I KNEW THAT KID WAS GOING TO BE A PROBLEM. WE SHOULD'VE LEFT HIM AT THE ACADEMY.
BUT DOES ANYONE LISTEN TO GOOD OL' BOUNCER? NO!
AND DO YOU KNOW WHY? BECAUSE I'M TOO NICE.
BOUNCER, I REALIZE BLADES IS DIFFICULT AT TIMES, BUT HOW WILL HE GROW INTO A GREAT SKYLANDER IF HE NEVER LEAVES THE ACADEMY?
BOP
HE'LL LEARN FROM MAKING MISTAKES.
RIGHT! JUST LOOK AT ME!
I WASN'T ALWAYS THIS CALM. I USED TO BE BANANA-CAKES CRAZY!
FINE!
KLONG

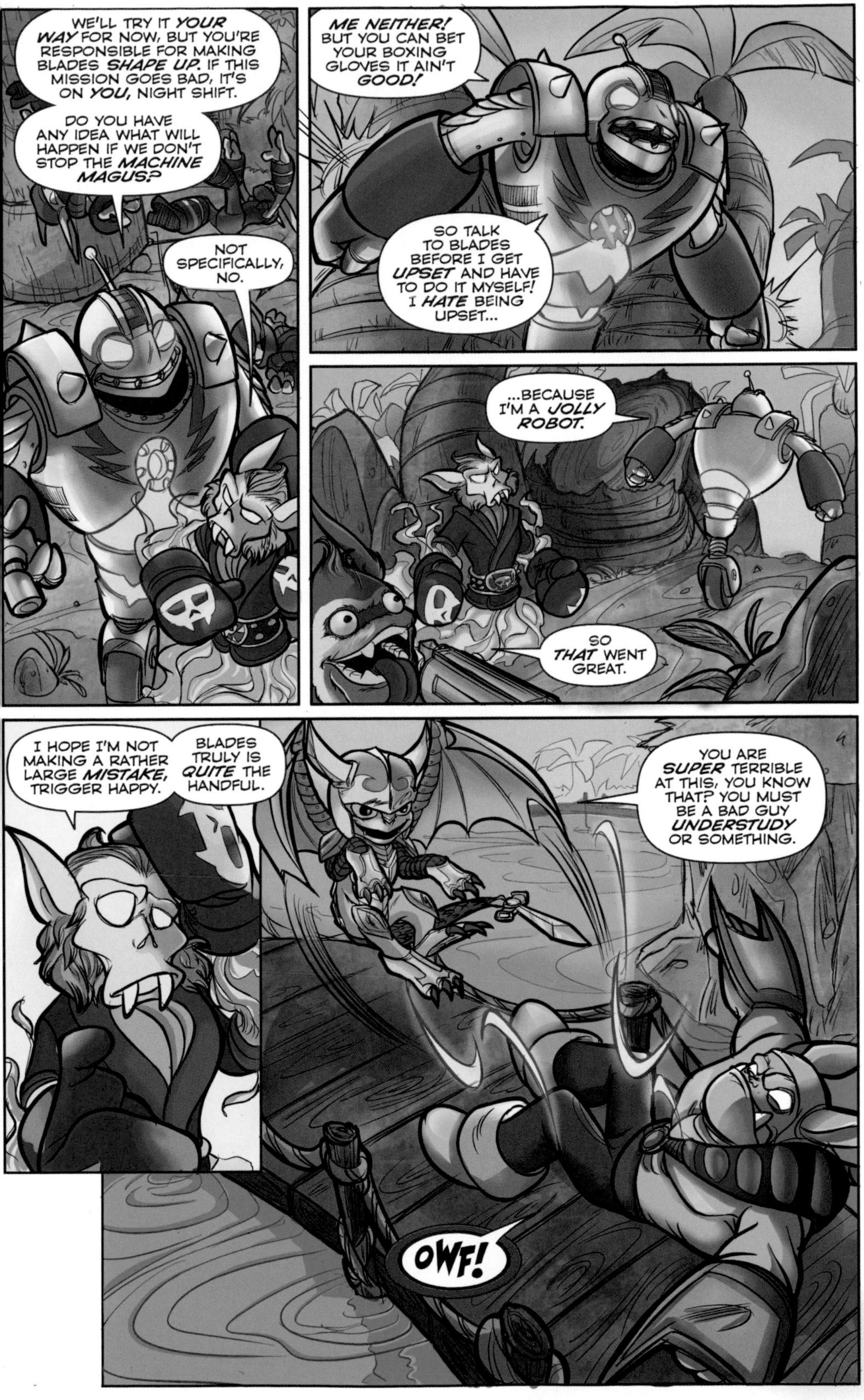
WE'LL TRY IT YOUR WAY FOR NOW, BUT YOU'RE RESPONSIBLE FOR MAKING BLADES SHAPE UP. IF THIS MISSION GOES BAD, IT'S ON YOU, NIGHT SHIFT.
DO YOU HAVE ANY IDEA WHAT WILL HAPPEN IF WE DON'T STOP THE MACHINE MAGUS?
NOT SPECIFICALLY, NO.
ME NEITHER! BUT YOU CAN BET YOUR BOXING GLOVES IT AIN'T GOOD!
SO TALK TO BLADES BEFORE I GET UPSET AND HAVE TO DO IT MYSELF! I HATE BEING UPSET...
...BECAUSE I'M A JOLLY ROBOT.
SO THAT WENT GREAT.
I HOPE I'M NOT MAKING A RATHER LARGE MISTAKE, TRIGGER HAPPY.
BLADES TRULY IS QUITE THE HANDFUL.
YOU ARE SUPER TERRIBLE AT THIS, YOU KNOW THAT? YOU MUST BE A BAD GUY UNDERSTUDY OR SOMETHING.
OWF!

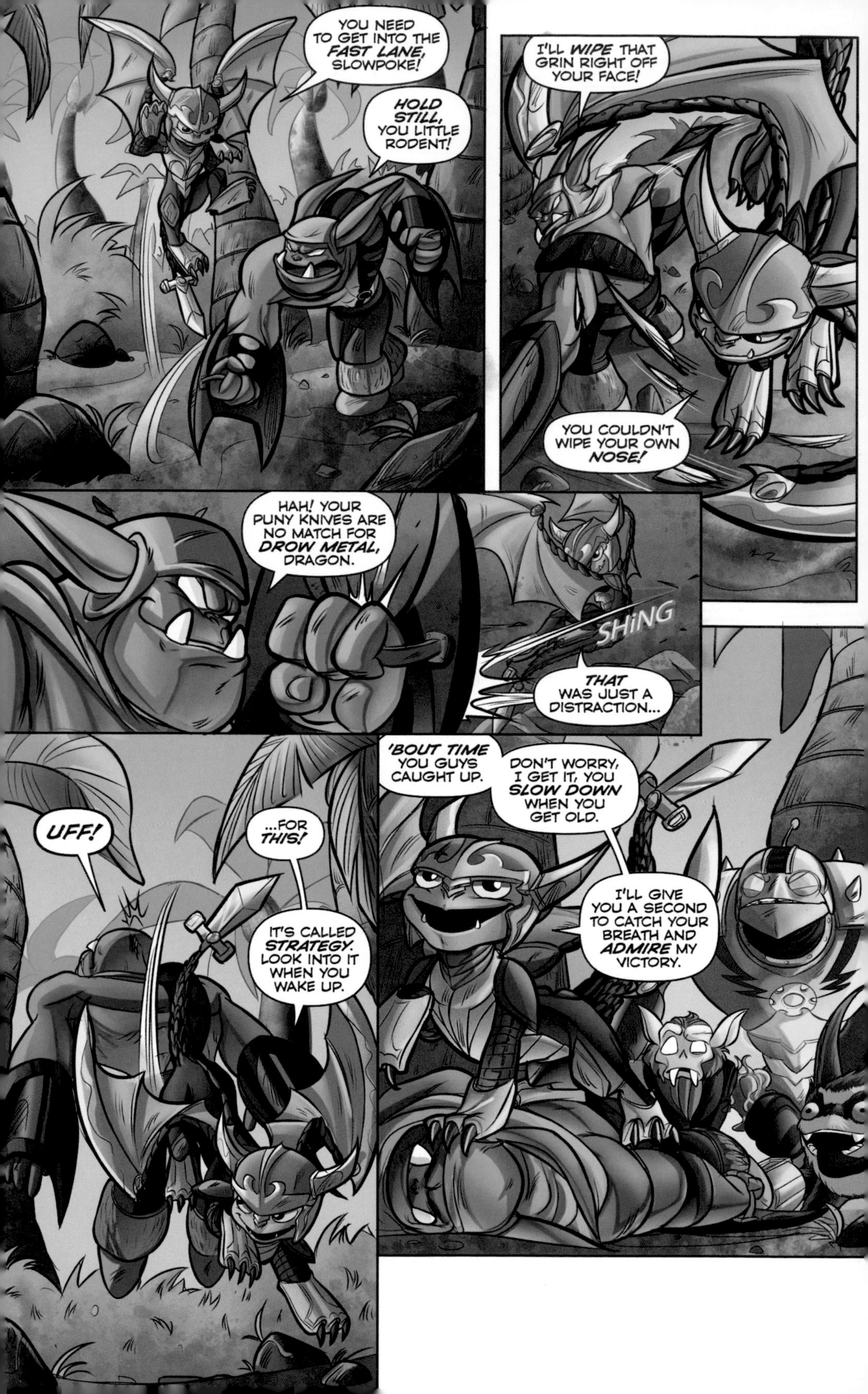
YOU NEED TO GET INTO THE FAST LANE, SLOWPOKE!
HOLD STILL, YOU LITTLE RODENT!
I'LL WIPE THAT GRIN RIGHT OFF YOUR FACE!
YOU COULDN'T WIPE YOUR OWN NOSE!
HAH! YOUR PUNY KNIVES ARE NO MATCH FOR DROW METAL, DRAGON.
SHING
THAT WAS JUST A DISTRACTION...
UFF!
...FOR THIS!
IT'S CALLED STRATEGY. LOOK INTO IT WHEN YOU WAKE UP.
'BOUT TIME YOU GUYS CAUGHT UP.
DON'T WORRY, I GET IT, YOU SLOW DOWN WHEN YOU GET OLD.
I'LL GIVE YOU A SECOND TO CATCH YOUR BREATH AND ADMIRE MY VICTORY.

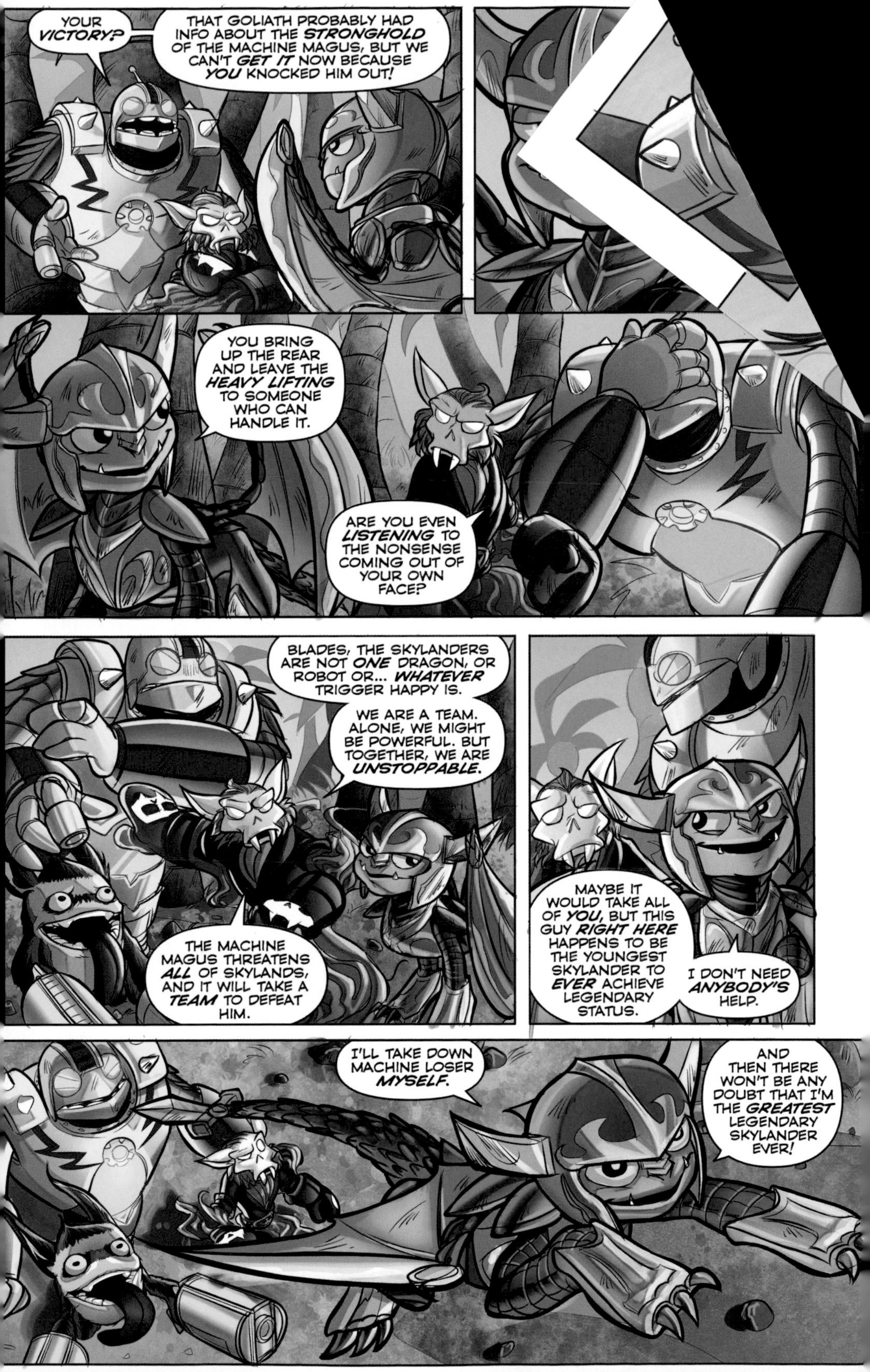
YOUR VICTORY?
THAT GOLIATH PROBABLY HAD INFO ABOUT THE STRONGHOLD OF THE MACHINE MAGUS, BUT WE CAN'T GET IT NOW BECAUSE YOU KNOCKED HIM OUT!
YOU BRING UP THE REAR AND LEAVE THE HEAVY LIFTING TO SOMEONE WHO CAN HANDLE IT.
ARE YOU EVEN LISTENING TO THE NONSENSE COMING OUT OF YOUR OWN FACE?
BLADES, THE SKYLANDERS ARE NOT ONE DRAGON, OR ROBOT OR... WHATEVER TRIGGER HAPPY IS.
WE ARE A TEAM. ALONE, WE MIGHT BE POWERFUL. BUT TOGETHER, WE ARE UNSTOPPABLE.
THE MACHINE MAGUS THREATENS ALL OF SKYLANDS, AND IT WILL TAKE A TEAM TO DEFEAT HIM.
MAYBE IT WOULD TAKE ALL OF YOU, BUT THIS GUY RIGHT HERE HAPPENS TO BE THE YOUNGEST SKYLANDER TO EVER ACHIEVE LEGENDARY STATUS.
I DON'T NEED ANYBODY'S HELP.
I'LL TAKE DOWN MACHINE LOSER MYSELF.
AND THEN THERE WON'T BE ANY DOUBT THAT I'M THE GREATEST LEGENDARY SKYLANDER EVER!

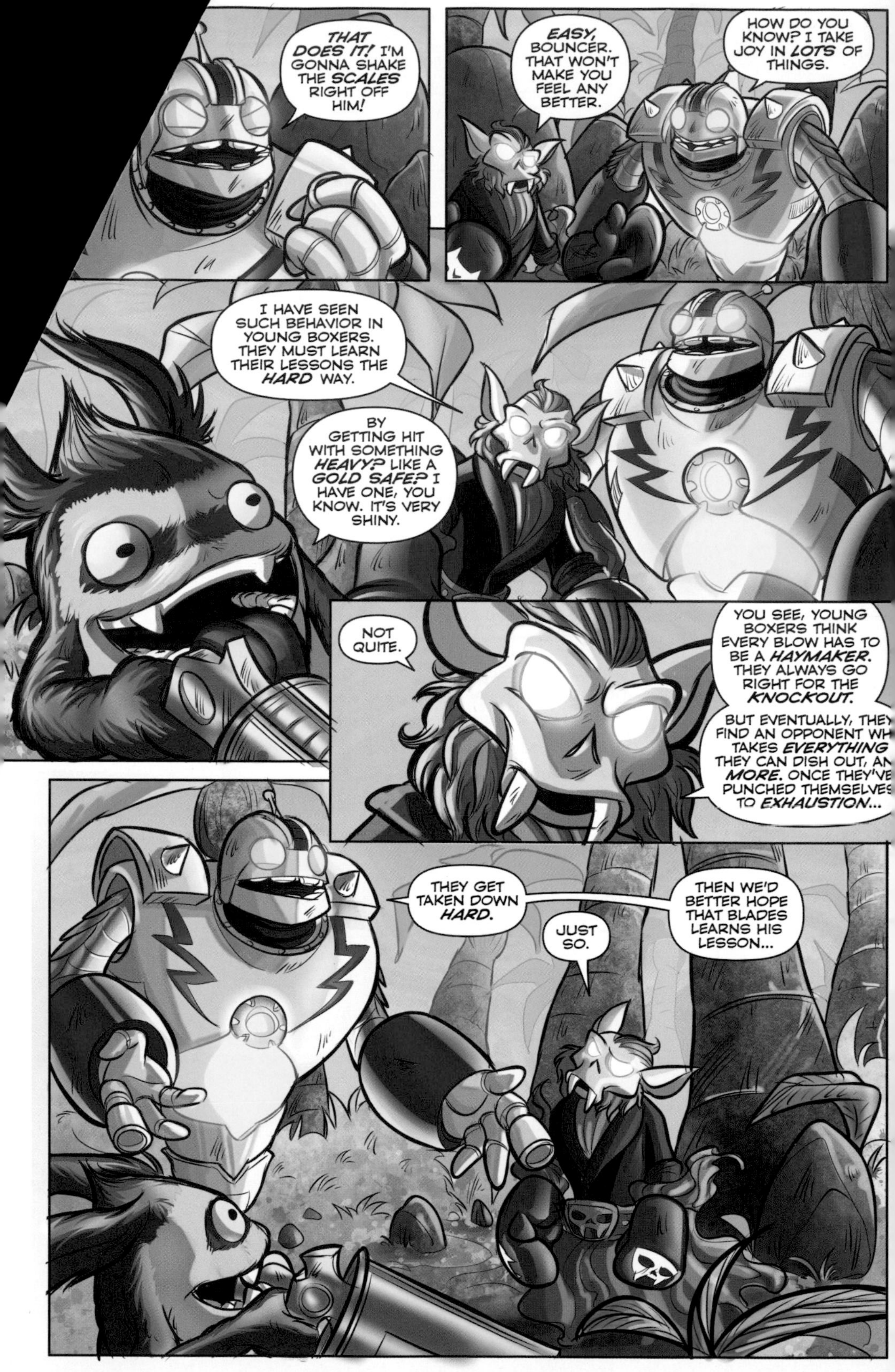
THAT DOES IT! I'M GONNA SHAKE THE SCALES RIGHT OFF HIM!
EASY, BOUNCER. THAT WON'T MAKE YOU FEEL ANY BETTER.
HOW DO YOU KNOW? I TAKE JOY IN LOTS OF THINGS.
I HAVE SEEN SUCH BEHAVIOR IN YOUNG BOXERS. THEY MUST LEARN THEIR LESSONS THE HARD WAY.
BY GETTING HIT WITH SOMETHING HEAVY? LIKE A GOLD SAFE? I HAVE ONE, YOU KNOW. IT'S VERY SHINY.
NOT QUITE.
YOU SEE, YOUNG BOXERS THINK EVERY BLOW HAS TO BE A HAYMAKER. THEY ALWAYS GO RIGHT FOR THE KNOCKOUT.
BUT EVENTUALLY, THEY FIND AN OPPONENT WHO TAKES EVERYTHING THEY CAN DISH OUT, AND MORE. ONCE THEY'VE PUNCHED THEMSELVES TO EXHAUSTION...
THEY GET TAKEN DOWN HARD.
JUST SO.
THEN WE'D BETTER HOPE THAT BLADES LEARNS HIS LESSON...

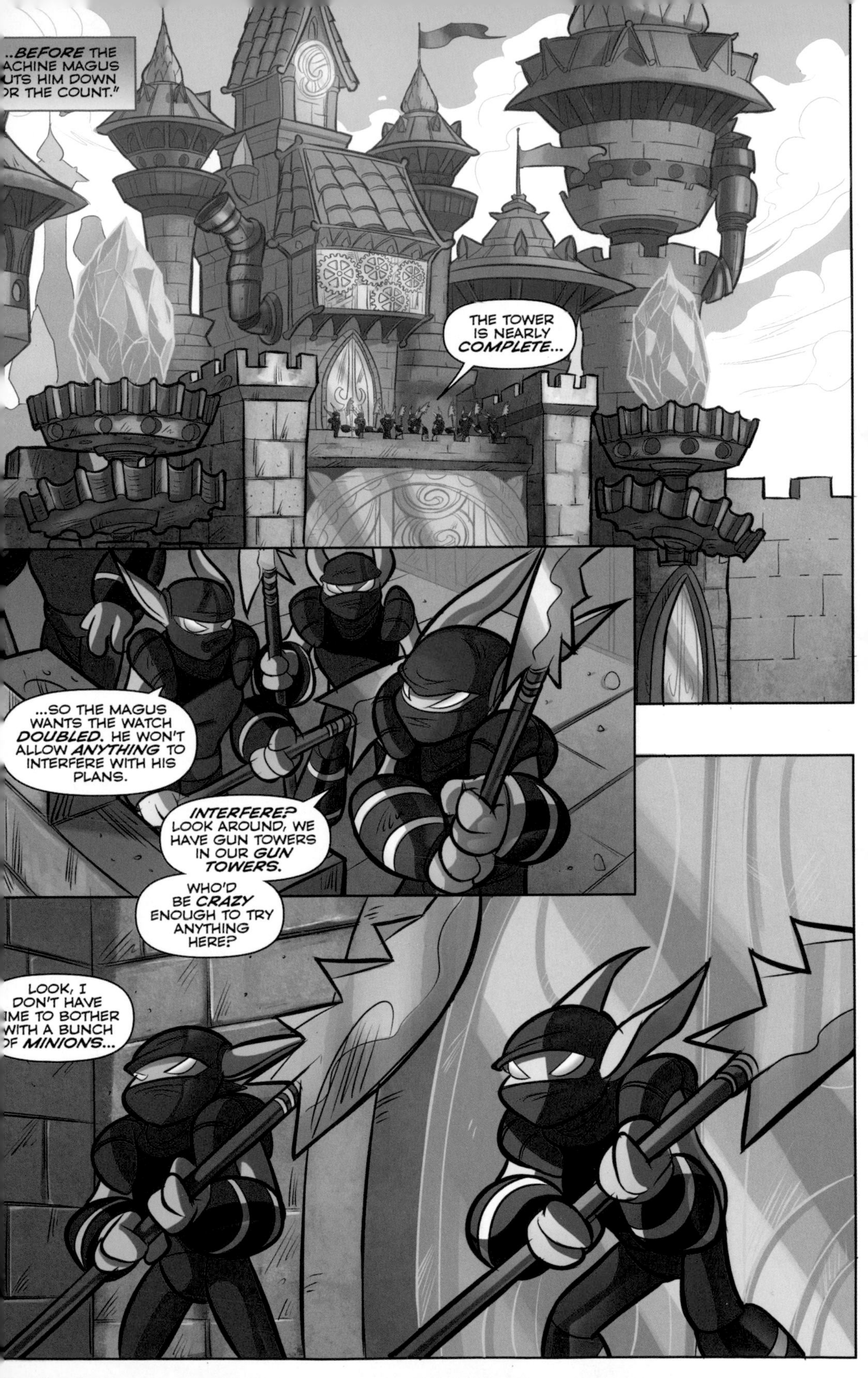

...BEFORE THE ACHINE MAGUS UTS HIM DOWN OR THE COUNT."
THE TOWER IS NEARLY COMPLETE...
...SO THE MAGUS WANTS THE WATCH DOUBLED. HE WON'T ALLOW ANYTHING TO INTERFERE WITH HIS PLANS.
INTERFERE? LOOK AROUND, WE HAVE GUN TOWERS IN OUR GUN TOWERS.
WHO'D BE CRAZY ENOUGH TO TRY ANYTHING HERE?
LOOK, I DON'T HAVE IME TO BOTHER WITH A BUNCH OF MINIONS...

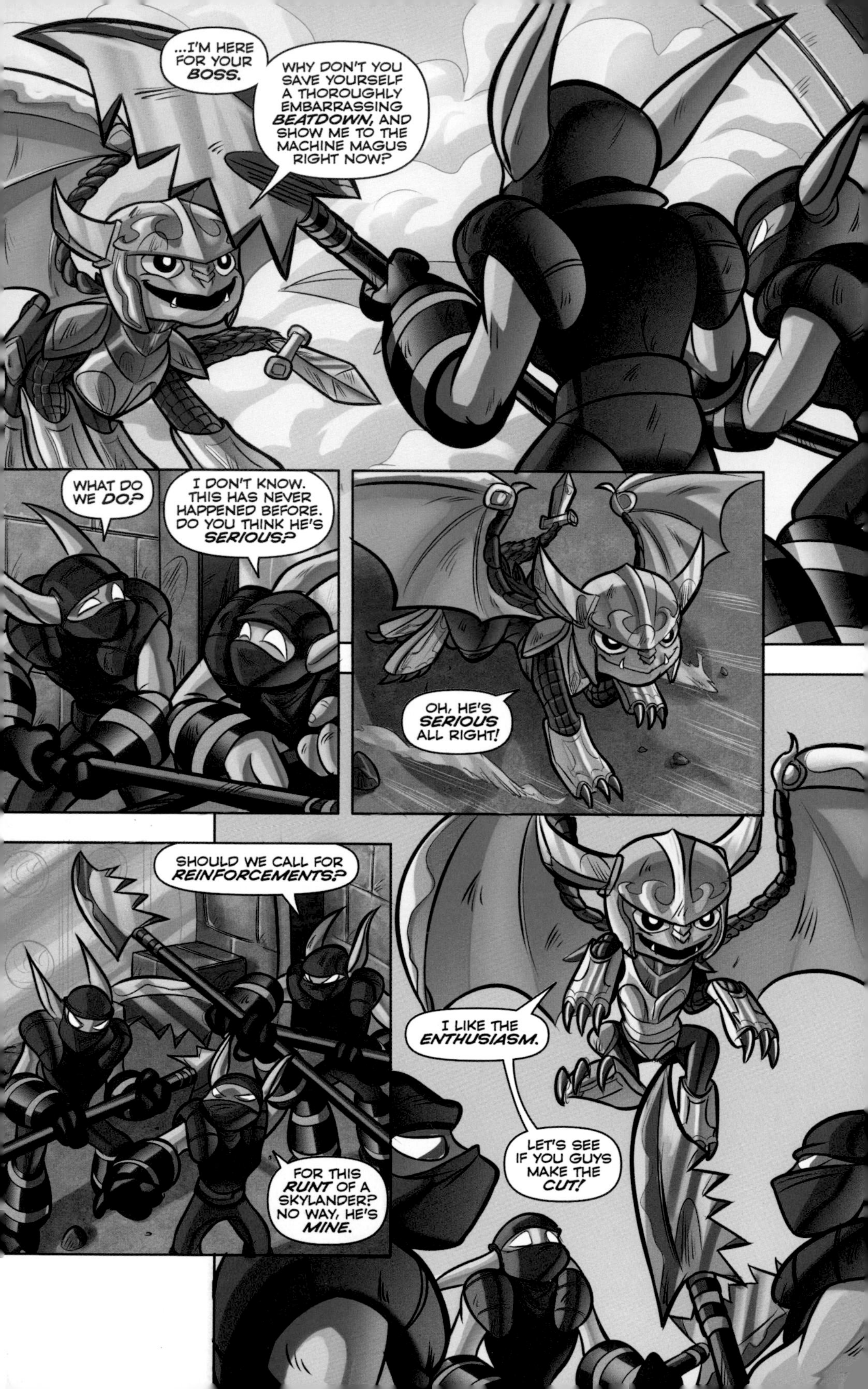
...I'M HERE FOR YOUR *BOSS*.
WHY DON'T YOU SAVE YOURSELF A THOROUGHLY EMBARRASSING *BEATDOWN*, AND SHOW ME TO THE MACHINE MAGUS RIGHT NOW?
WHAT DO WE *DO*?
I DON'T KNOW. THIS HAS NEVER HAPPENED BEFORE. DO YOU THINK HE'S *SERIOUS*?
OH, HE'S *SERIOUS* ALL RIGHT!
SHOULD WE CALL FOR *REINFORCEMENTS*?
FOR THIS *RUNT* OF A SKYLANDER? NO WAY, HE'S *MINE*.
I LIKE THE *ENTHUSIASM*.
LET'S SEE IF YOU GUYS MAKE THE *CUT*!

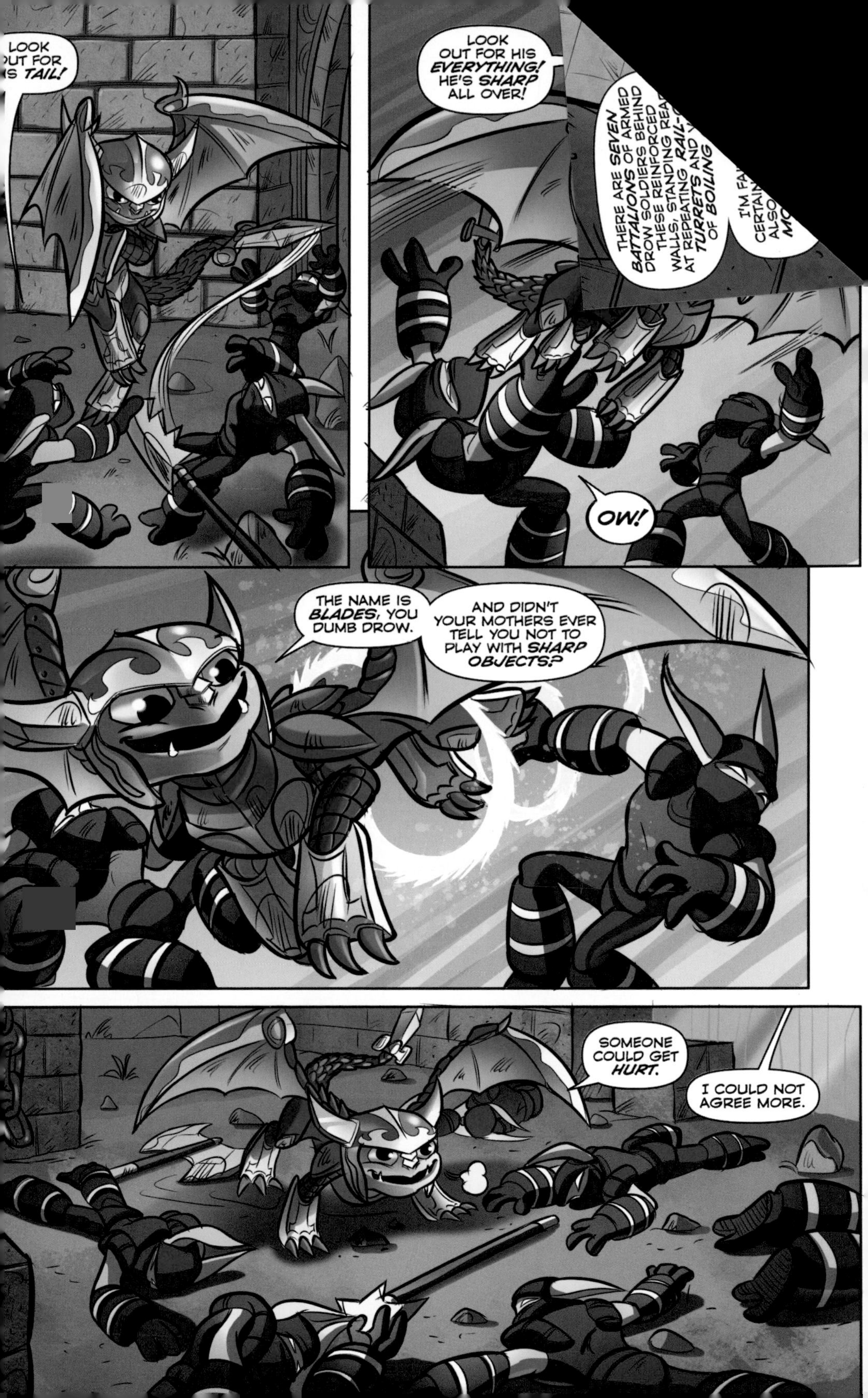

LOOK OUT FOR S TAIL!
LOOK OUT FOR HIS EVERYTHING! HE'S SHARP ALL OVER!
OW!
THE NAME IS BLADES, YOU DUMB DROW.
AND DIDN'T YOUR MOTHERS EVER TELL YOU NOT TO PLAY WITH SHARP OBJECTS?
SOMEONE COULD GET HURT.
I COULD NOT AGREE MORE.

...BY ...GUN ...ATS ...OIL.

...RLY ...THERE'S A *METAL-INGER* TANK BACK THERE SOMEPLACE.

DID YOU REALLY THINK YOU WERE GOING TO TAKE THE STRONGHOLD OF THE *MACHINE MAGUS* ALL BY YOURSELF?

WELL, SURE, IT SOUNDS CRAZY WHEN YOU SAY IT LIKE *THAT*.

STILL *BRASH* EVEN IN THE FACE OF OVERWHELMING ODDS AND CERTAIN DEFEAT.

YOU'RE A *LEGEND* IN YOUR OWN MIND, SKYLANDER.

THANKS!

IT *WASN'T* A COMPLIMENT!

PERHAPS A *TEAM* OF SKYLANDERS MIGHT HAVE HAD A CHANCE AGAINST ME *BEFORE* MY *OMNI-DIS-RUPTOR* WAS FULLY OPERATIONAL...

...BUT NOW AN ENTIRE *ARMY* WON'T BE ABLE TO STOP ME!

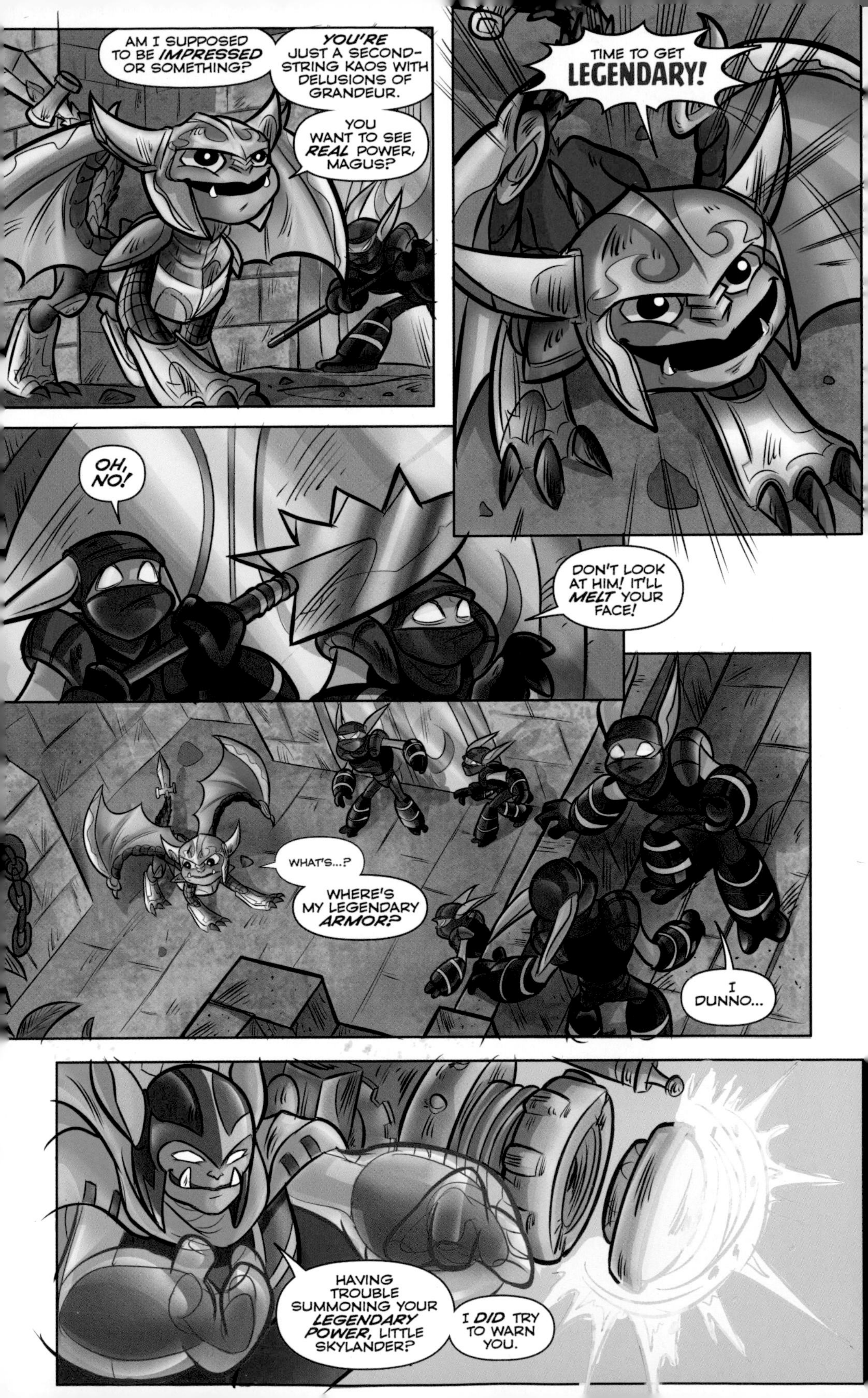
AM I SUPPOSED TO BE *IMPRESSED* OR SOMETHING?
YOU'RE JUST A SECOND-STRING KAOS WITH DELUSIONS OF GRANDEUR.
YOU WANT TO SEE *REAL* POWER, MAGUS?
TIME TO GET LEGENDARY!
OH, NO!
DON'T LOOK AT HIM! IT'LL *MELT* YOUR FACE!
WHAT'S...?
WHERE'S MY LEGENDARY *ARMOR?*
I DUNNO...
HAVING TROUBLE SUMMONING YOUR *LEGENDARY POWER,* LITTLE SKYLANDER?
I *DID* TRY TO WARN YOU.

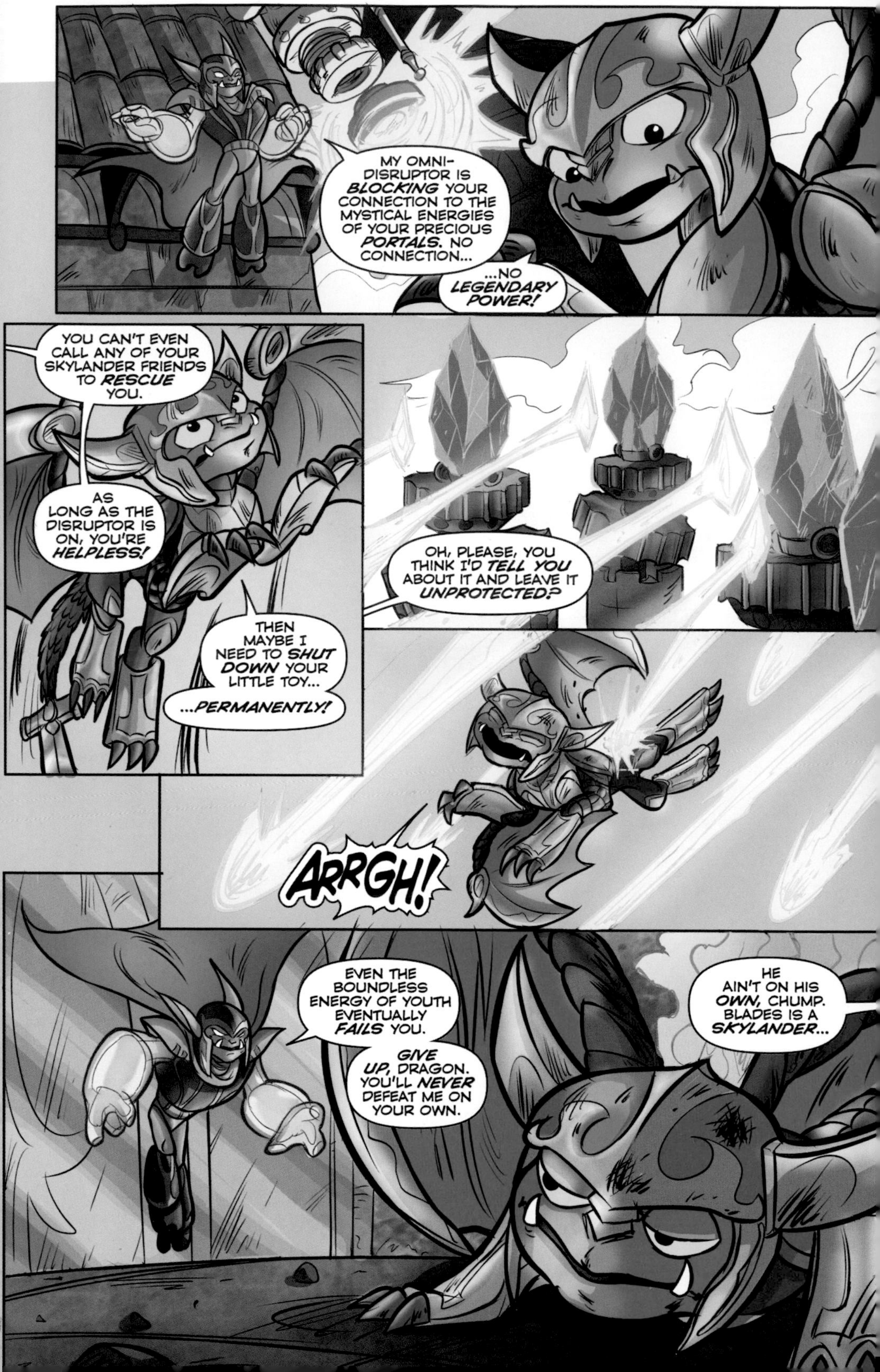
MY OMNI-DISRUPTOR IS BLOCKING YOUR CONNECTION TO THE MYSTICAL ENERGIES OF YOUR PRECIOUS PORTALS. NO CONNECTION...
...NO LEGENDARY POWER!
YOU CAN'T EVEN CALL ANY OF YOUR SKYLANDER FRIENDS TO RESCUE YOU.
AS LONG AS THE DISRUPTOR IS ON, YOU'RE HELPLESS!
THEN MAYBE I NEED TO SHUT DOWN YOUR LITTLE TOY...
...PERMANENTLY!
OH, PLEASE, YOU THINK I'D TELL YOU ABOUT IT AND LEAVE IT UNPROTECTED?
ARRGH!
EVEN THE BOUNDLESS ENERGY OF YOUTH EVENTUALLY FAILS YOU.
GIVE UP, DRAGON. YOU'LL NEVER DEFEAT ME ON YOUR OWN.
HE AIN'T ON HIS OWN, CHUMP. BLADES IS A SKYLANDER...

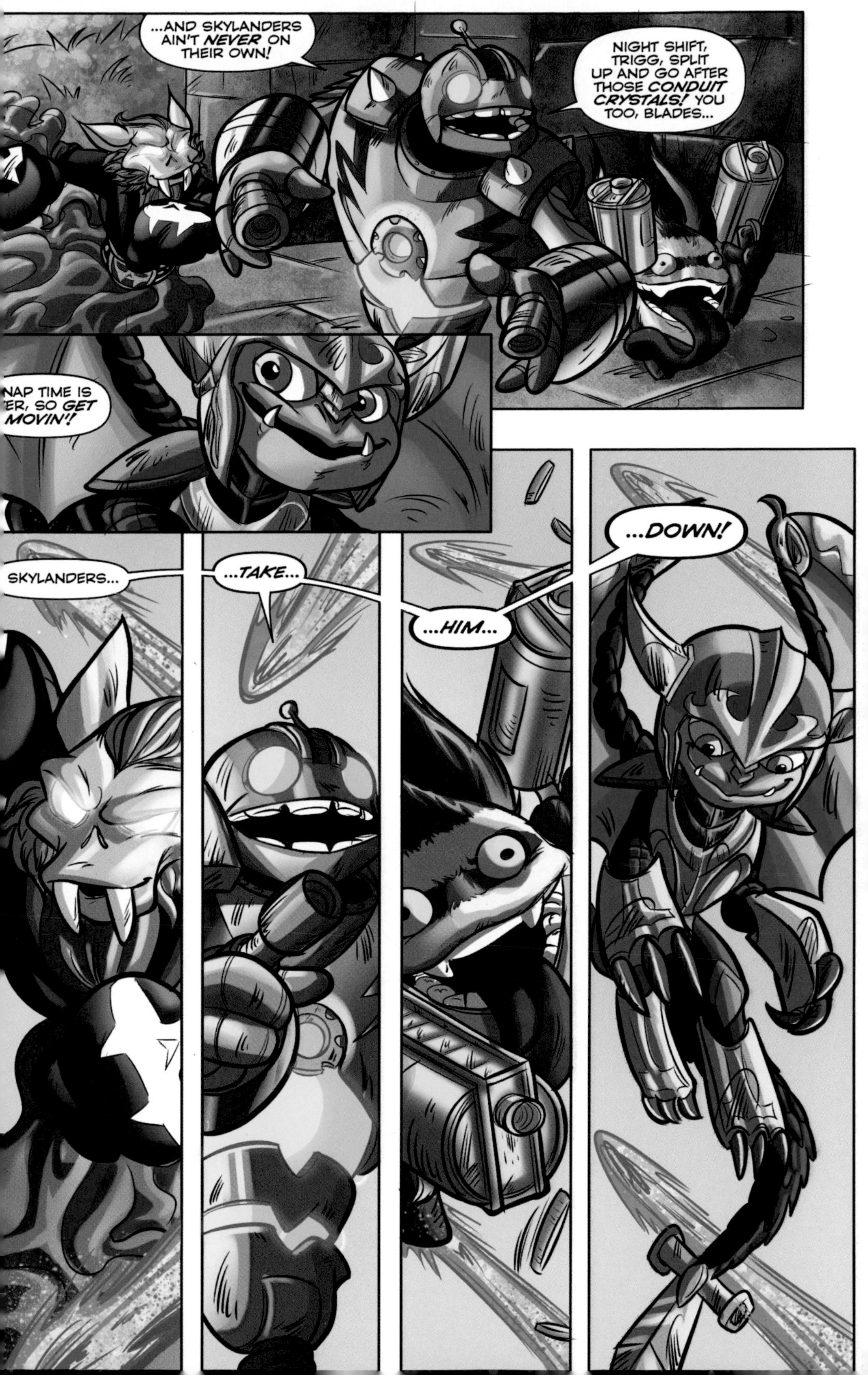
...AND SKYLANDERS AIN'T NEVER ON THEIR OWN!
NIGHT SHIFT, TRIGG, SPLIT UP AND GO AFTER THOSE CONDUIT CRYSTALS! YOU TOO, BLADES...
NAP TIME IS ER, SO GET MOVIN'!
SKYLANDERS...
...TAKE...
...HIM...
...DOWN!

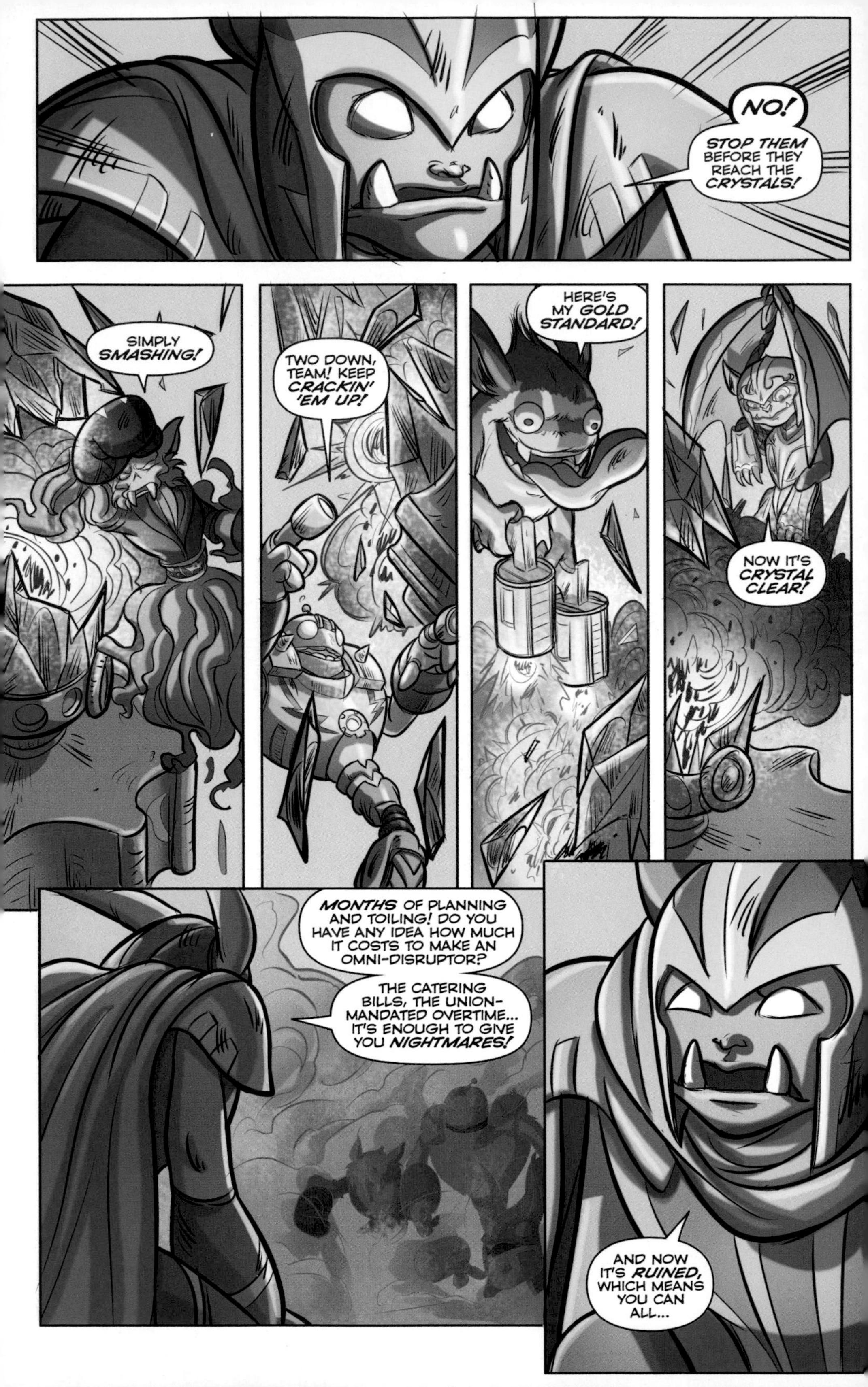
NO!
STOP THEM BEFORE THEY REACH THE CRYSTALS!
SIMPLY SMASHING!
TWO DOWN, TEAM! KEEP CRACKIN' 'EM UP!
HERE'S MY GOLD STANDARD!
NOW IT'S CRYSTAL CLEAR!
MONTHS OF PLANNING AND TOILING! DO YOU HAVE ANY IDEA HOW MUCH IT COSTS TO MAKE AN OMNI-DISRUPTOR?
THE CATERING BILLS, THE UNION-MANDATED OVERTIME... IT'S ENOUGH TO GIVE YOU NIGHTMARES!
AND NOW IT'S RUINED, WHICH MEANS YOU CAN ALL...

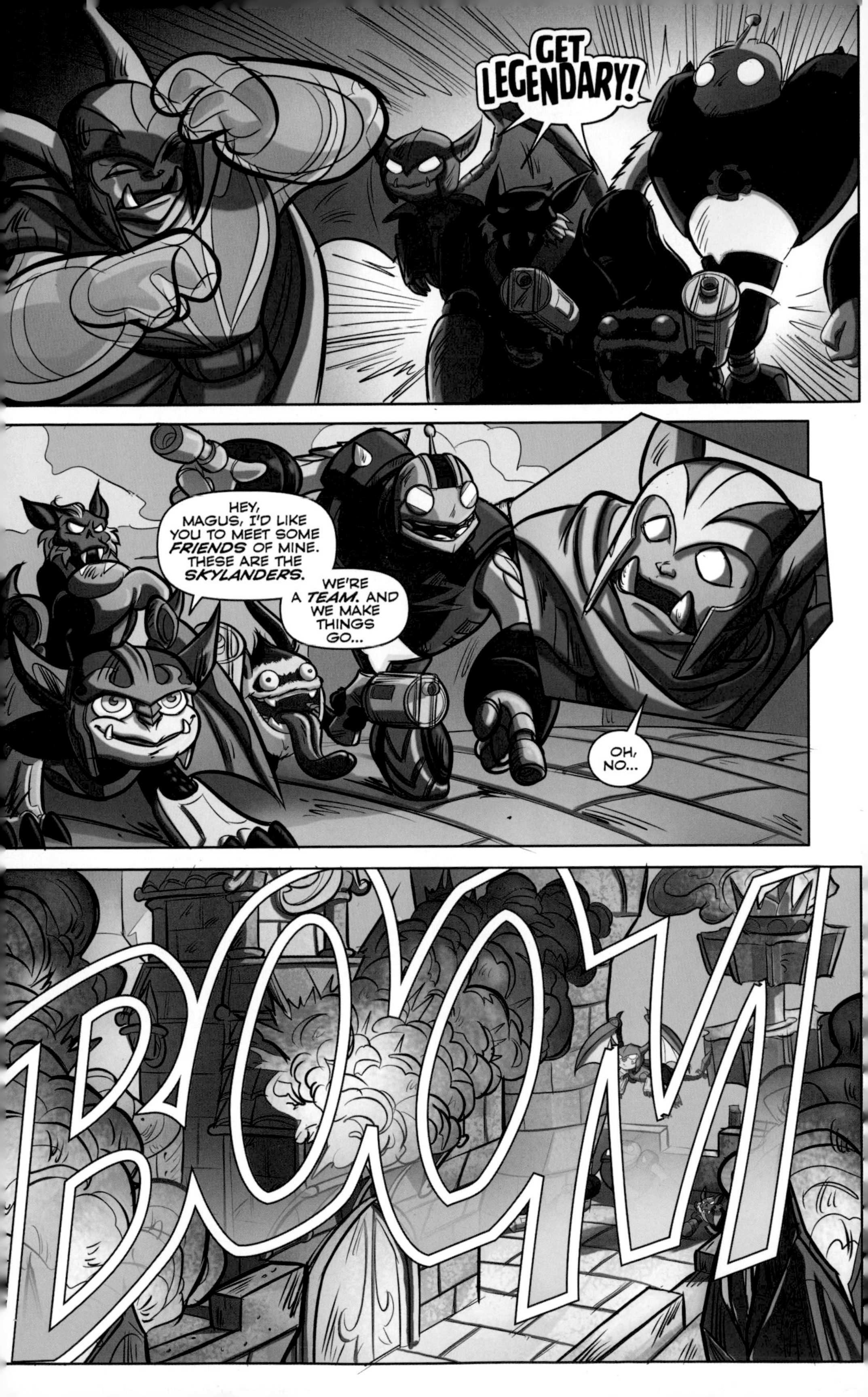
GET LEGENDARY!
HEY, MAGUS, I'D LIKE YOU TO MEET SOME *FRIENDS* OF MINE. THESE ARE THE *SKYLANDERS.*
WE'RE A *TEAM.* AND WE MAKE THINGS GO...
OH, NO...
BOOM

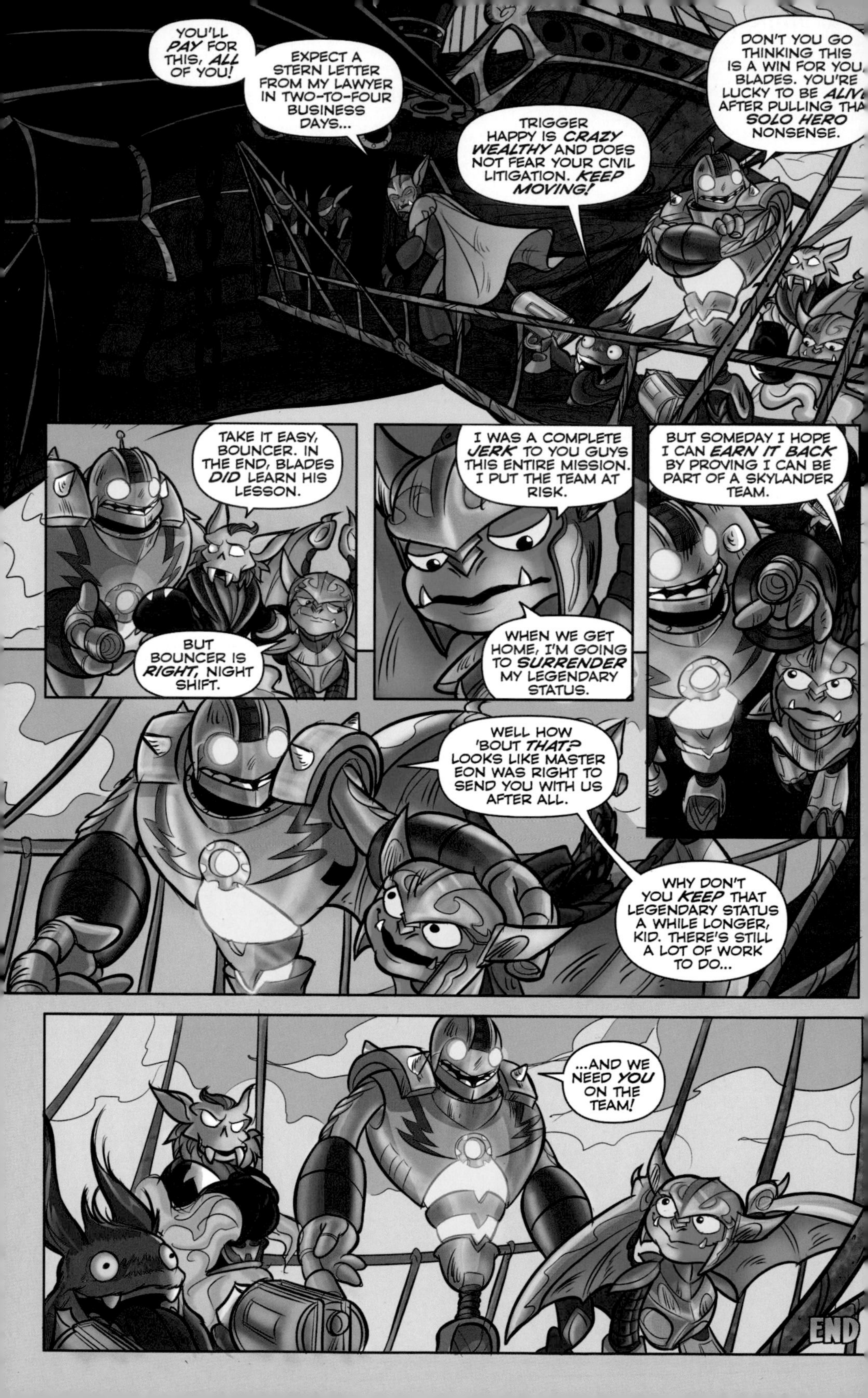
YOU'LL PAY FOR THIS, ALL OF YOU!
EXPECT A STERN LETTER FROM MY LAWYER IN TWO-TO-FOUR BUSINESS DAYS...
TRIGGER HAPPY IS CRAZY WEALTHY AND DOES NOT FEAR YOUR CIVIL LITIGATION. KEEP MOVING!
DON'T YOU GO THINKING THIS IS A WIN FOR YOU, BLADES. YOU'RE LUCKY TO BE ALIVE AFTER PULLING THAT SOLO HERO NONSENSE.
TAKE IT EASY, BOUNCER. IN THE END, BLADES DID LEARN HIS LESSON.
BUT BOUNCER IS RIGHT, NIGHT SHIFT.
I WAS A COMPLETE JERK TO YOU GUYS THIS ENTIRE MISSION. I PUT THE TEAM AT RISK.
WHEN WE GET HOME, I'M GOING TO SURRENDER MY LEGENDARY STATUS.
BUT SOMEDAY I HOPE I CAN EARN IT BACK BY PROVING I CAN BE PART OF A SKYLANDER TEAM.
WELL HOW 'BOUT THAT? LOOKS LIKE MASTER EON WAS RIGHT TO SEND YOU WITH US AFTER ALL.
WHY DON'T YOU KEEP THAT LEGENDARY STATUS A WHILE LONGER, KID. THERE'S STILL A LOT OF WORK TO DO...
...AND WE NEED YOU ON THE TEAM!
END

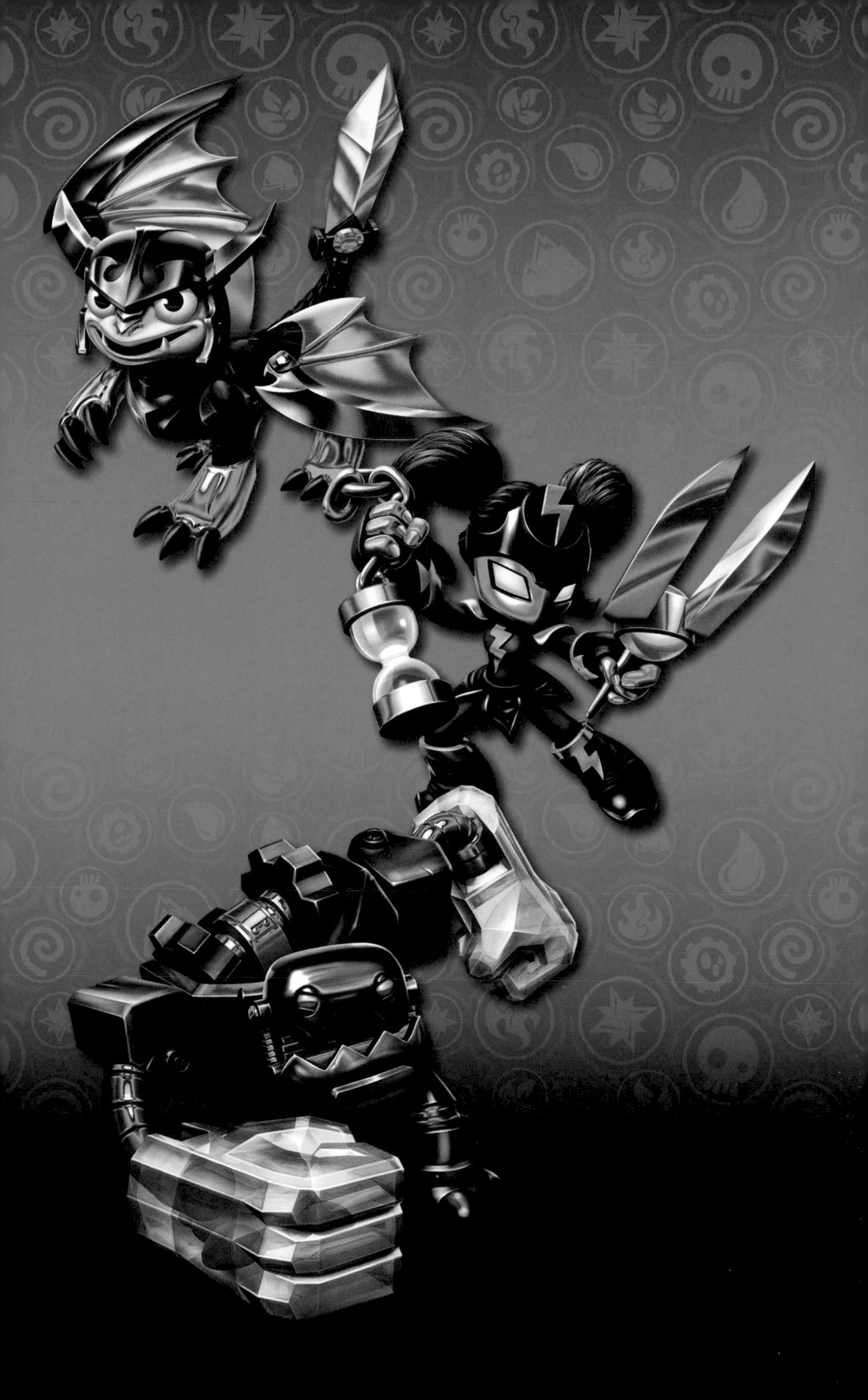

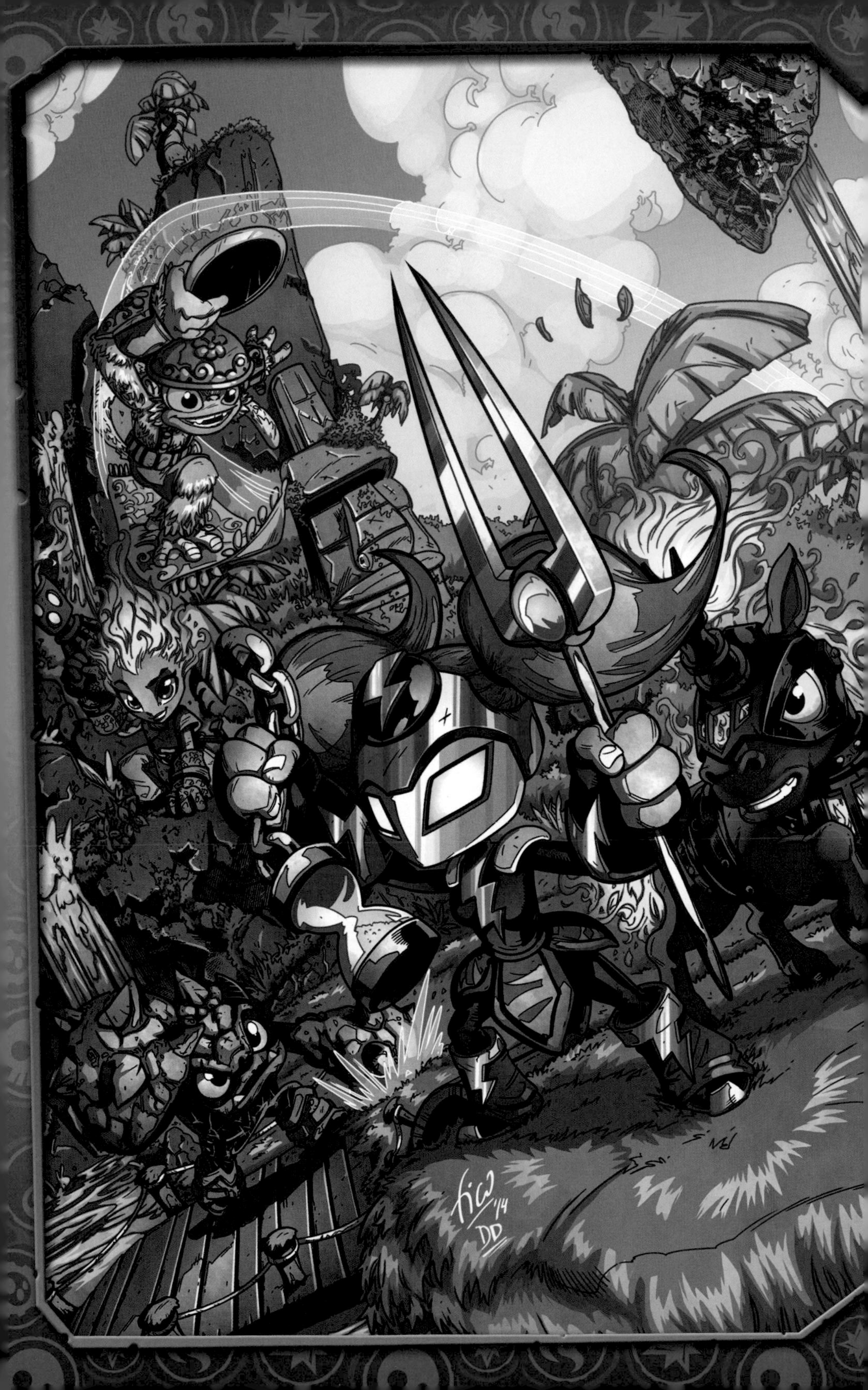

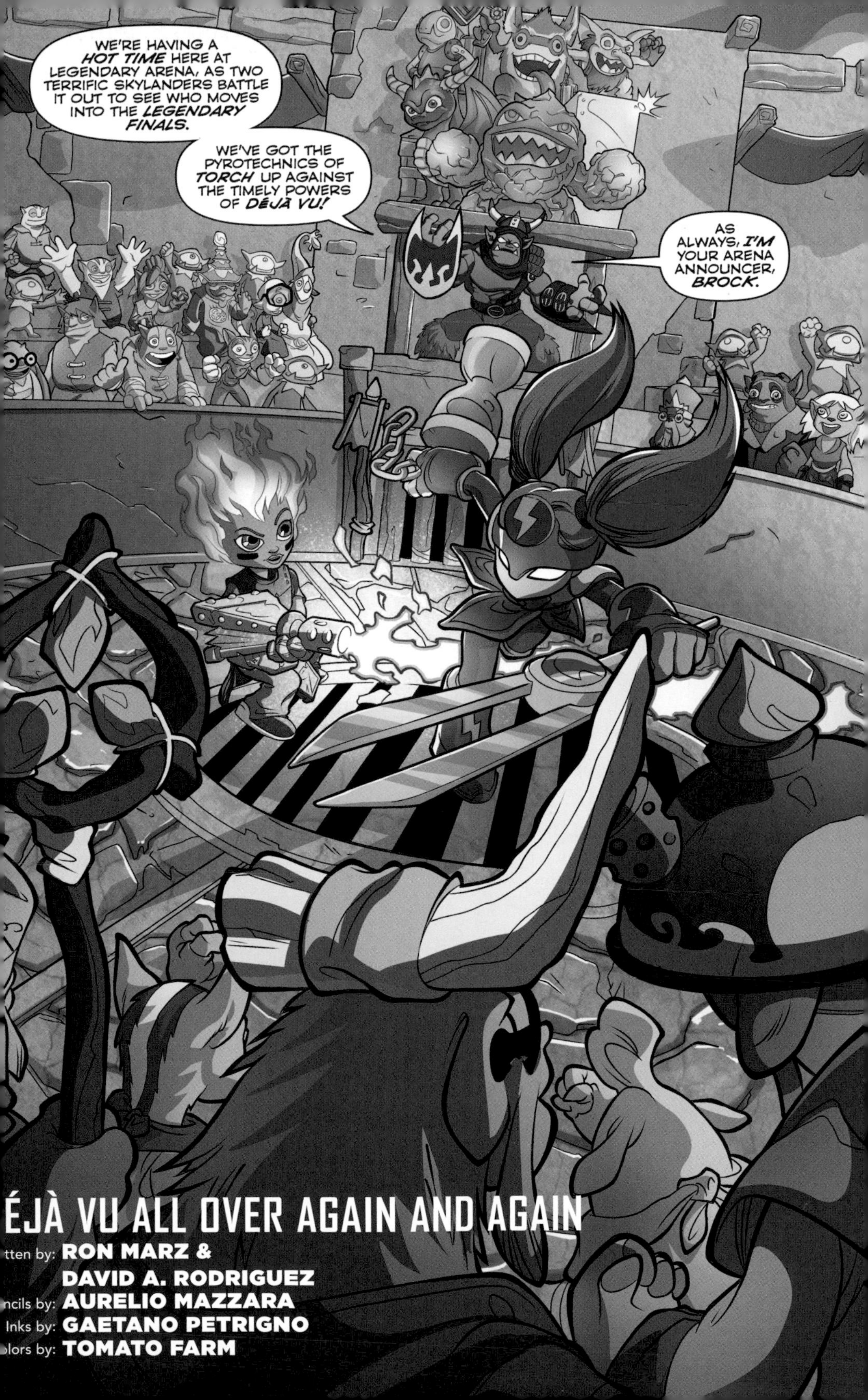
WE'RE HAVING A HOT TIME HERE AT LEGENDARY ARENA, AS TWO TERRIFIC SKYLANDERS BATTLE IT OUT TO SEE WHO MOVES INTO THE LEGENDARY FINALS.
WE'VE GOT THE PYROTECHNICS OF TORCH UP AGAINST THE TIMELY POWERS OF DÉJÀ VU!
AS ALWAYS, I'M YOUR ARENA ANNOUNCER, BROCK.
ÉJÀ VU ALL OVER AGAIN AND AGAIN
tten by: RON MARZ &
DAVID A. RODRIGUEZ
ncils by: AURELIO MAZZARA
Inks by: GAETANO PETRIGNO
olors by: TOMATO FARM

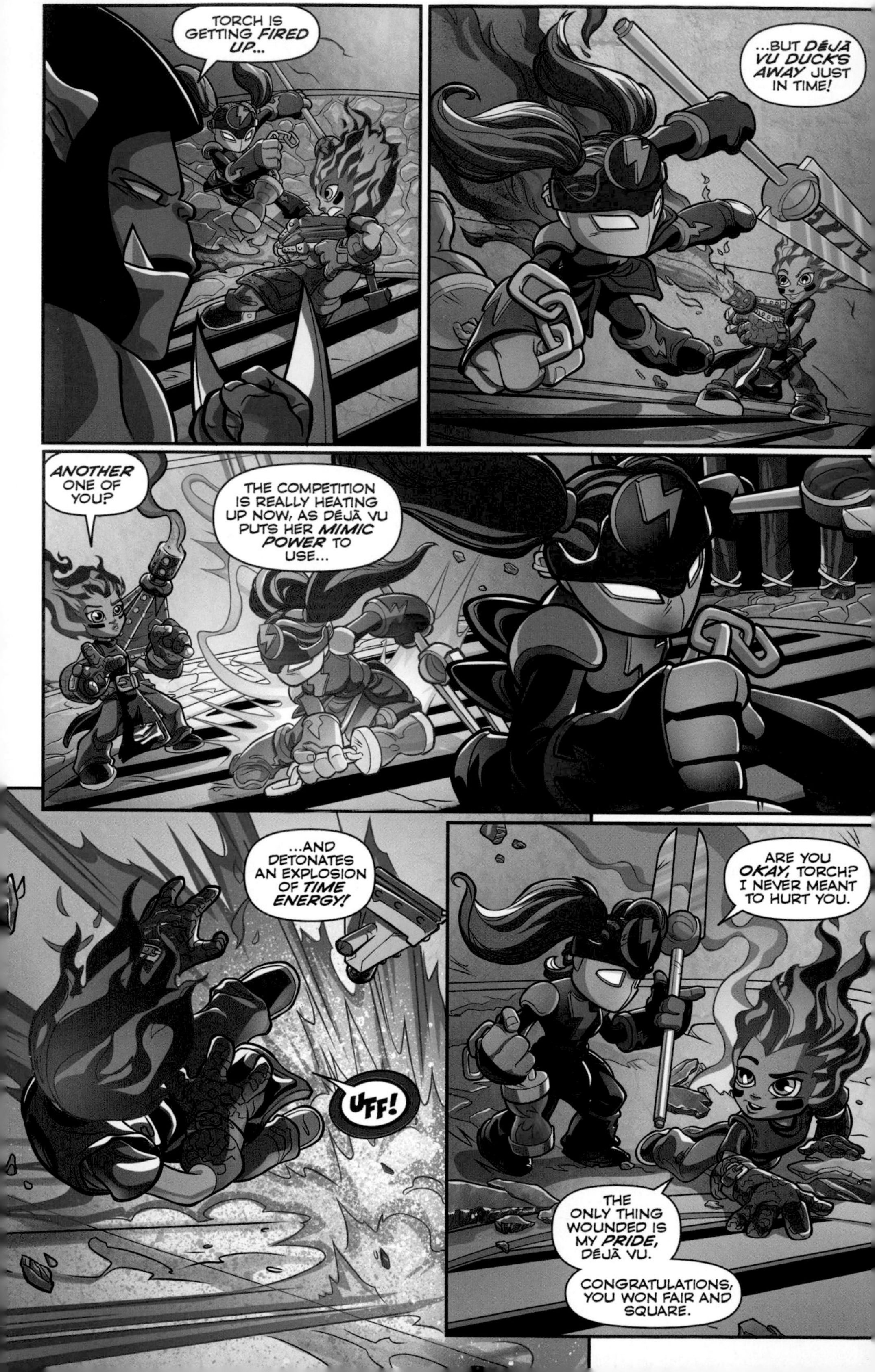
TORCH IS GETTING *FIRED UP*...
...BUT *DÉJÀ VU DUCKS AWAY* JUST IN TIME!
ANOTHER ONE OF YOU?
THE COMPETITION IS REALLY HEATING UP NOW, AS DÉJÀ VU PUTS HER *MIMIC POWER* TO USE...
...AND DETONATES AN EXPLOSION OF *TIME ENERGY!*
UFF!
ARE YOU *OKAY,* TORCH? I NEVER MEANT TO HURT YOU.
THE ONLY THING WOUNDED IS MY *PRIDE,* DÉJÀ VU.
CONGRATULATIONS, YOU WON FAIR AND SQUARE.

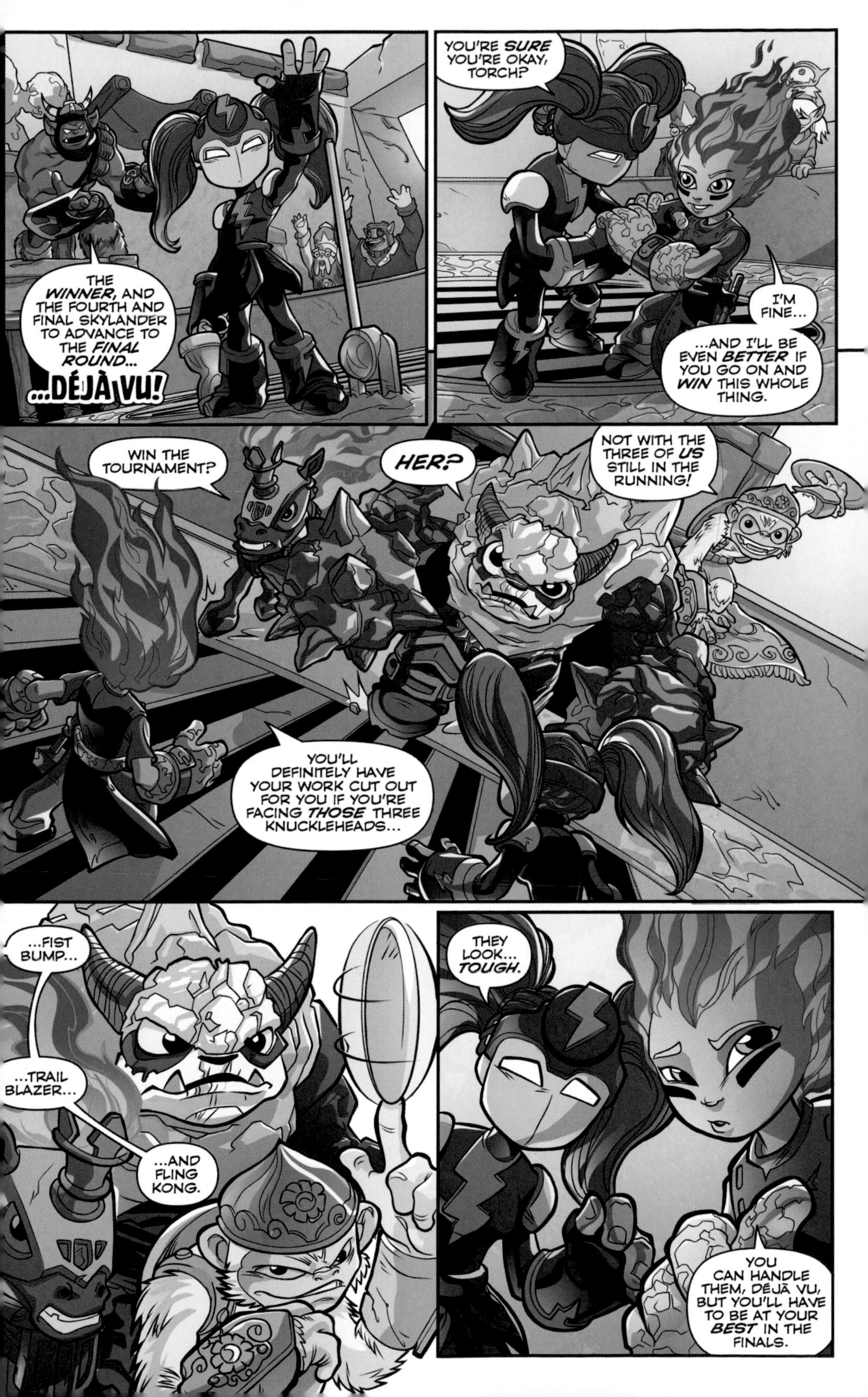
THE WINNER, AND THE FOURTH AND FINAL SKYLANDER TO ADVANCE TO THE FINAL ROUND...
...DÉJÀ VU!
YOU'RE SURE YOU'RE OKAY, TORCH?
I'M FINE...
...AND I'LL BE EVEN BETTER IF YOU GO ON AND WIN THIS WHOLE THING.
WIN THE TOURNAMENT?
HER?
NOT WITH THE THREE OF US STILL IN THE RUNNING!
YOU'LL DEFINITELY HAVE YOUR WORK CUT OUT FOR YOU IF YOU'RE FACING THOSE THREE KNUCKLEHEADS...
...FIST BUMP...
...TRAIL BLAZER...
...AND FLING KONG.
THEY LOOK... TOUGH.
YOU CAN HANDLE THEM, DÉJÀ VU, BUT YOU'LL HAVE TO BE AT YOUR BEST IN THE FINALS.

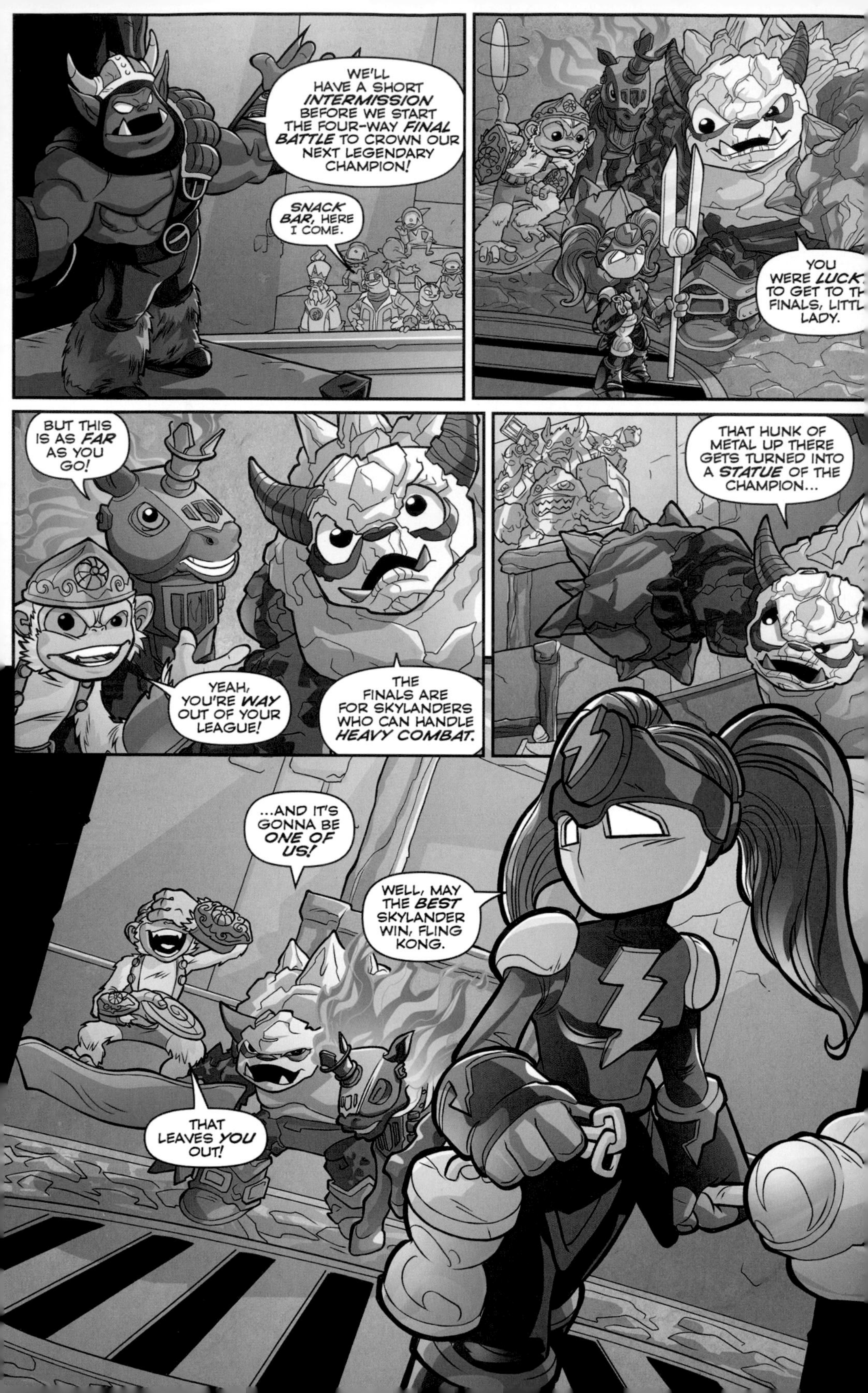
WE'LL HAVE A SHORT *INTERMISSION* BEFORE WE START THE FOUR-WAY *FINAL BATTLE* TO CROWN OUR NEXT LEGENDARY CHAMPION!
SNACK BAR, HERE I COME.
YOU WERE *LUCK*... TO GET TO TH... FINALS, LITTL... LADY.
BUT THIS IS AS *FAR* AS YOU GO!
YEAH, YOU'RE *WAY* OUT OF YOUR LEAGUE!
THE FINALS ARE FOR SKYLANDERS WHO CAN HANDLE *HEAVY COMBAT.*
THAT HUNK OF METAL UP THERE GETS TURNED INTO A *STATUE* OF THE CHAMPION...
...AND IT'S GONNA BE *ONE OF US!*
WELL, MAY THE *BEST* SKYLANDER WIN, FLING KONG.
THAT LEAVES *YOU* OUT!

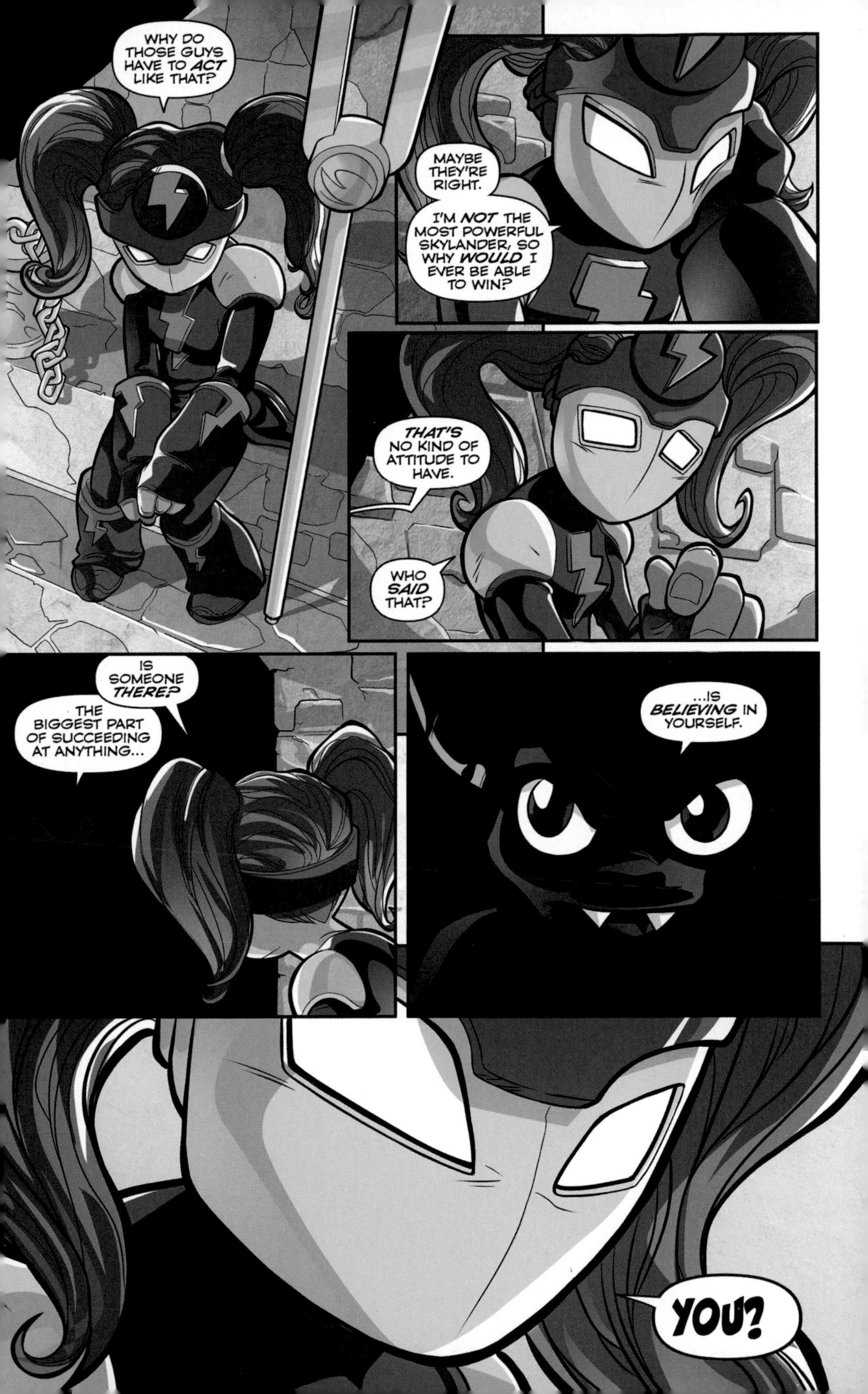
WHY DO THOSE GUYS HAVE TO *ACT* LIKE THAT?
MAYBE THEY'RE RIGHT.
I'M *NOT* THE MOST POWERFUL SKYLANDER, SO WHY *WOULD* I EVER BE ABLE TO WIN?
THAT'S NO KIND OF ATTITUDE TO HAVE.
WHO *SAID* THAT?
IS SOMEONE *THERE?*
THE BIGGEST PART OF SUCCEEDING AT ANYTHING...
...IS *BELIEVING* IN YOURSELF.
YOU?

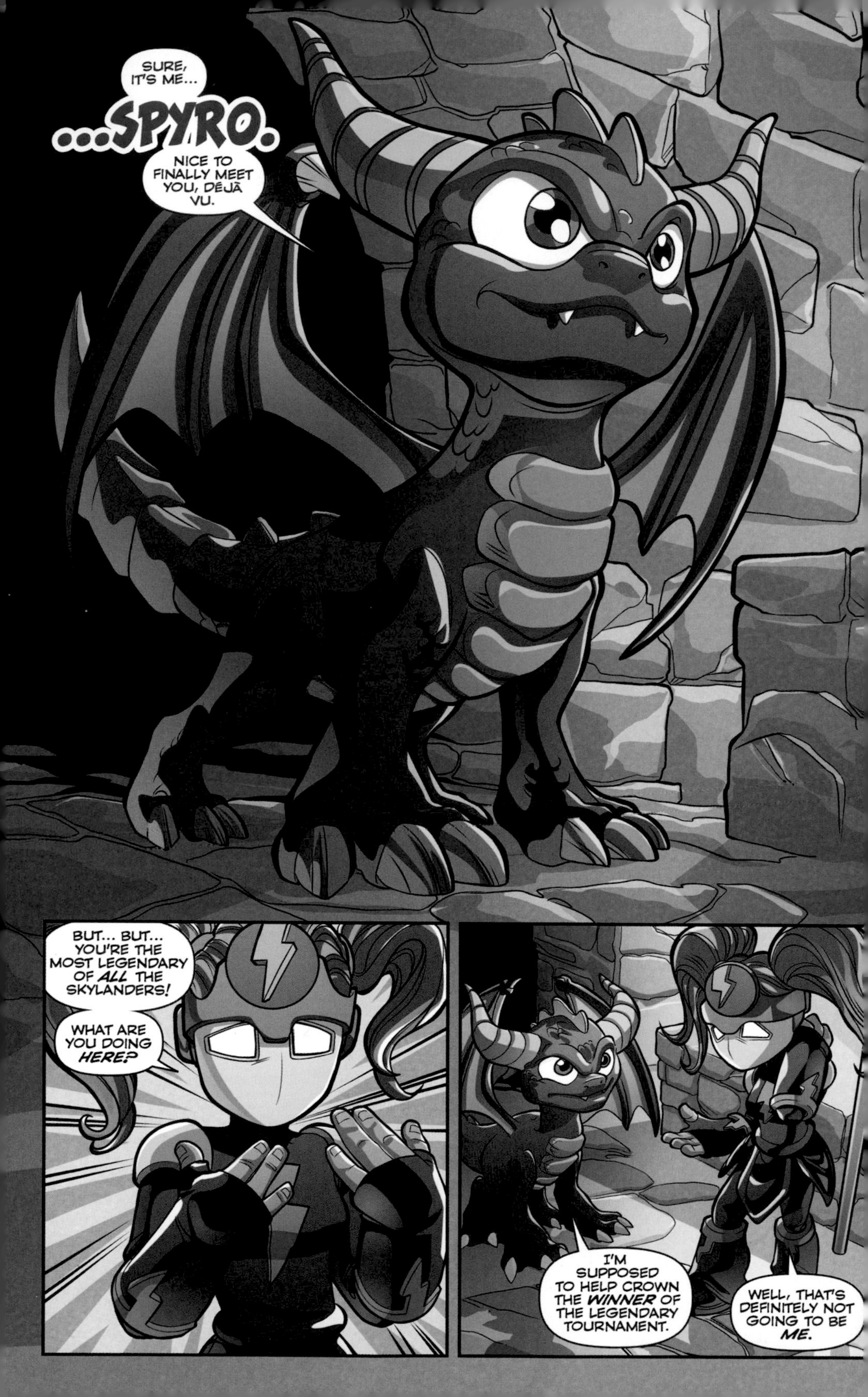
SURE, IT'S ME...
...SPYRO.
NICE TO FINALLY MEET YOU, DÉJÀ VU.
BUT... BUT... YOU'RE THE MOST LEGENDARY OF *ALL* THE SKYLANDERS!
WHAT ARE YOU DOING *HERE?*
I'M SUPPOSED TO HELP CROWN THE *WINNER* OF THE LEGENDARY TOURNAMENT.
WELL, THAT'S DEFINITELY NOT GOING TO BE *ME*.

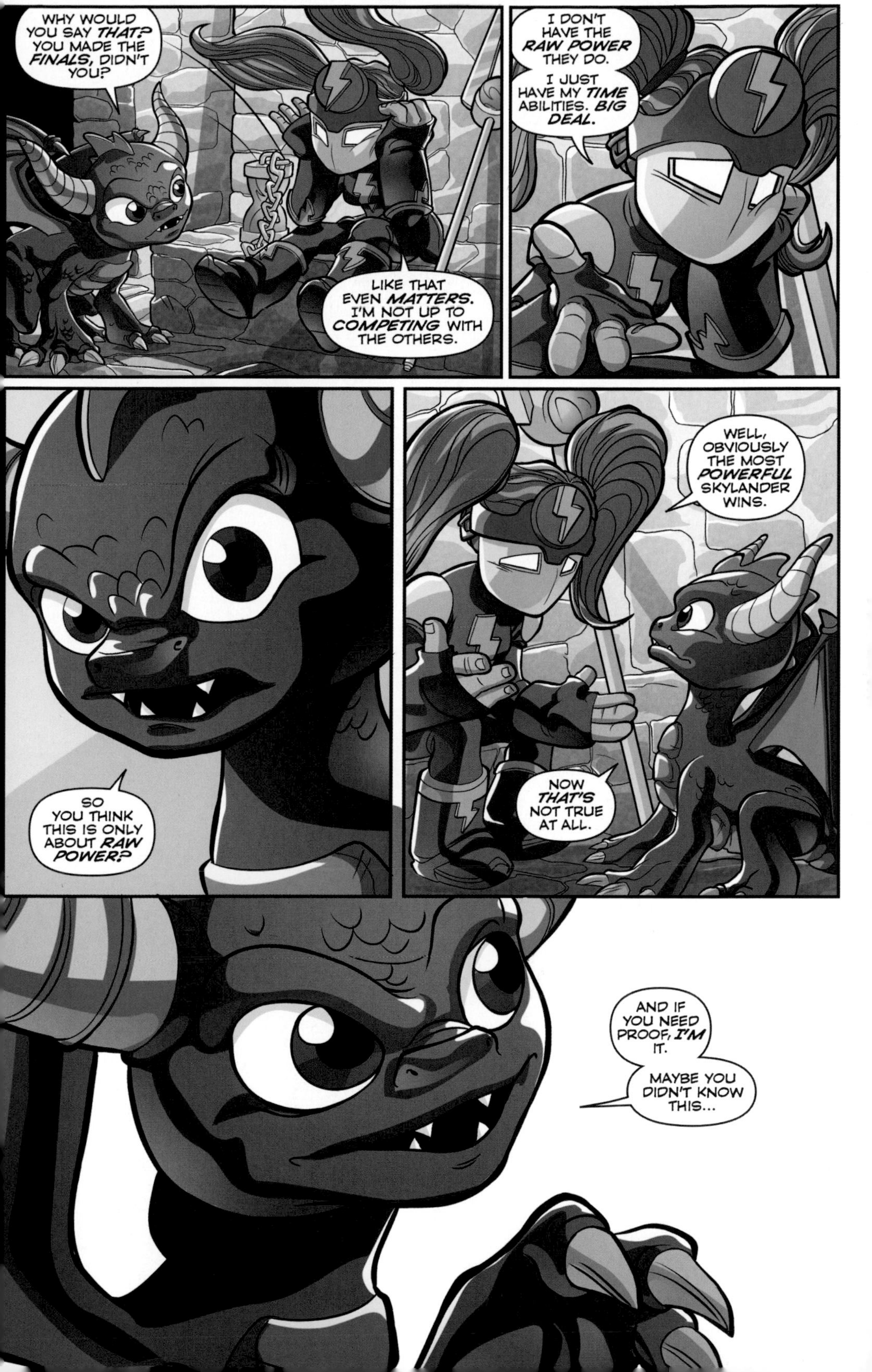
WHY WOULD YOU SAY *THAT?* YOU MADE THE *FINALS,* DIDN'T YOU?
LIKE THAT EVEN *MATTERS.* I'M NOT UP TO *COMPETING* WITH THE OTHERS.
I DON'T HAVE THE *RAW POWER* THEY DO.
I JUST HAVE MY *TIME* ABILITIES. *BIG DEAL.*
SO YOU THINK THIS IS ONLY ABOUT *RAW POWER?*
WELL, OBVIOUSLY THE MOST *POWERFUL* SKYLANDER WINS.
NOW *THAT'S* NOT TRUE AT ALL.
AND IF YOU NEED PROOF, *I'M* IT.
MAYBE YOU DIDN'T KNOW THIS...

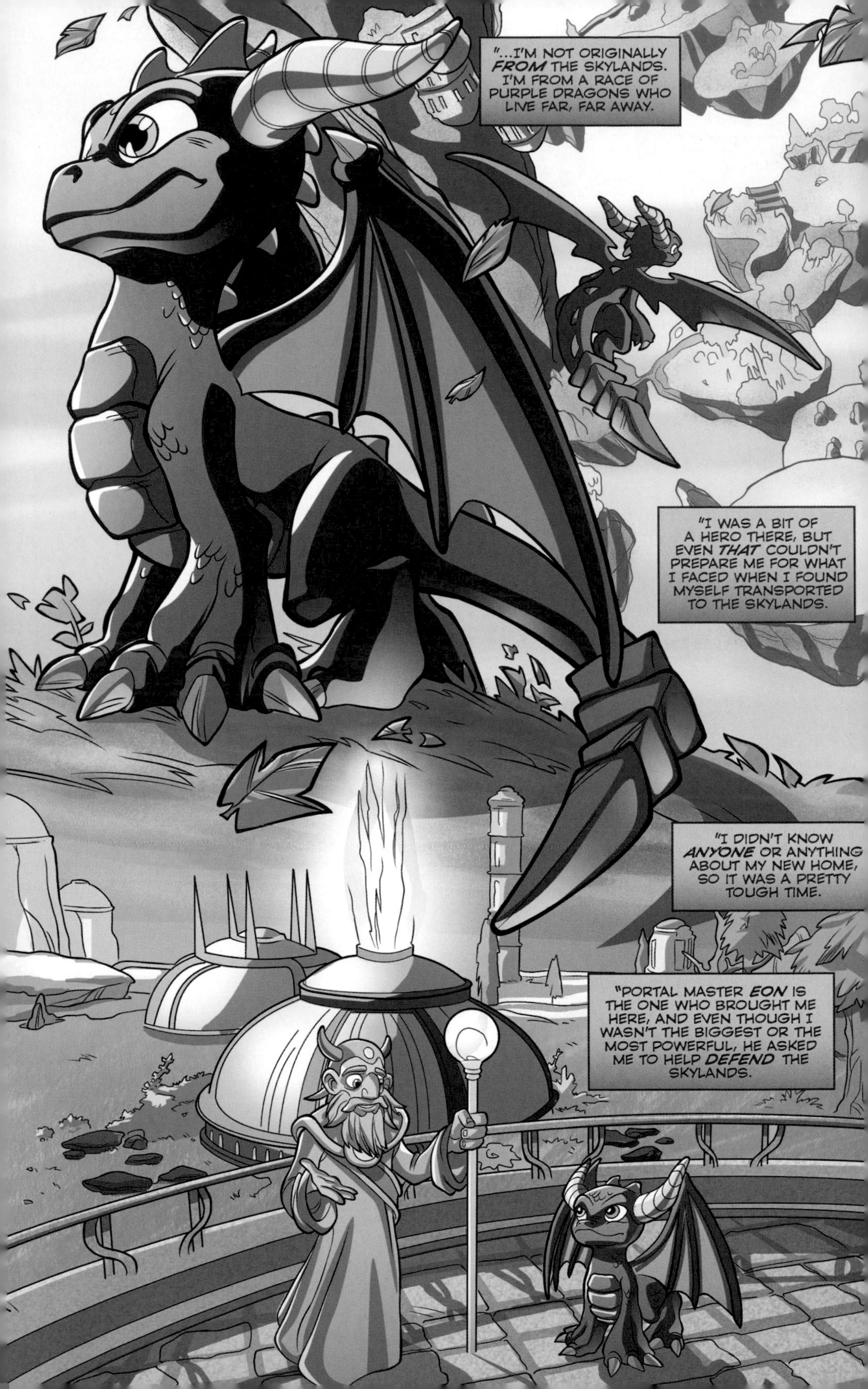
"...I'M NOT ORIGINALLY *FROM* THE SKYLANDS. I'M FROM A RACE OF PURPLE DRAGONS WHO LIVE FAR, FAR AWAY.
"I WAS A BIT OF A HERO THERE, BUT EVEN *THAT* COULDN'T PREPARE ME FOR WHAT I FACED WHEN I FOUND MYSELF TRANSPORTED TO THE SKYLANDS.
"I DIDN'T KNOW *ANYONE* OR ANYTHING ABOUT MY NEW HOME, SO IT WAS A PRETTY TOUGH TIME.
"PORTAL MASTER *EON* IS THE ONE WHO BROUGHT ME HERE, AND EVEN THOUGH I WASN'T THE BIGGEST OR THE MOST POWERFUL, HE ASKED ME TO HELP *DEFEND* THE SKYLANDS.

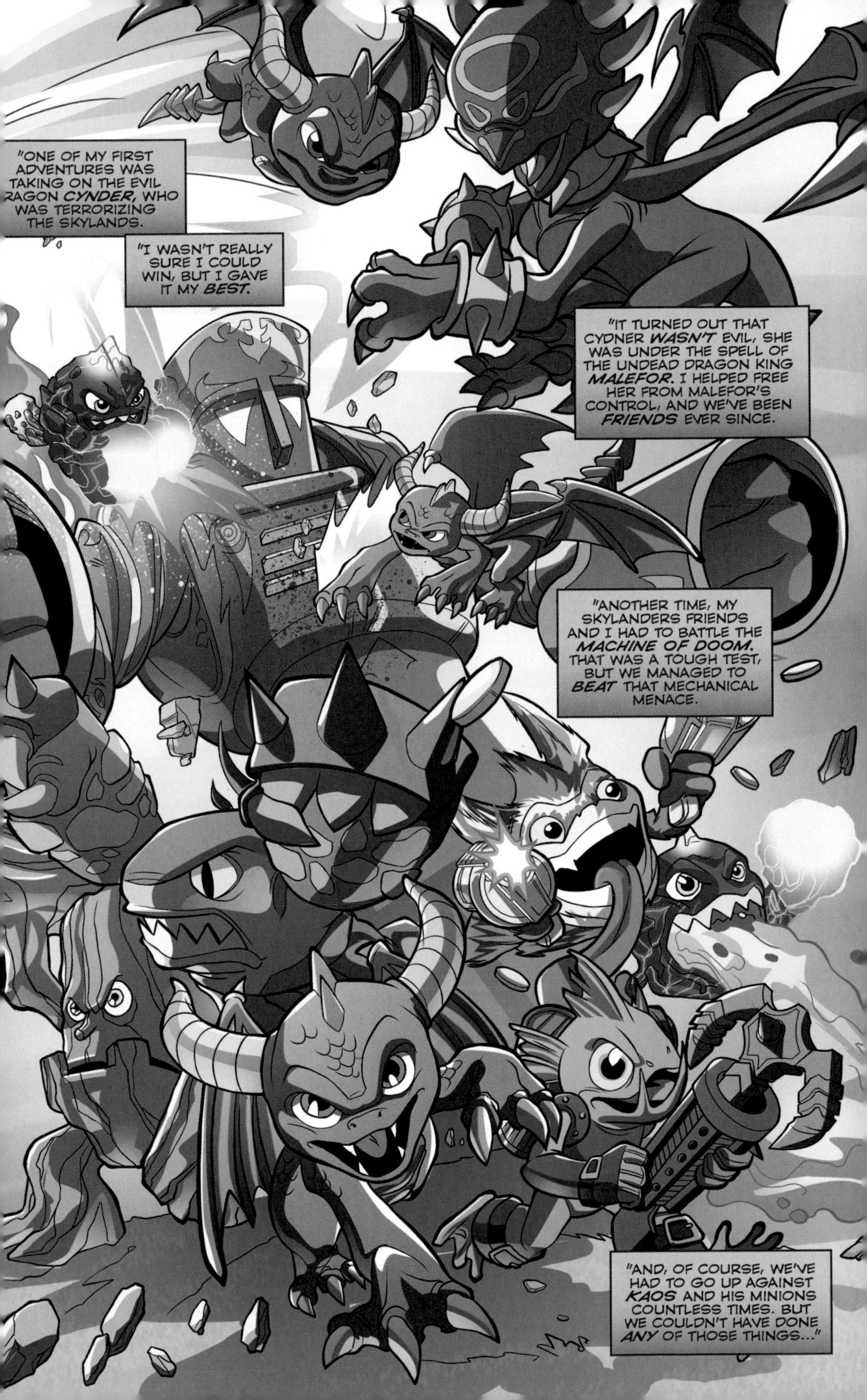
"ONE OF MY FIRST ADVENTURES WAS TAKING ON THE EVIL DRAGON CYNDER, WHO WAS TERRORIZING THE SKYLANDS.
"I WASN'T REALLY SURE I COULD WIN, BUT I GAVE IT MY BEST.
"IT TURNED OUT THAT CYDNER WASN'T EVIL, SHE WAS UNDER THE SPELL OF THE UNDEAD DRAGON KING MALEFOR. I HELPED FREE HER FROM MALEFOR'S CONTROL, AND WE'VE BEEN FRIENDS EVER SINCE.
"ANOTHER TIME, MY SKYLANDERS FRIENDS AND I HAD TO BATTLE THE MACHINE OF DOOM. THAT WAS A TOUGH TEST, BUT WE MANAGED TO BEAT THAT MECHANICAL MENACE.
"AND, OF COURSE, WE'VE HAD TO GO UP AGAINST KAOS AND HIS MINIONS COUNTLESS TIMES. BUT WE COULDN'T HAVE DONE ANY OF THOSE THINGS..."

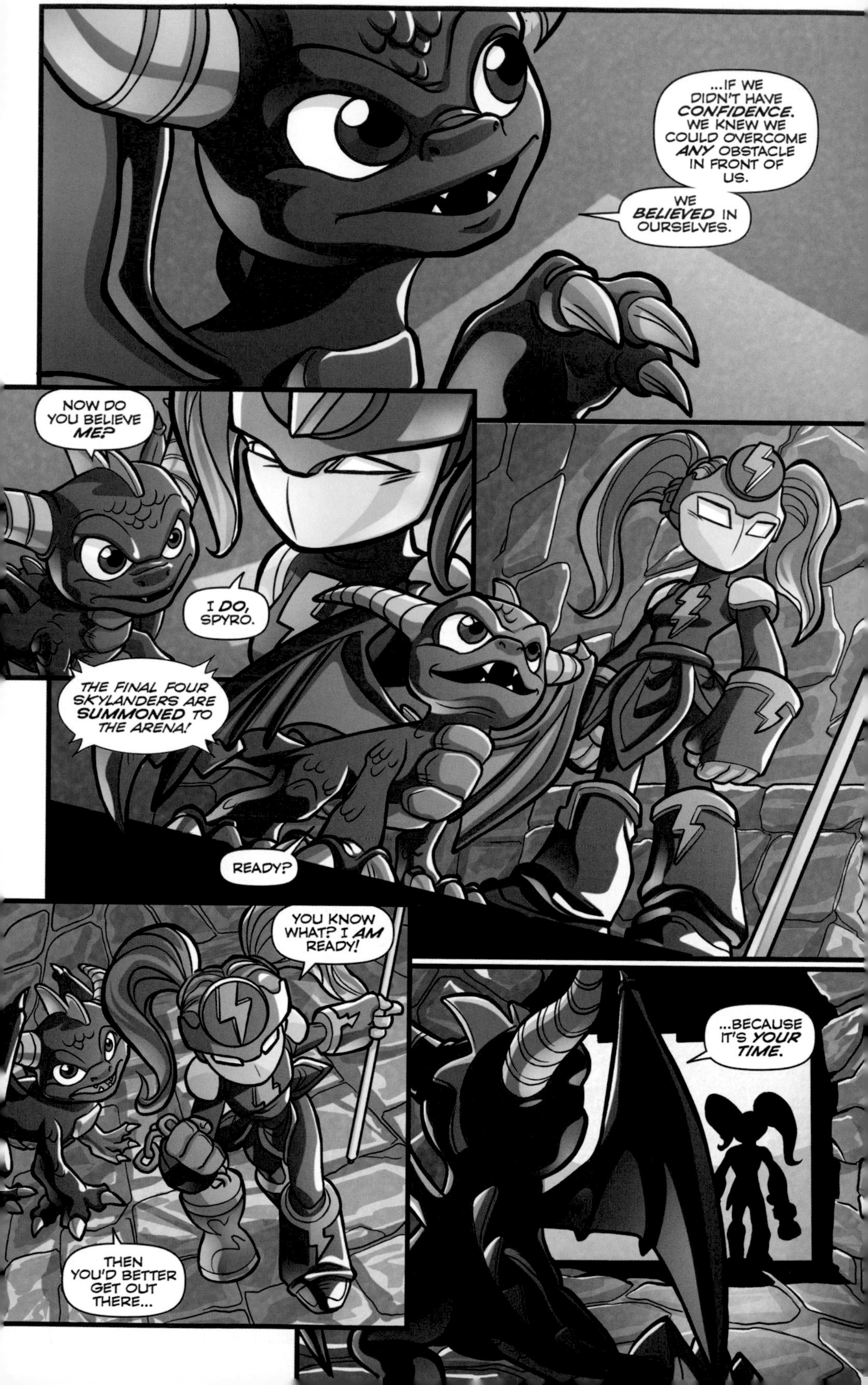
...IF WE DIDN'T HAVE CONFIDENCE. WE KNEW WE COULD OVERCOME ANY OBSTACLE IN FRONT OF US.
WE BELIEVED IN OURSELVES.
NOW DO YOU BELIEVE ME?
I DO, SPYRO.
THE FINAL FOUR SKYLANDERS ARE SUMMONED TO THE ARENA!
READY?
YOU KNOW WHAT? I AM READY!
THEN YOU'D BETTER GET OUT THERE...
...BECAUSE IT'S YOUR TIME.

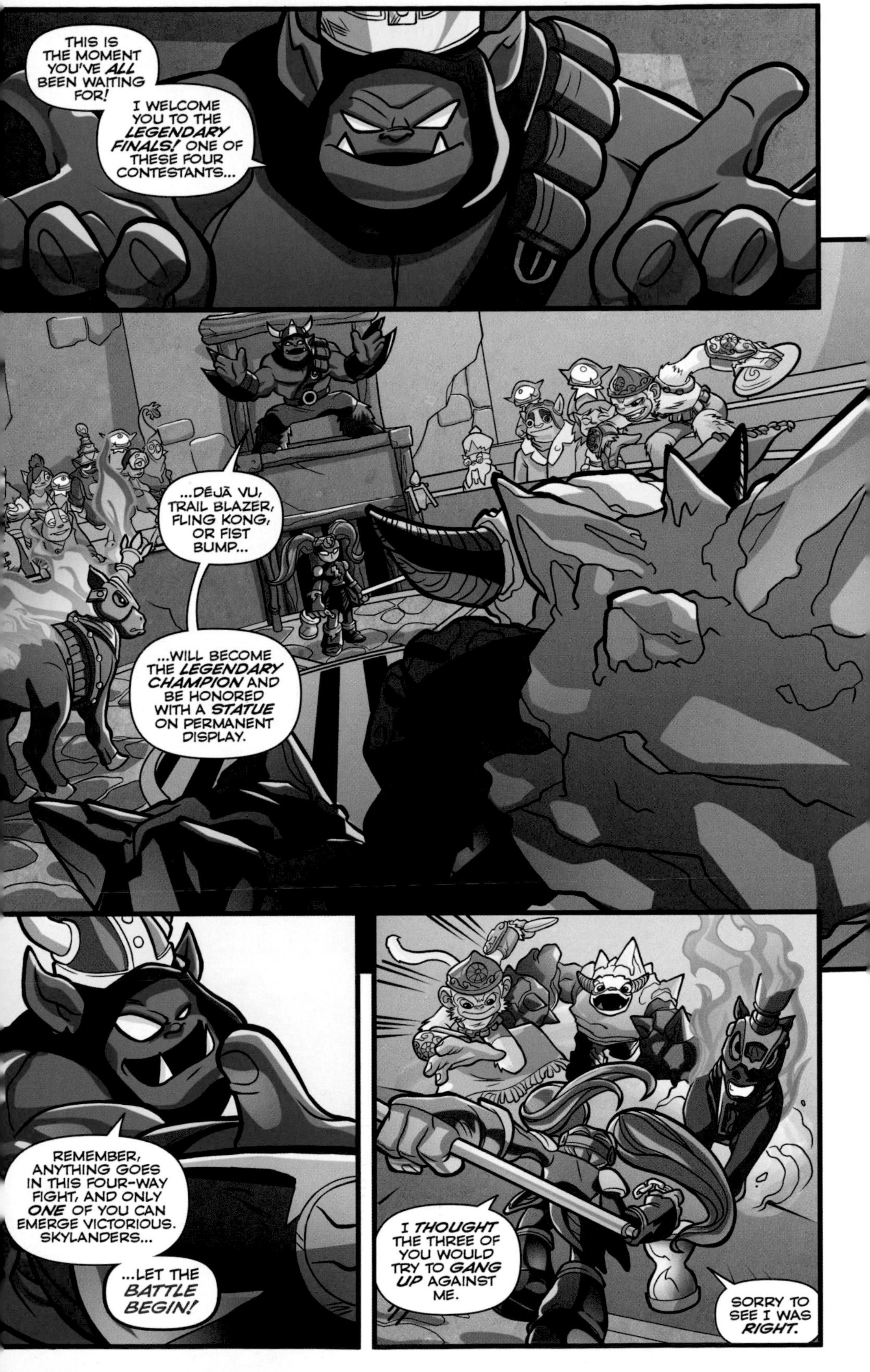
THIS IS THE MOMENT YOU'VE *ALL* BEEN WAITING FOR!
I WELCOME YOU TO THE ***LEGENDARY FINALS!*** ONE OF THESE FOUR CONTESTANTS...
...DÉJÀ VU, TRAIL BLAZER, FLING KONG, OR FIST BUMP...
...WILL BECOME THE ***LEGENDARY CHAMPION*** AND BE HONORED WITH A ***STATUE*** ON PERMANENT DISPLAY.
REMEMBER, ANYTHING GOES IN THIS FOUR-WAY FIGHT, AND ONLY ***ONE*** OF YOU CAN EMERGE VICTORIOUS. SKYLANDERS...
...LET THE ***BATTLE BEGIN!***
I ***THOUGHT*** THE THREE OF YOU WOULD TRY TO ***GANG UP*** AGAINST ME.
SORRY TO SEE I WAS ***RIGHT.***

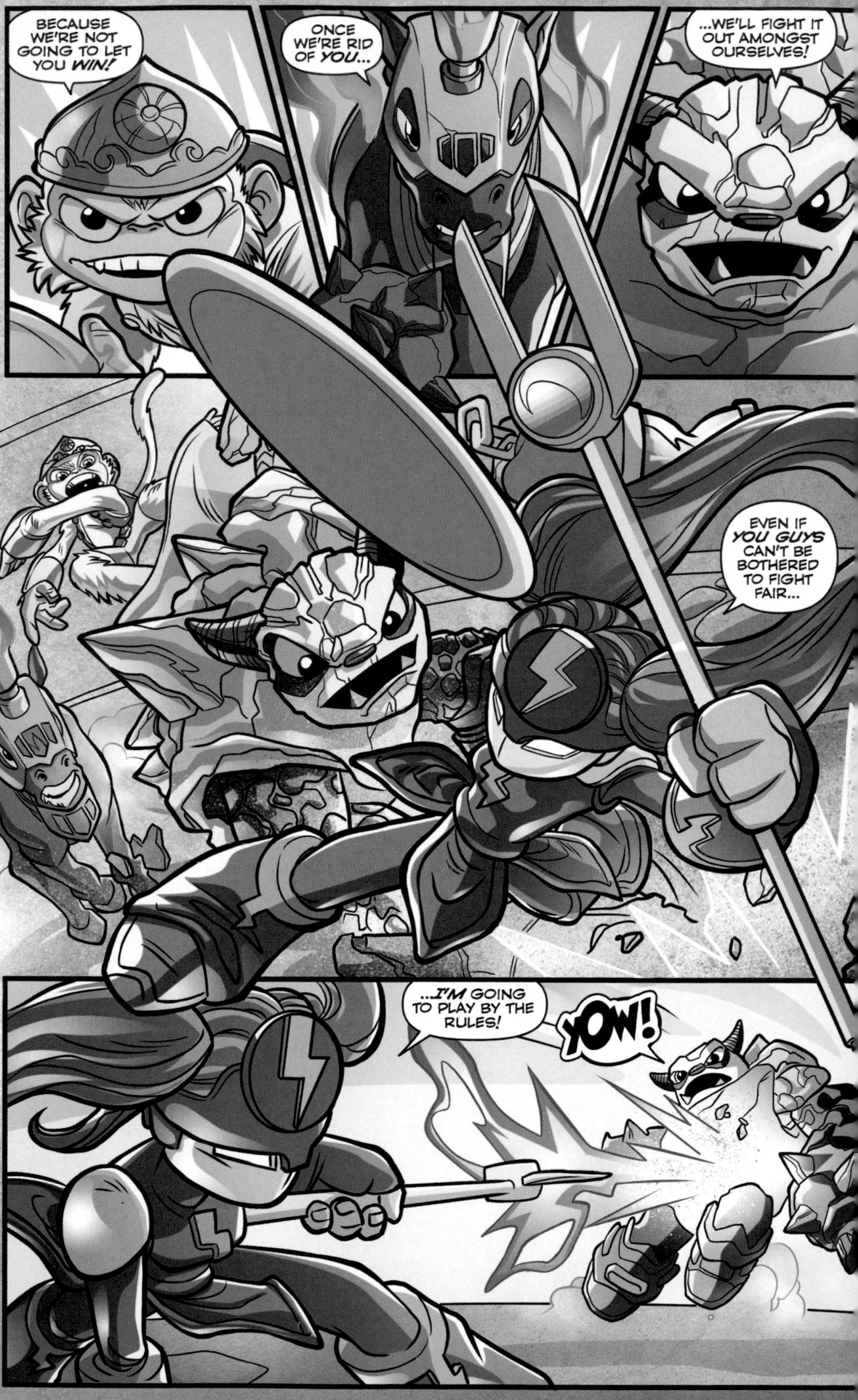
BECAUSE WE'RE NOT GOING TO LET YOU *WIN!*
ONCE WE'RE RID OF *YOU*...
...WE'LL FIGHT IT OUT AMONGST OURSELVES!
EVEN IF *YOU GUYS* CAN'T BE BOTHERED TO FIGHT FAIR...
...*I'M* GOING TO PLAY BY THE RULES!
YOW!

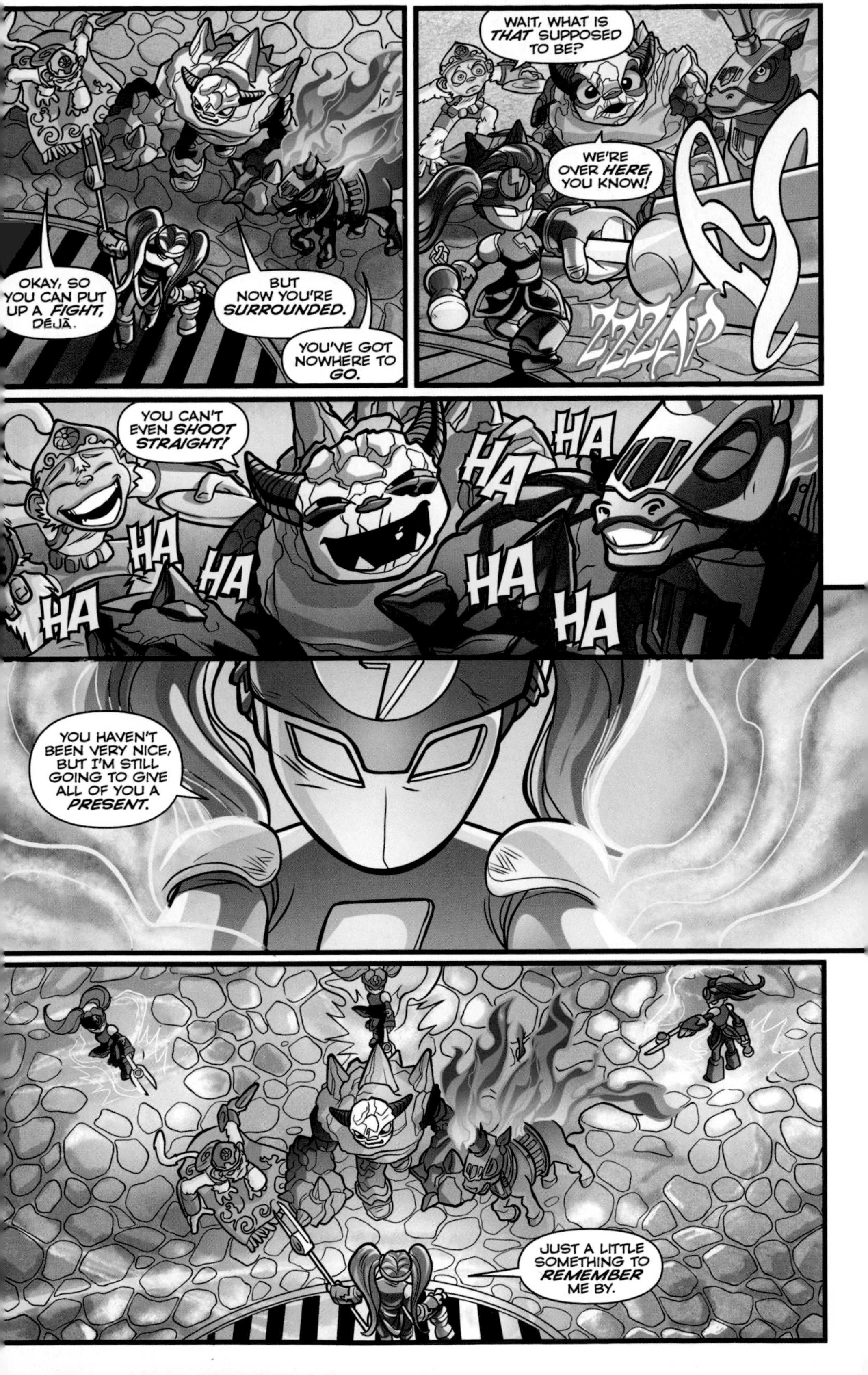
OKAY, SO YOU CAN PUT UP A *FIGHT*, DÉJÀ.
BUT NOW YOU'RE *SURROUNDED*.
YOU'VE GOT NOWHERE TO *GO*.
WAIT, WHAT IS *THAT* SUPPOSED TO BE?
WE'RE OVER *HERE*, YOU KNOW!
ZZZAP
YOU CAN'T EVEN *SHOOT STRAIGHT!*
HA HA HA HA HA HA HA
YOU HAVEN'T BEEN VERY NICE, BUT I'M STILL GOING TO GIVE ALL OF YOU A *PRESENT*.
JUST A LITTLE SOMETHING TO *REMEMBER* ME BY.

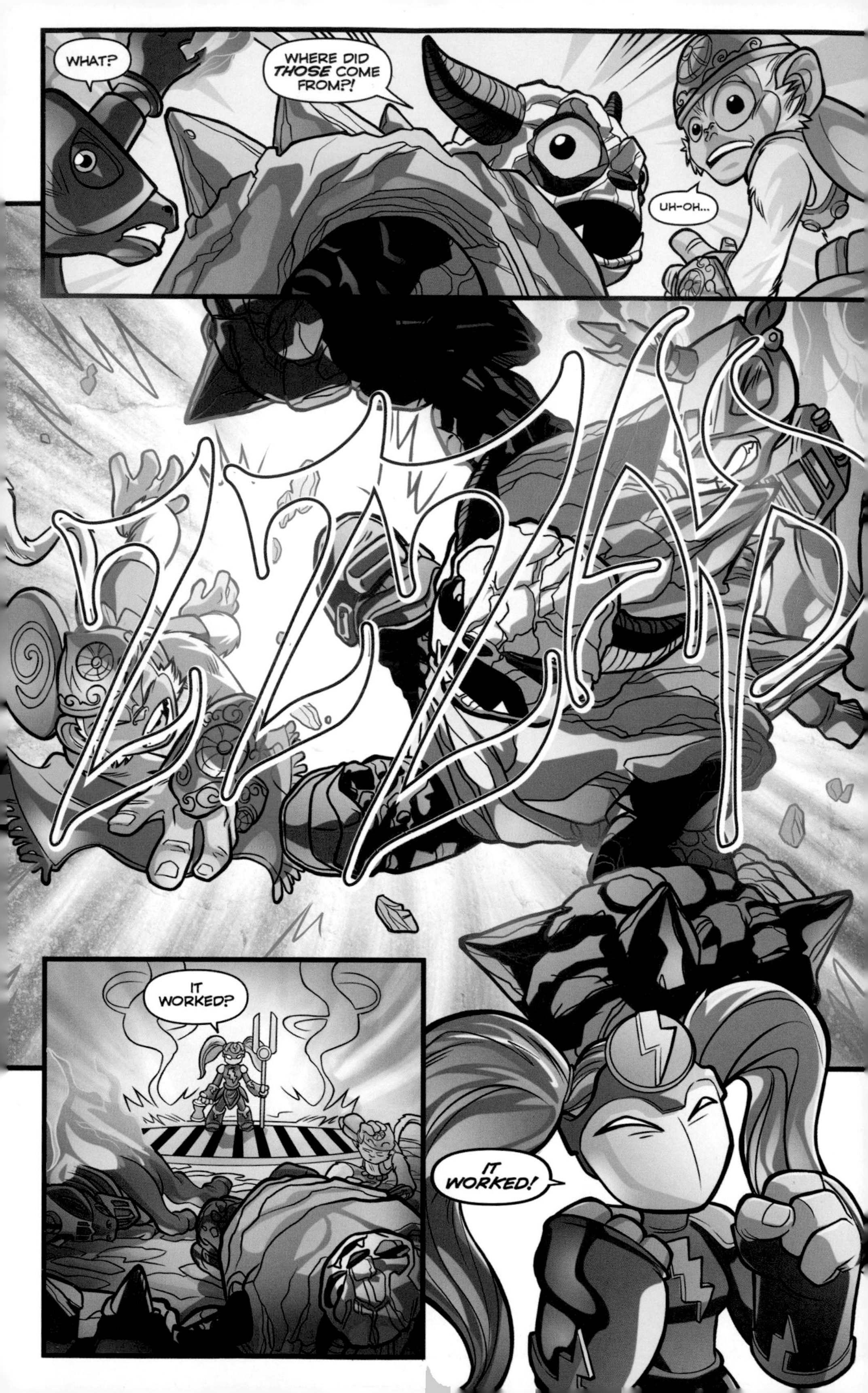
WHAT?
WHERE DID *THOSE* COME FROM?!
UH-OH...
ZZZAP
IT WORKED?
IT WORKED!

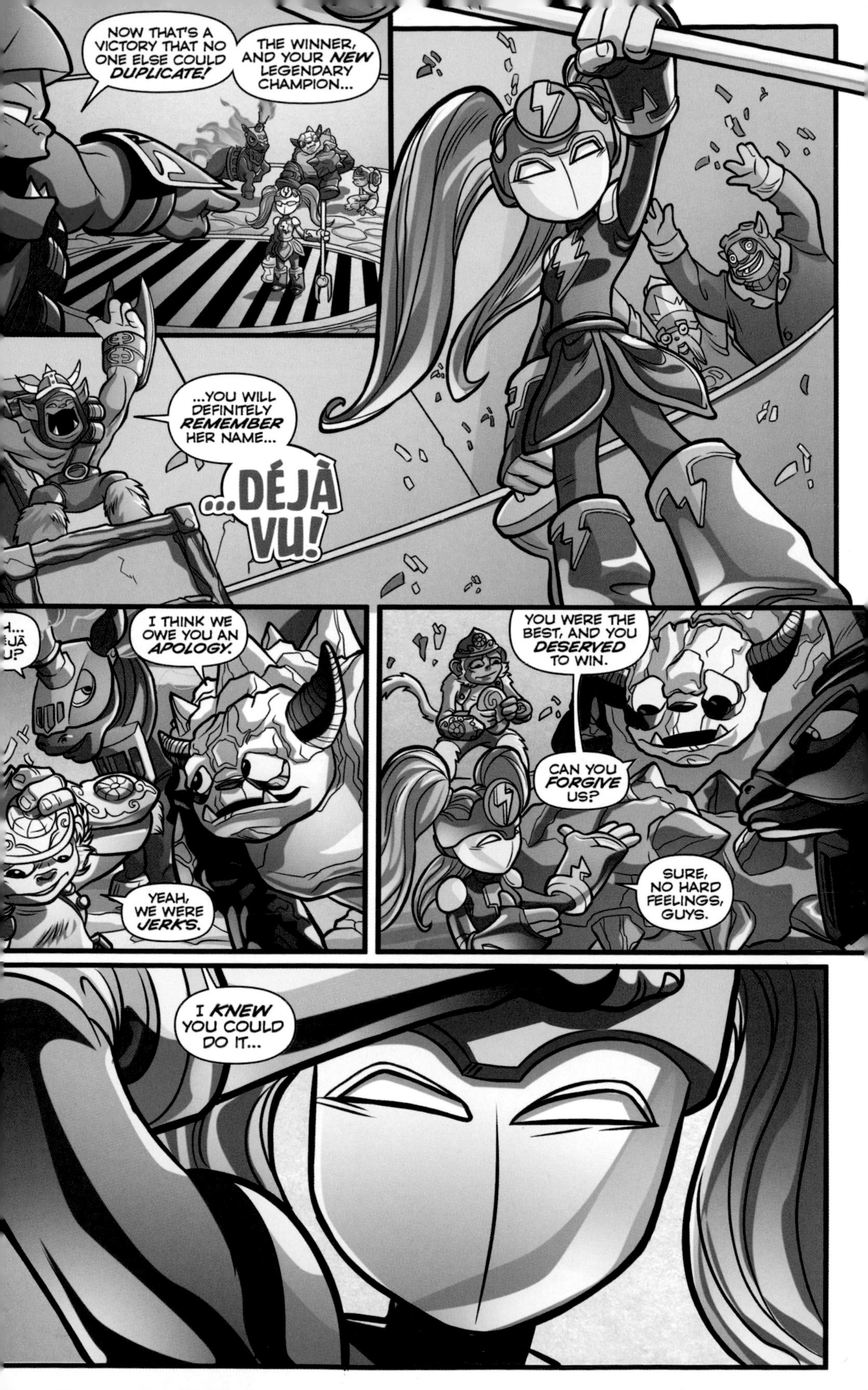
NOW THAT'S A VICTORY THAT NO ONE ELSE COULD *DUPLICATE!*
THE WINNER, AND YOUR *NEW* LEGENDARY CHAMPION...
...YOU WILL DEFINITELY *REMEMBER* HER NAME...
...DÉJÀ VU!
I THINK WE OWE YOU AN *APOLOGY.*
YEAH, WE WERE *JERKS.*
YOU WERE THE BEST, AND YOU *DESERVED* TO WIN.
CAN YOU *FORGIVE* US?
SURE, NO HARD FEELINGS, GUYS.
I *KNEW* YOU COULD DO IT...

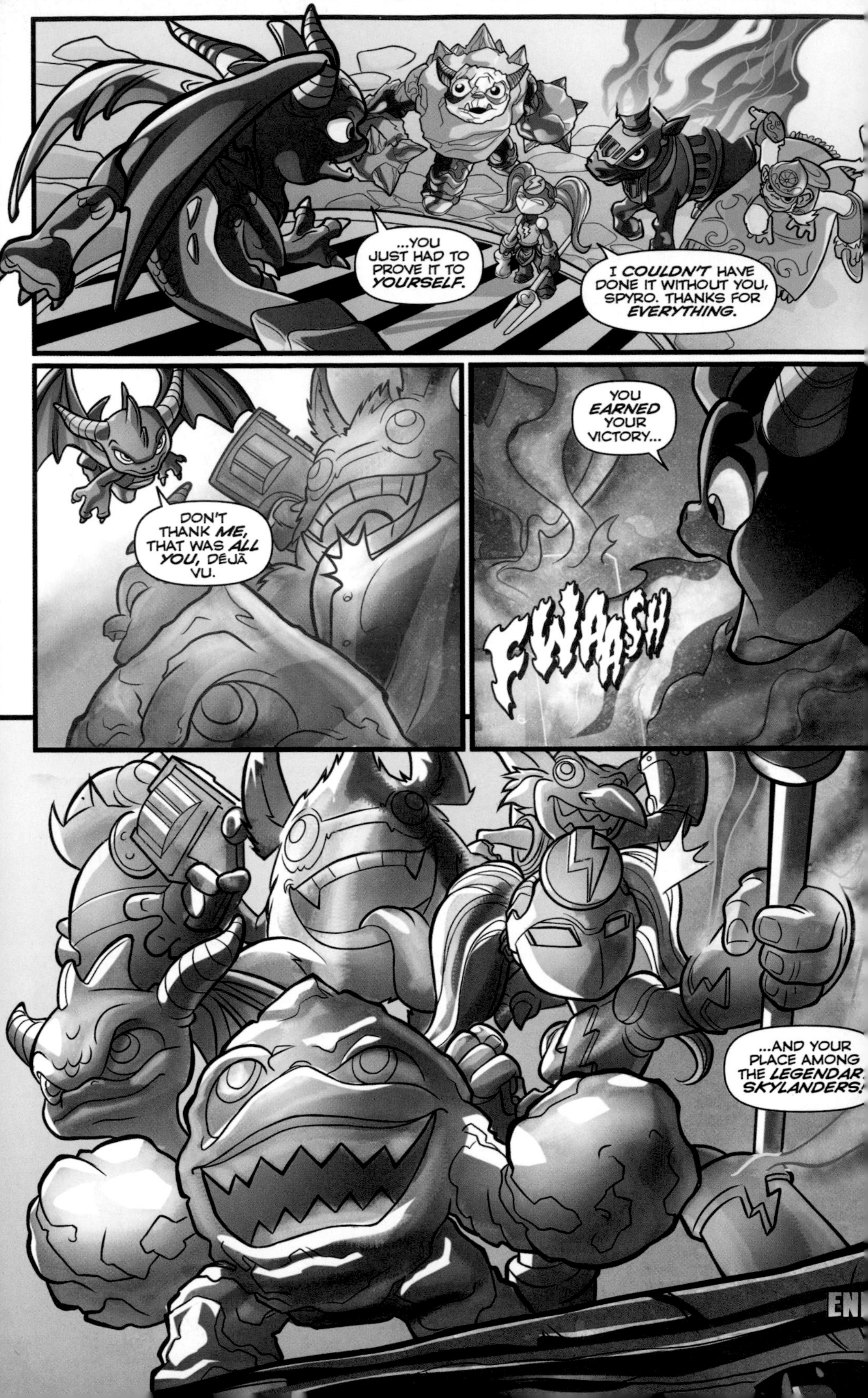
...YOU JUST HAD TO PROVE IT TO *YOURSELF*.
I *COULDN'T* HAVE DONE IT WITHOUT YOU, SPYRO. THANKS FOR *EVERYTHING*.
DON'T THANK *ME*, THAT WAS *ALL YOU*, DÉJÀ VU.
YOU *EARNED* YOUR VICTORY...
FWAASH
...AND YOUR PLACE AMONG THE *LEGENDAR* *SKYLANDERS!*
EN

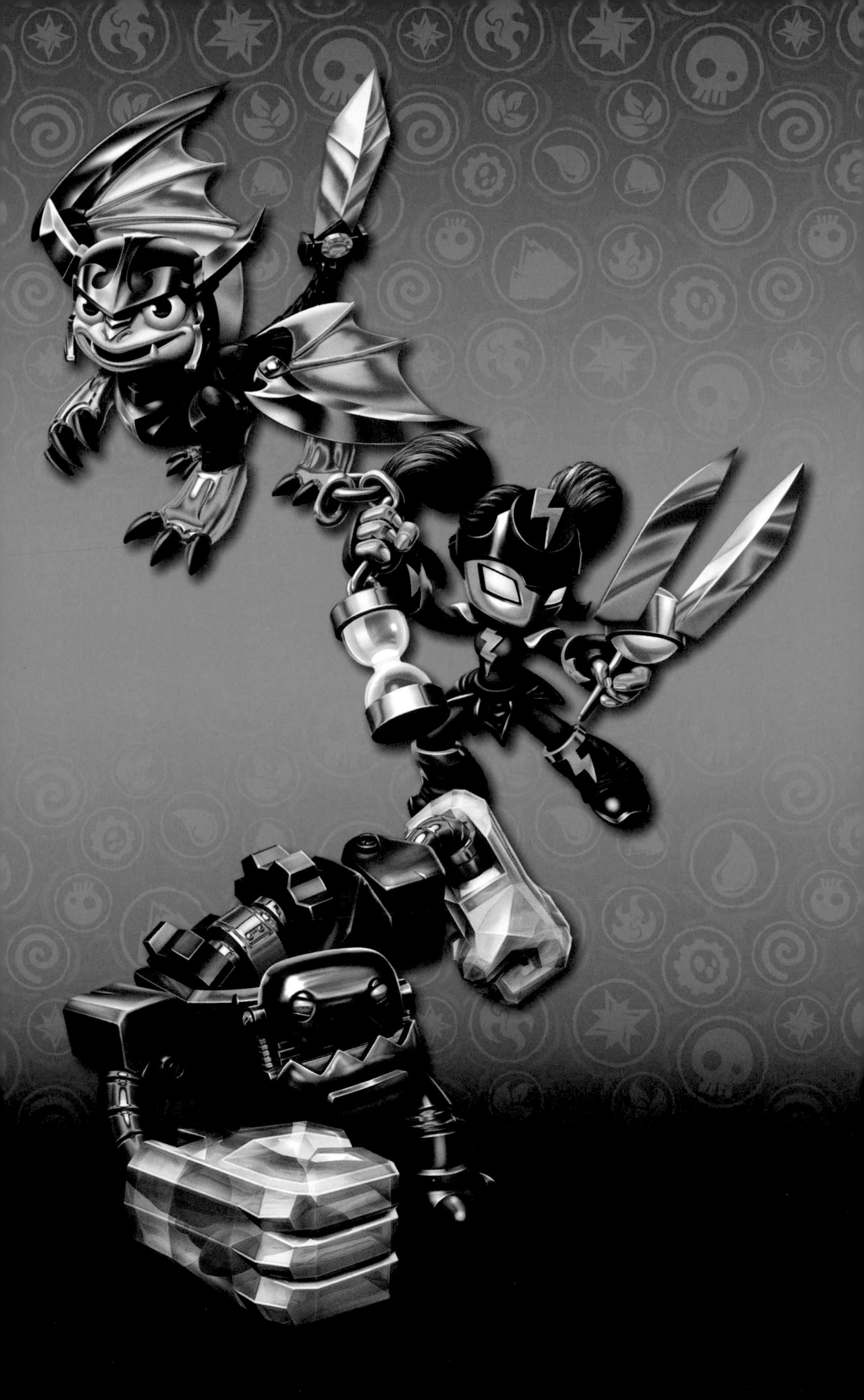

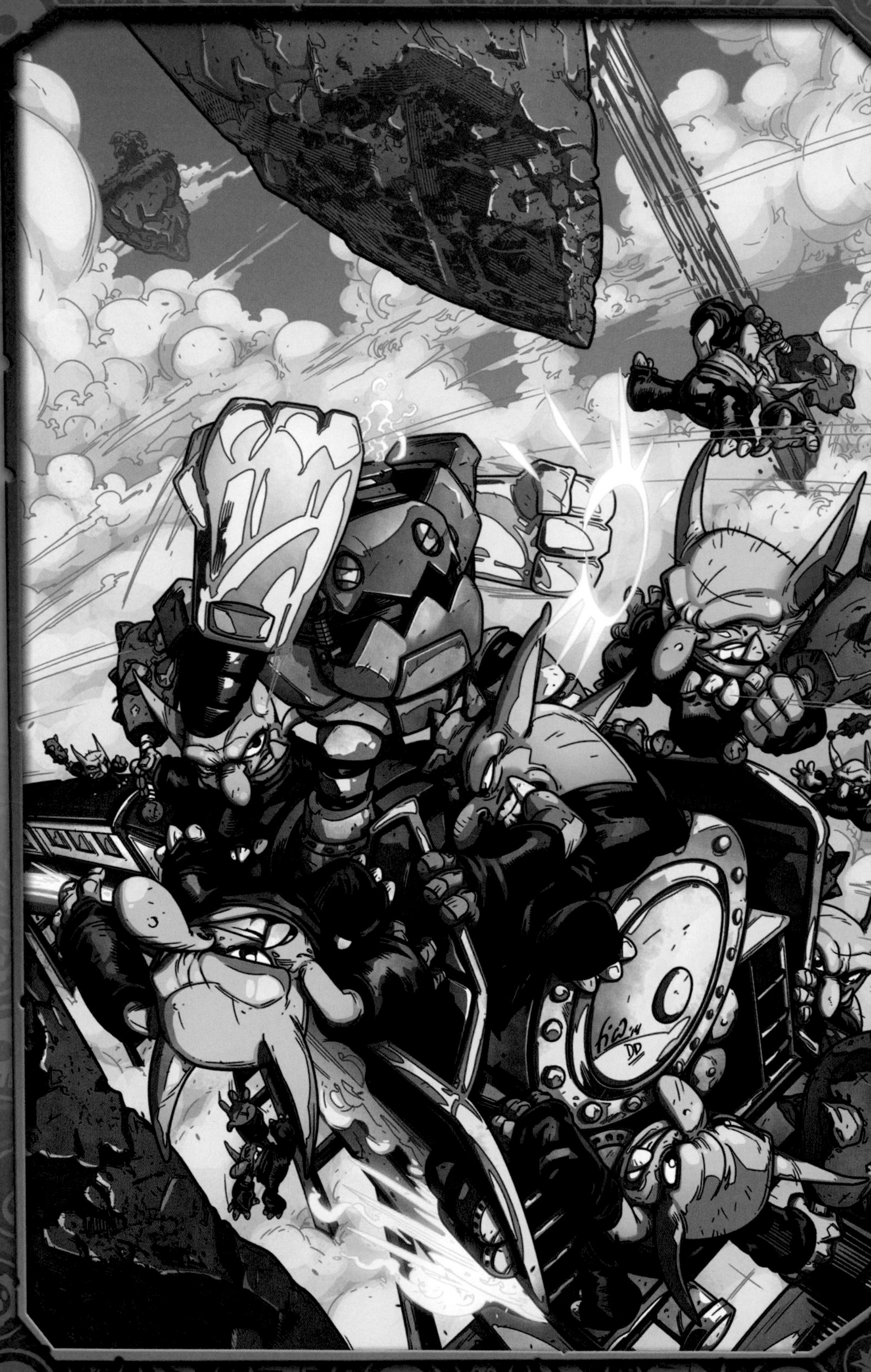

LAME IT ON THE TRAIN

tten by: RON MARZ &
DAVID A. RODRIGUEZ
Art by: SALVATORE COSTANZA
lors by: TOMATO FARM
ters by: DERON BENNETT

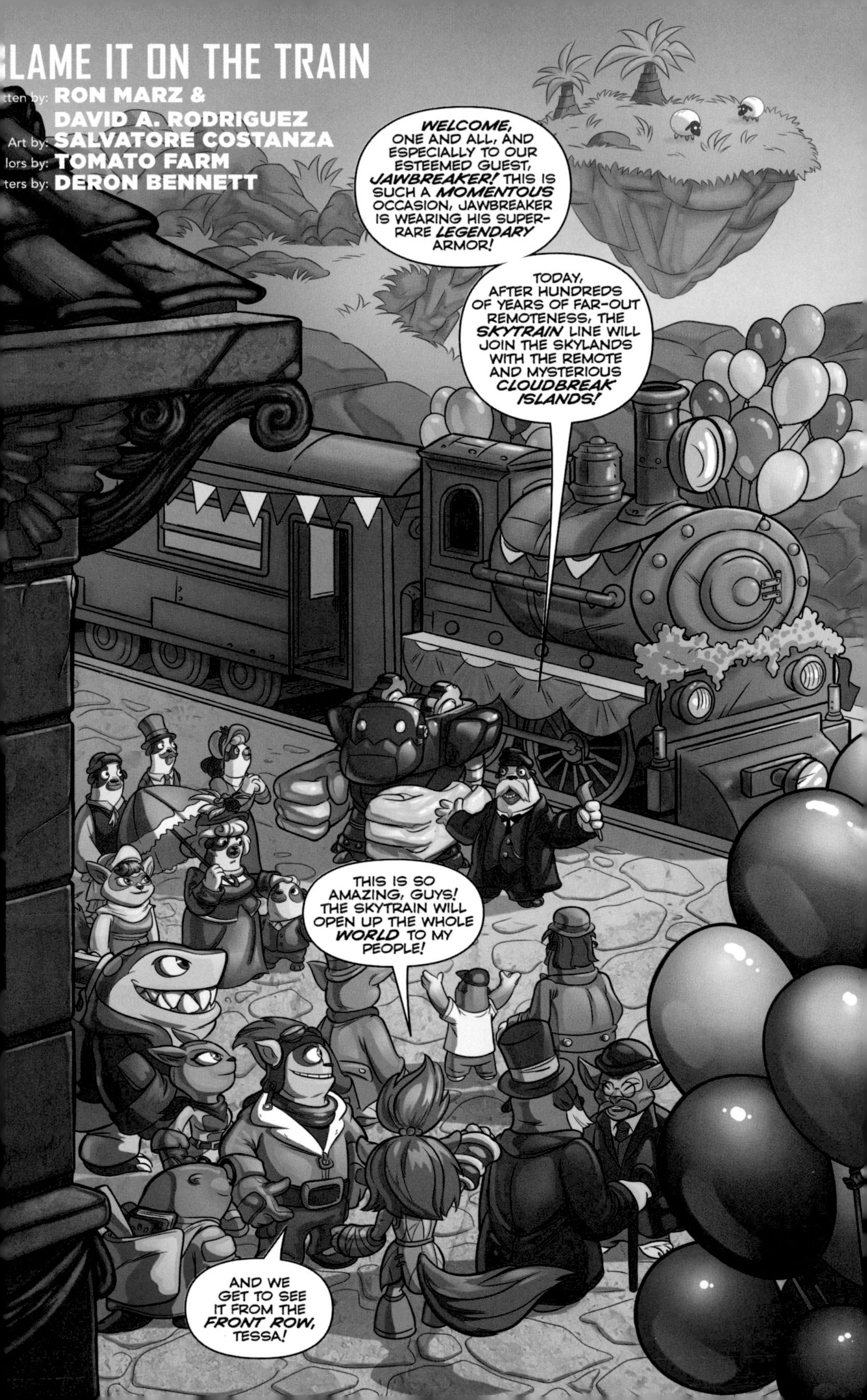
WELCOME, ONE AND ALL, AND ESPECIALLY TO OUR ESTEEMED GUEST, JAWBREAKER! THIS IS SUCH A MOMENTOUS OCCASION, JAWBREAKER IS WEARING HIS SUPER-RARE LEGENDARY ARMOR!
TODAY, AFTER HUNDREDS OF YEARS OF FAR-OUT REMOTENESS, THE SKYTRAIN LINE WILL JOIN THE SKYLANDS WITH THE REMOTE AND MYSTERIOUS CLOUDBREAK ISLANDS!
THIS IS SO AMAZING, GUYS! THE SKYTRAIN WILL OPEN UP THE WHOLE WORLD TO MY PEOPLE!
AND WE GET TO SEE IT FROM THE FRONT ROW, TESSA!

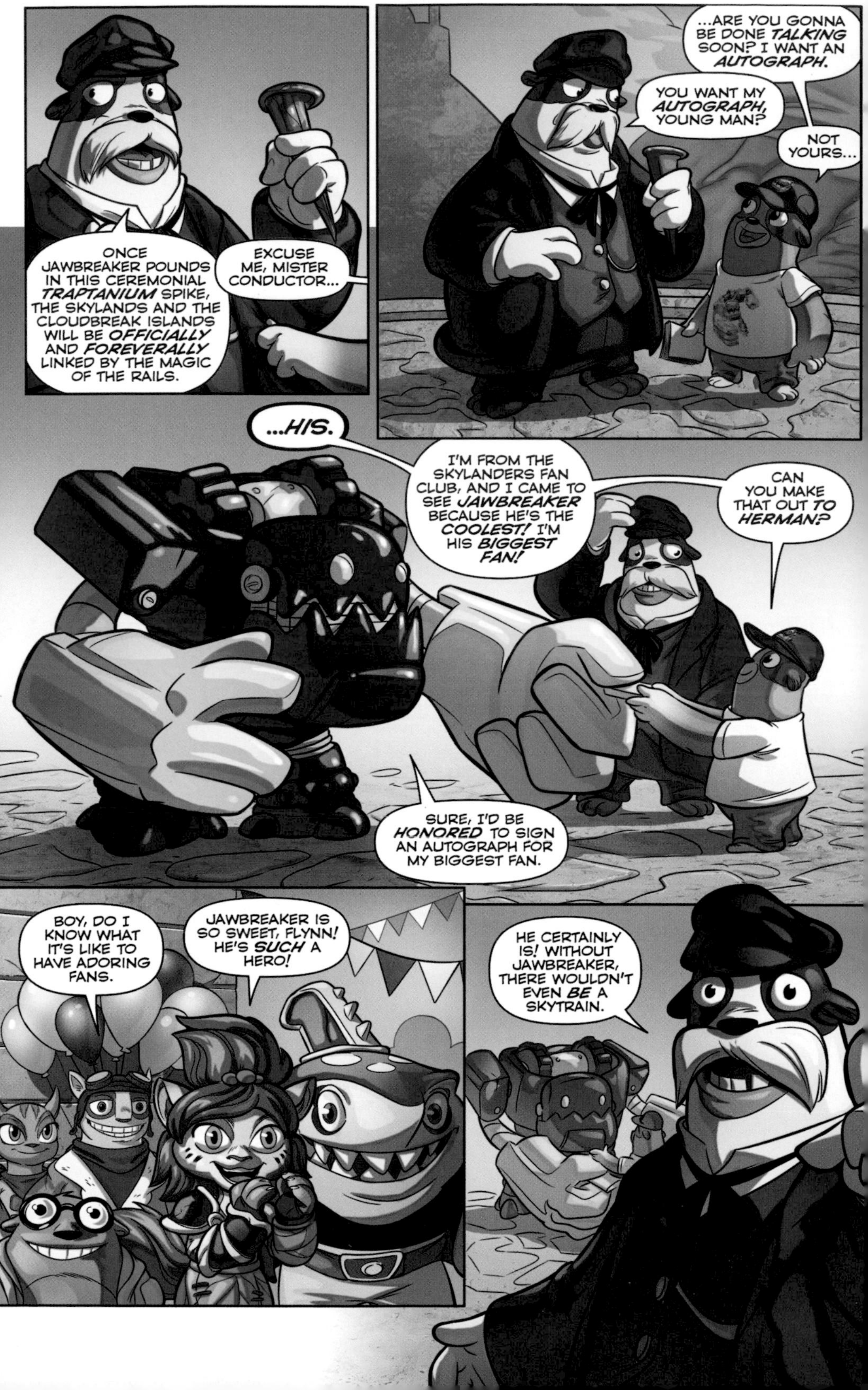
ONCE JAWBREAKER POUNDS IN THIS CEREMONIAL TRAPTANIUM SPIKE, THE SKYLANDS AND THE CLOUDBREAK ISLANDS WILL BE OFFICIALLY AND FOREVERALLY LINKED BY THE MAGIC OF THE RAILS.
EXCUSE ME, MISTER CONDUCTOR...
...ARE YOU GONNA BE DONE TALKING SOON? I WANT AN AUTOGRAPH.
YOU WANT MY AUTOGRAPH, YOUNG MAN?
NOT YOURS...
...HIS.
I'M FROM THE SKYLANDERS FAN CLUB, AND I CAME TO SEE JAWBREAKER BECAUSE HE'S THE COOLEST! I'M HIS BIGGEST FAN!
CAN YOU MAKE THAT OUT TO HERMAN?
SURE, I'D BE HONORED TO SIGN AN AUTOGRAPH FOR MY BIGGEST FAN.
BOY, DO I KNOW WHAT IT'S LIKE TO HAVE ADORING FANS.
JAWBREAKER IS SO SWEET, FLYNN! HE'S SUCH A HERO!
HE CERTAINLY IS! WITHOUT JAWBREAKER, THERE WOULDN'T EVEN BE A SKYTRAIN.

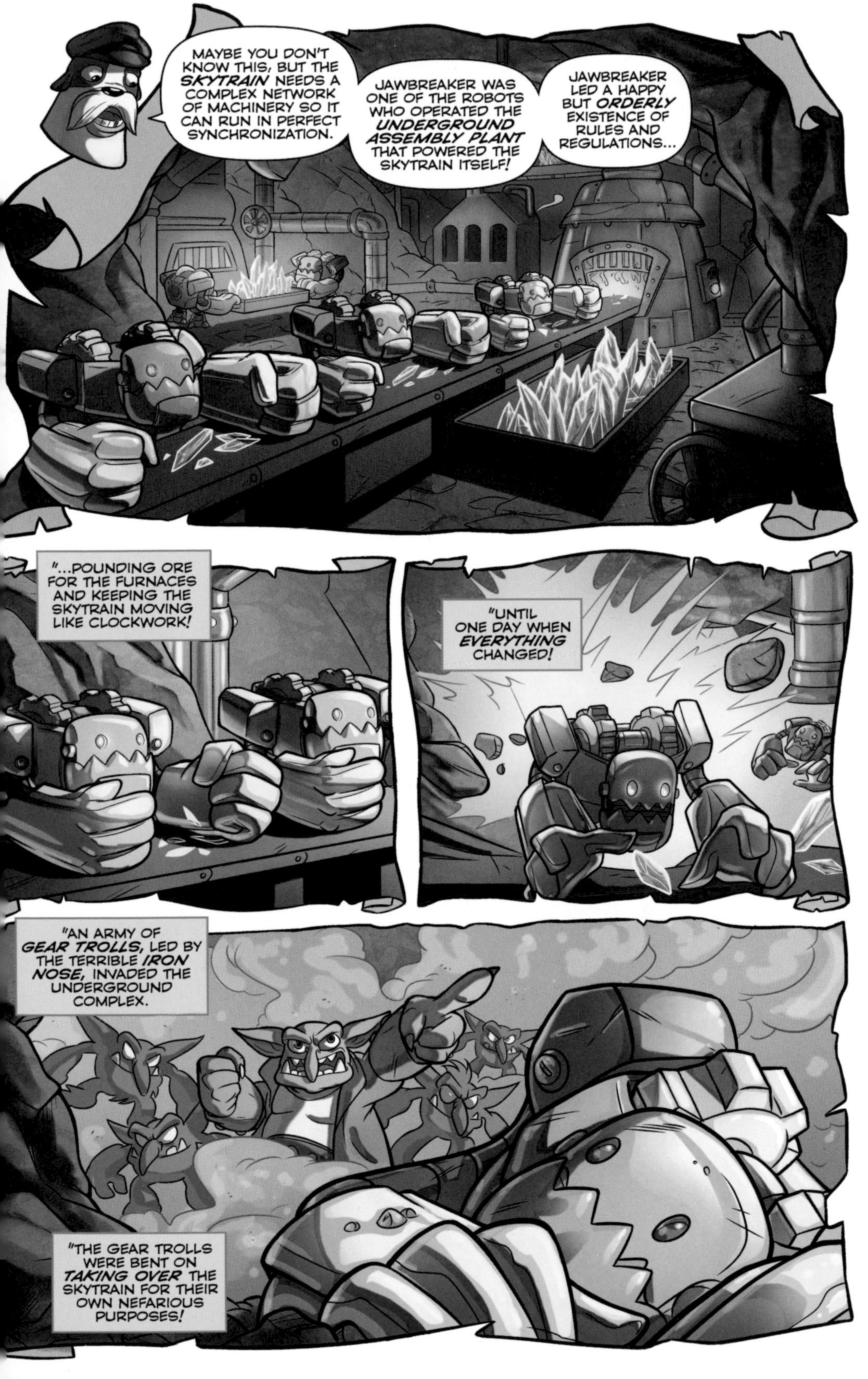
MAYBE YOU DON'T KNOW THIS, BUT THE SKYTRAIN NEEDS A COMPLEX NETWORK OF MACHINERY SO IT CAN RUN IN PERFECT SYNCHRONIZATION.
JAWBREAKER WAS ONE OF THE ROBOTS WHO OPERATED THE UNDERGROUND ASSEMBLY PLANT THAT POWERED THE SKYTRAIN ITSELF!
JAWBREAKER LED A HAPPY BUT ORDERLY EXISTENCE OF RULES AND REGULATIONS...
"...POUNDING ORE FOR THE FURNACES AND KEEPING THE SKYTRAIN MOVING LIKE CLOCKWORK!
"UNTIL ONE DAY WHEN EVERYTHING CHANGED!
"AN ARMY OF GEAR TROLLS, LED BY THE TERRIBLE IRON NOSE, INVADED THE UNDERGROUND COMPLEX.
"THE GEAR TROLLS WERE BENT ON TAKING OVER THE SKYTRAIN FOR THEIR OWN NEFARIOUS PURPOSES!

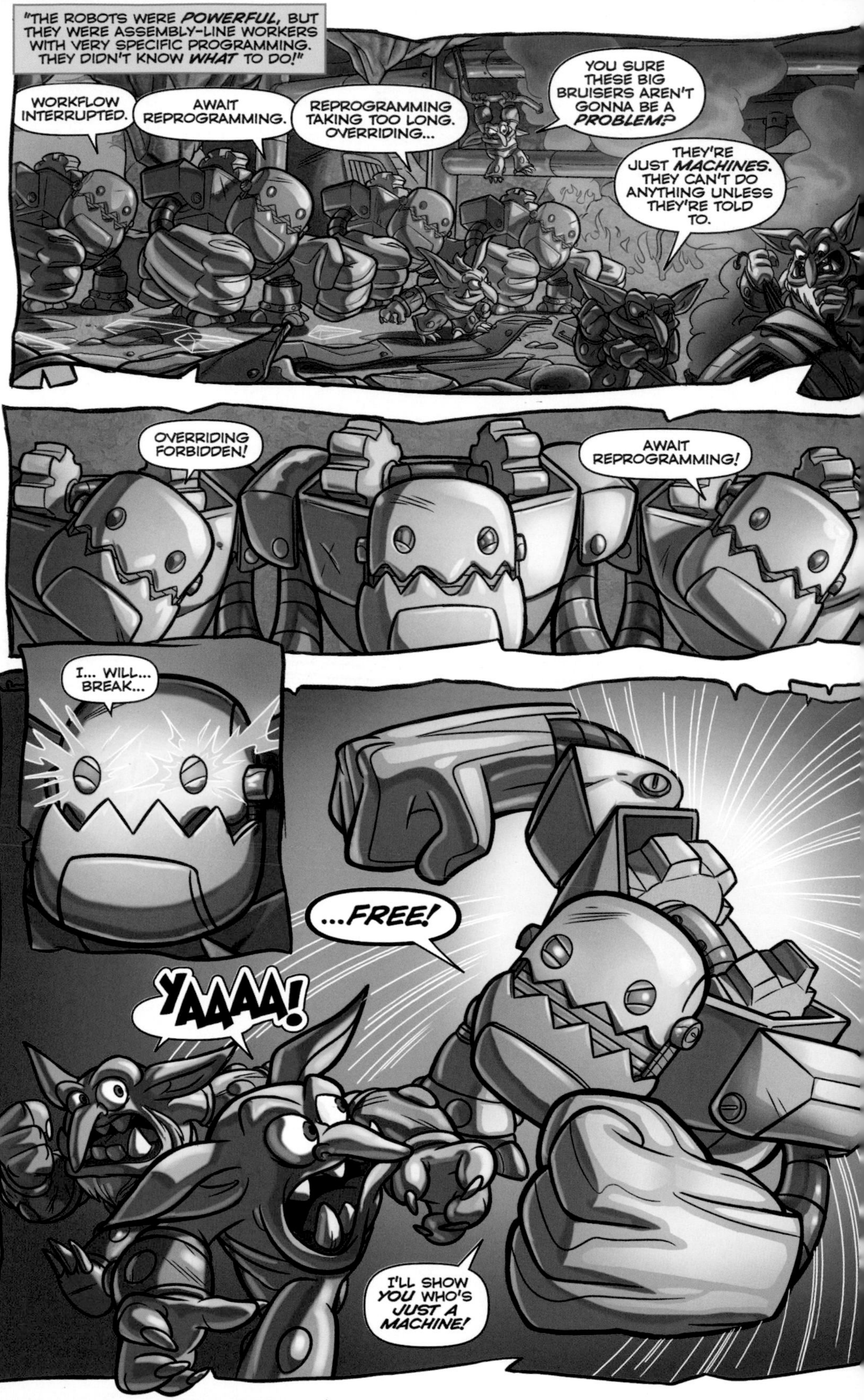
"THE ROBOTS WERE POWERFUL, BUT THEY WERE ASSEMBLY-LINE WORKERS WITH VERY SPECIFIC PROGRAMMING. THEY DIDN'T KNOW WHAT TO DO!"
WORKFLOW INTERRUPTED.
AWAIT REPROGRAMMING.
REPROGRAMMING TAKING TOO LONG. OVERRIDING...
YOU SURE THESE BIG BRUISERS AREN'T GONNA BE A PROBLEM?
THEY'RE JUST MACHINES. THEY CAN'T DO ANYTHING UNLESS THEY'RE TOLD TO.
OVERRIDING FORBIDDEN!
AWAIT REPROGRAMMING!
I... WILL... BREAK...
...FREE!
YAAAA!
I'LL SHOW YOU WHO'S JUST A MACHINE!

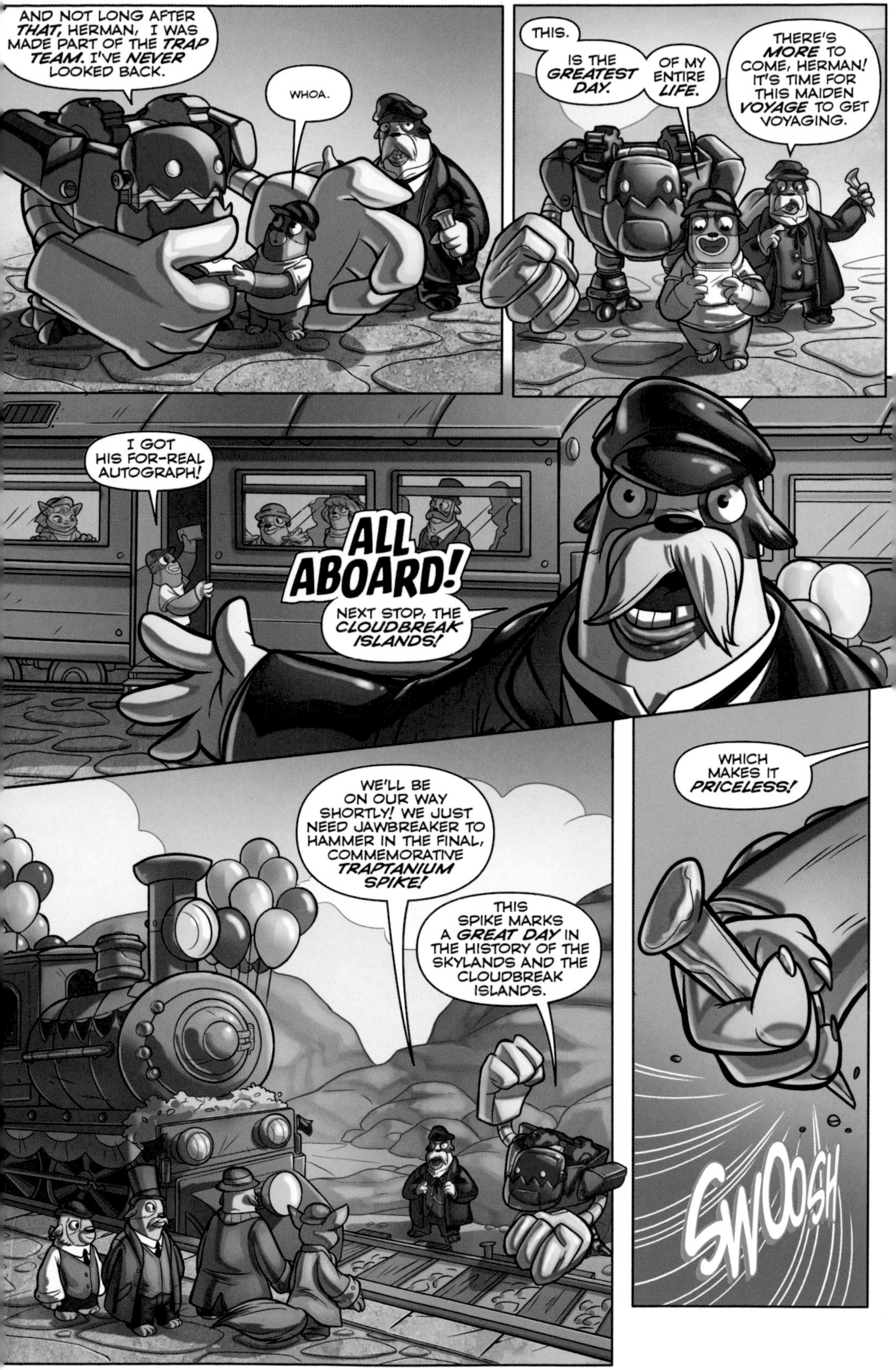
AND NOT LONG AFTER THAT, HERMAN, I WAS MADE PART OF THE TRAP TEAM. I'VE NEVER LOOKED BACK.
WHOA.
THIS.
IS THE GREATEST DAY.
OF MY ENTIRE LIFE.
THERE'S MORE TO COME, HERMAN! IT'S TIME FOR THIS MAIDEN VOYAGE TO GET VOYAGING.
I GOT HIS FOR-REAL AUTOGRAPH!
ALL ABOARD!
NEXT STOP, THE CLOUDBREAK ISLANDS!
WE'LL BE ON OUR WAY SHORTLY! WE JUST NEED JAWBREAKER TO HAMMER IN THE FINAL, COMMEMORATIVE TRAPTANIUM SPIKE!
THIS SPIKE MARKS A GREAT DAY IN THE HISTORY OF THE SKYLANDS AND THE CLOUDBREAK ISLANDS.
WHICH MAKES IT PRICELESS!
SWOOSH

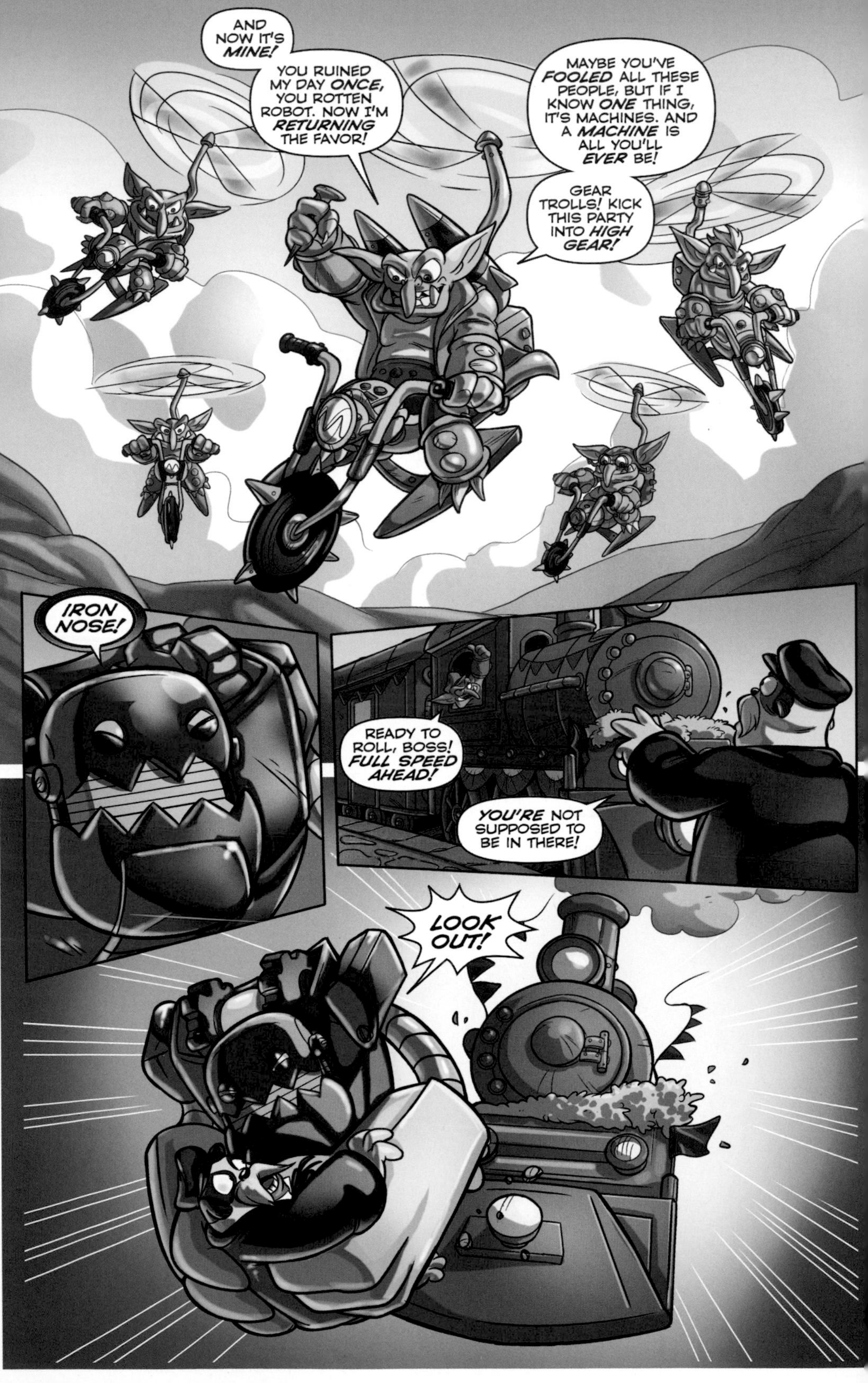
AND NOW IT'S MINE!
YOU RUINED MY DAY ONCE, YOU ROTTEN ROBOT. NOW I'M RETURNING THE FAVOR!
MAYBE YOU'VE FOOLED ALL THESE PEOPLE, BUT IF I KNOW ONE THING, IT'S MACHINES. AND A MACHINE IS ALL YOU'LL EVER BE!
GEAR TROLLS! KICK THIS PARTY INTO HIGH GEAR!
IRON NOSE!
READY TO ROLL, BOSS! FULL SPEED AHEAD!
YOU'RE NOT SUPPOSED TO BE IN THERE!
LOOK OUT!

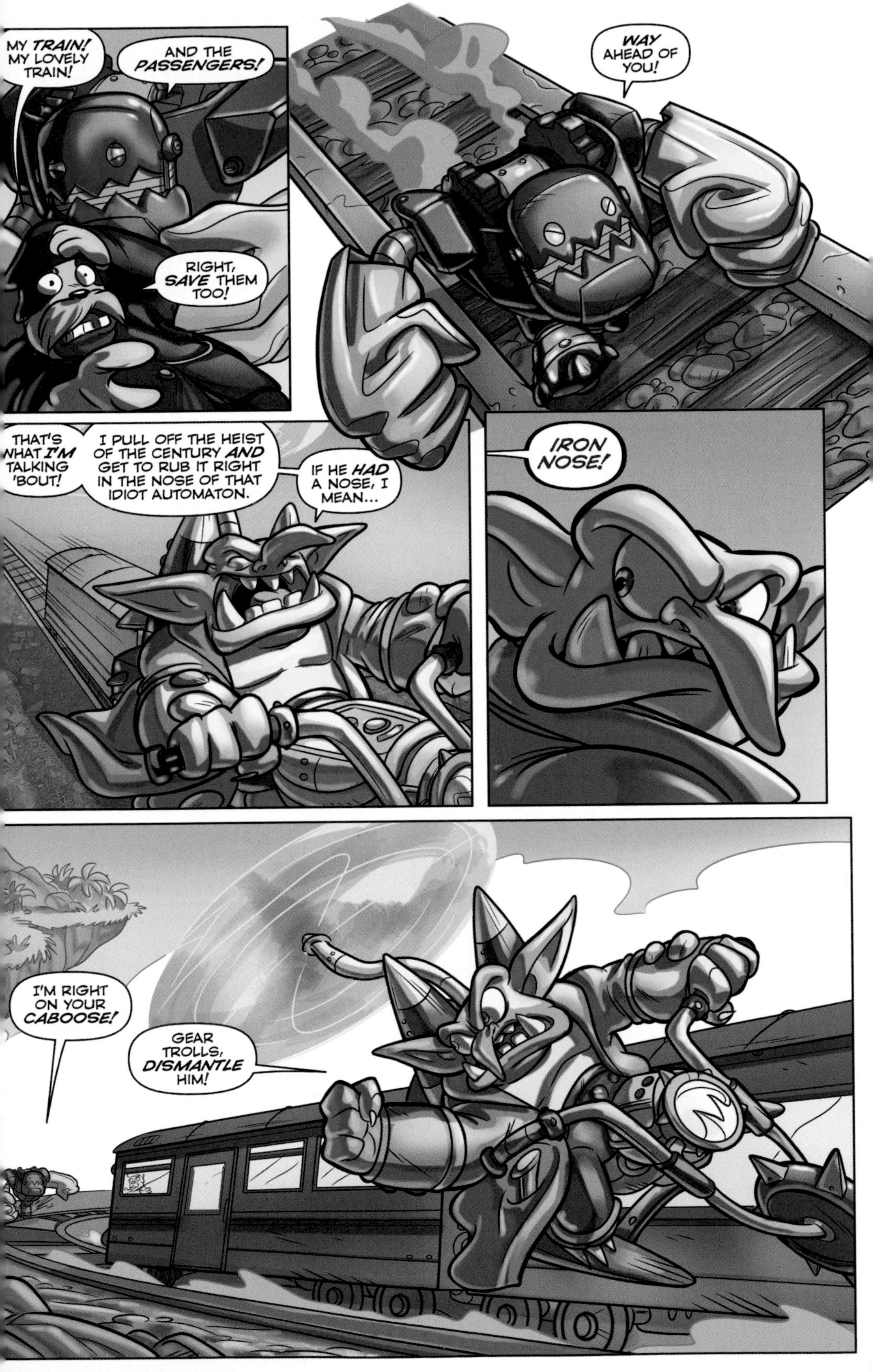
MY TRAIN! MY LOVELY TRAIN!
AND THE PASSENGERS!
RIGHT, SAVE THEM TOO!
WAY AHEAD OF YOU!
THAT'S WHAT I'M TALKING 'BOUT!
I PULL OFF THE HEIST OF THE CENTURY AND GET TO RUB IT RIGHT IN THE NOSE OF THAT IDIOT AUTOMATON.
IF HE HAD A NOSE, I MEAN...
IRON NOSE!
I'M RIGHT ON YOUR CABOOSE!
GEAR TROLLS, DISMANTLE HIM!

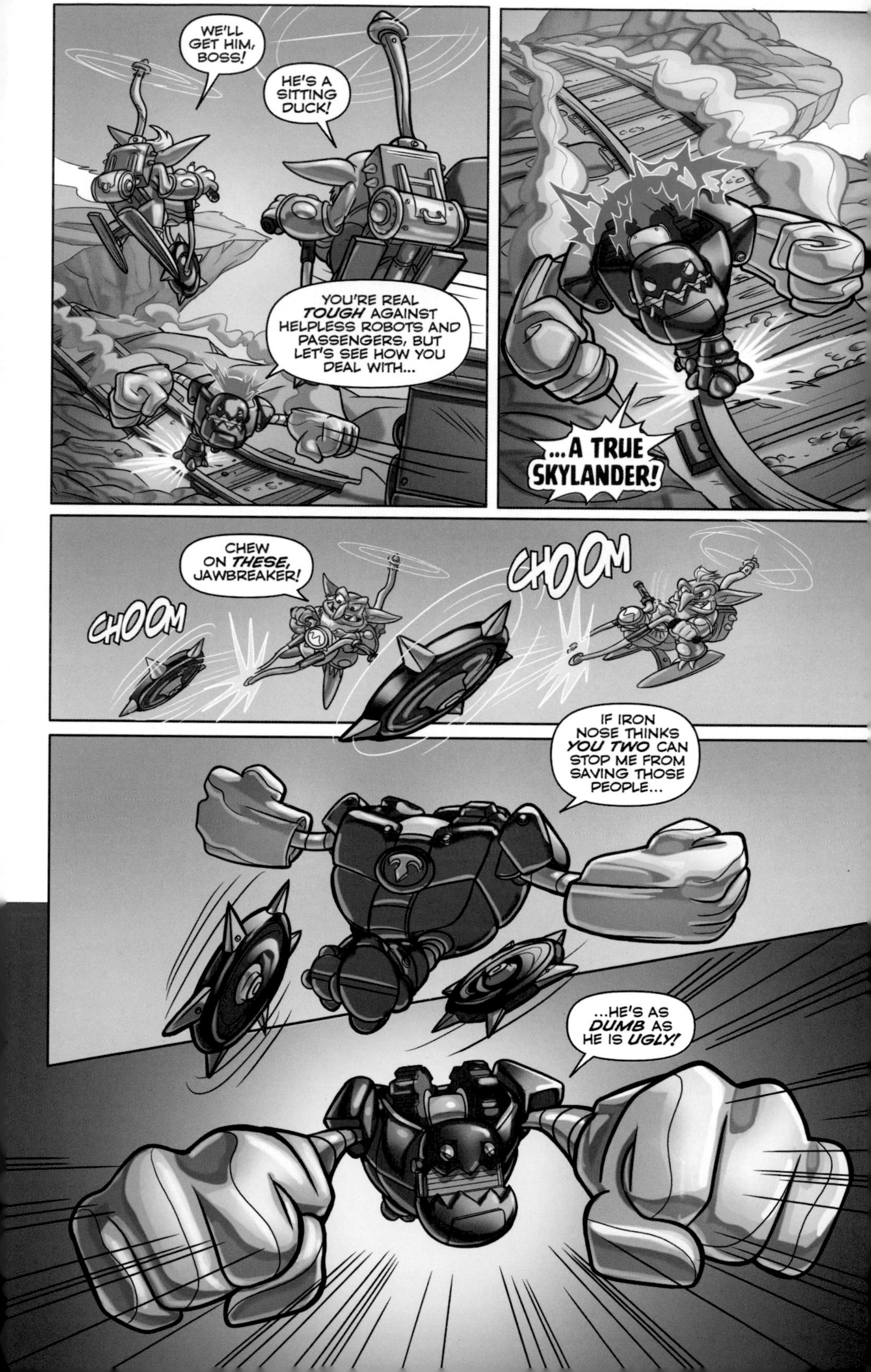
WE'LL GET HIM, BOSS!
HE'S A SITTING DUCK!
YOU'RE REAL TOUGH AGAINST HELPLESS ROBOTS AND PASSENGERS, BUT LET'S SEE HOW YOU DEAL WITH...
...A TRUE SKYLANDER!
CHEW ON THESE, JAWBREAKER!
CHOOM
CHOOM
IF IRON NOSE THINKS YOU TWO CAN STOP ME FROM SAVING THOSE PEOPLE...
...HE'S AS DUMB AS HE IS UGLY!

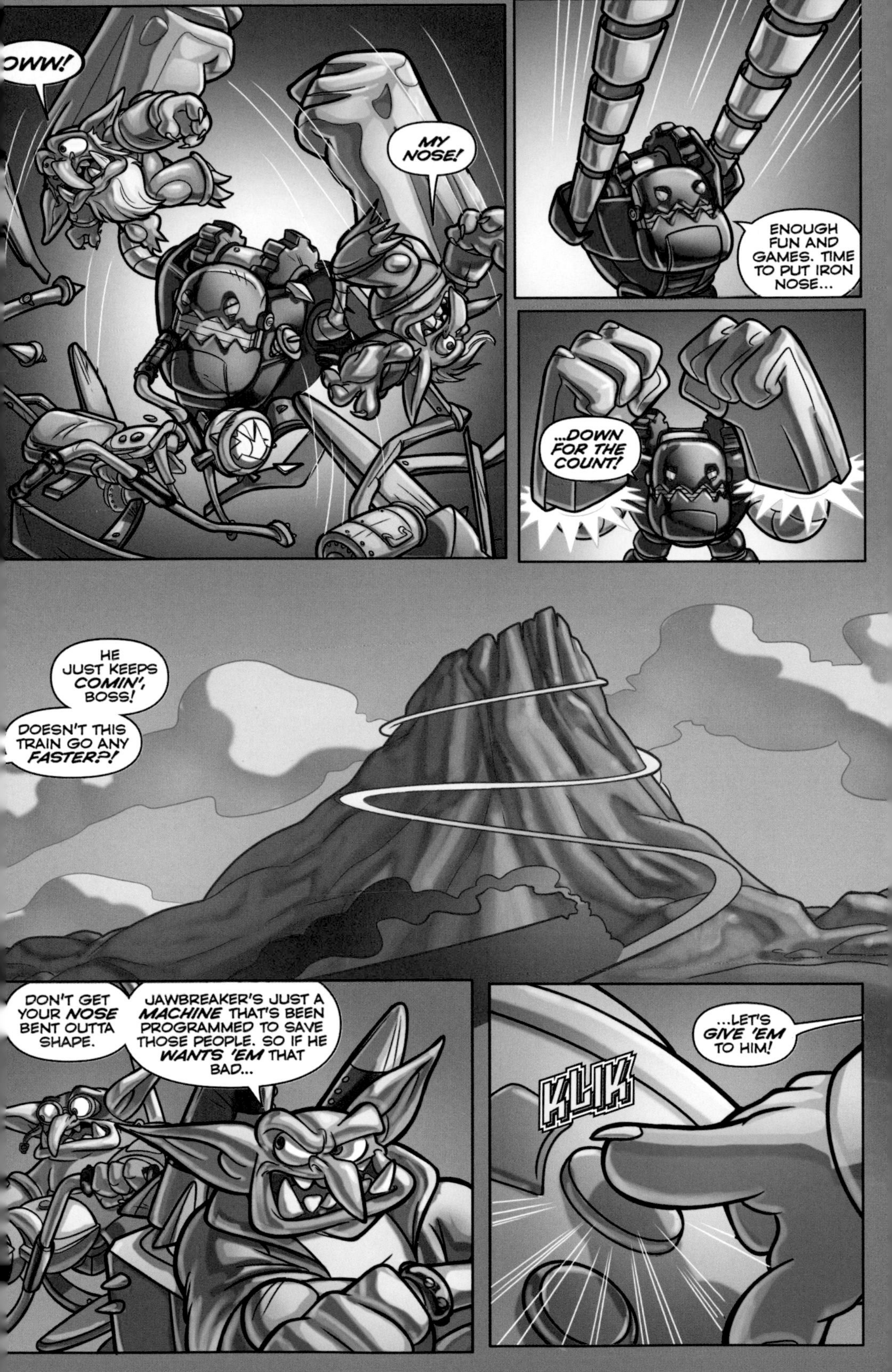
OWW!
MY NOSE!
ENOUGH FUN AND GAMES. TIME TO PUT IRON NOSE...
...DOWN FOR THE COUNT!
HE JUST KEEPS COMIN', BOSS!
DOESN'T THIS TRAIN GO ANY FASTER?!
DON'T GET YOUR NOSE BENT OUTTA SHAPE.
JAWBREAKER'S JUST A MACHINE THAT'S BEEN PROGRAMMED TO SAVE THOSE PEOPLE. SO IF HE WANTS 'EM THAT BAD...
KLIK
...LET'S GIVE 'EM TO HIM!

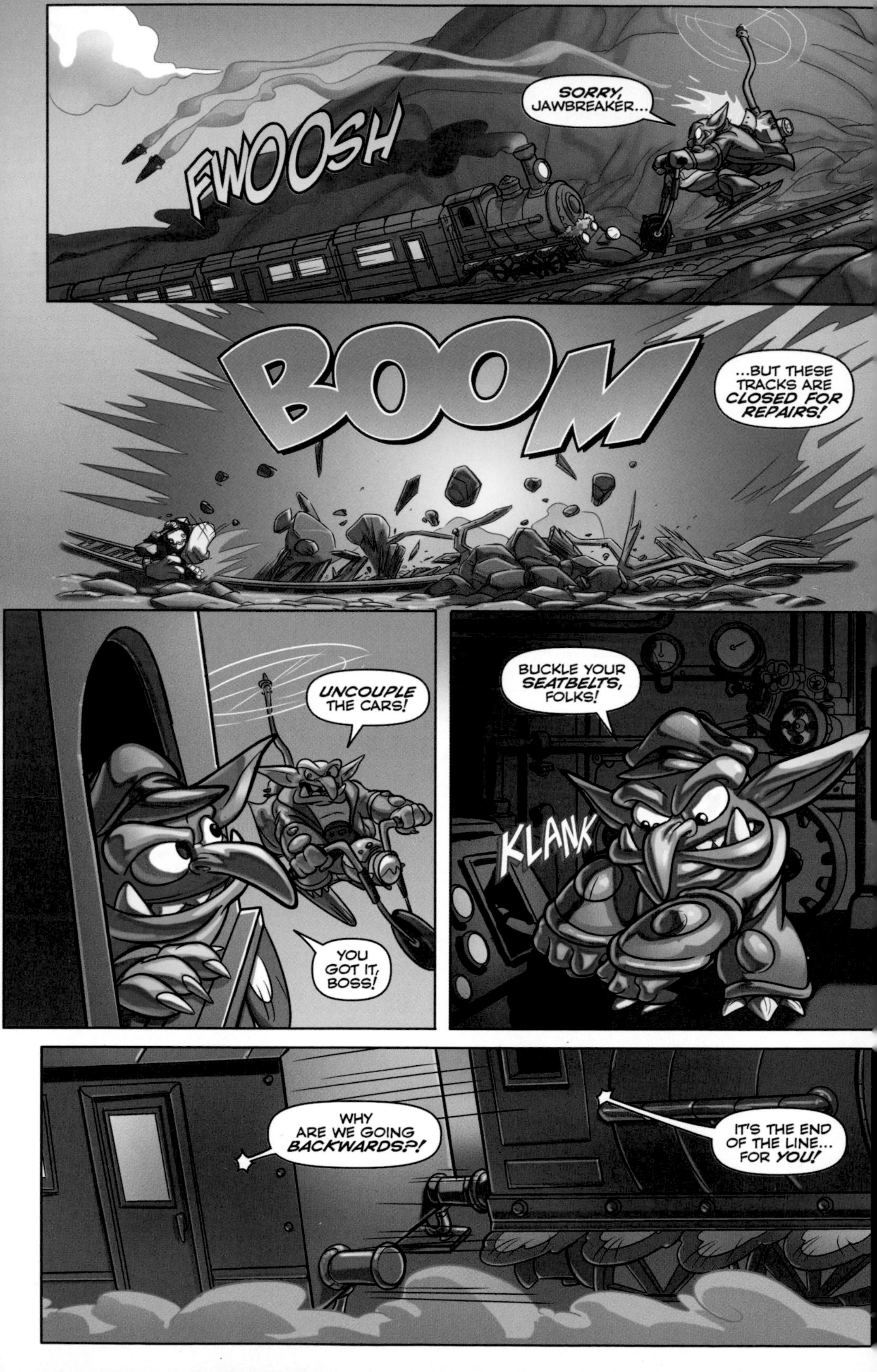
SORRY, JAWBREAKER...
FWOOSH
BOOM
...BUT THESE TRACKS ARE CLOSED FOR REPAIRS!
UNCOUPLE THE CARS!
YOU GOT IT, BOSS!
BUCKLE YOUR SEATBELTS, FOLKS!
KLANK
WHY ARE WE GOING BACKWARDS?!
IT'S THE END OF THE LINE... FOR YOU!

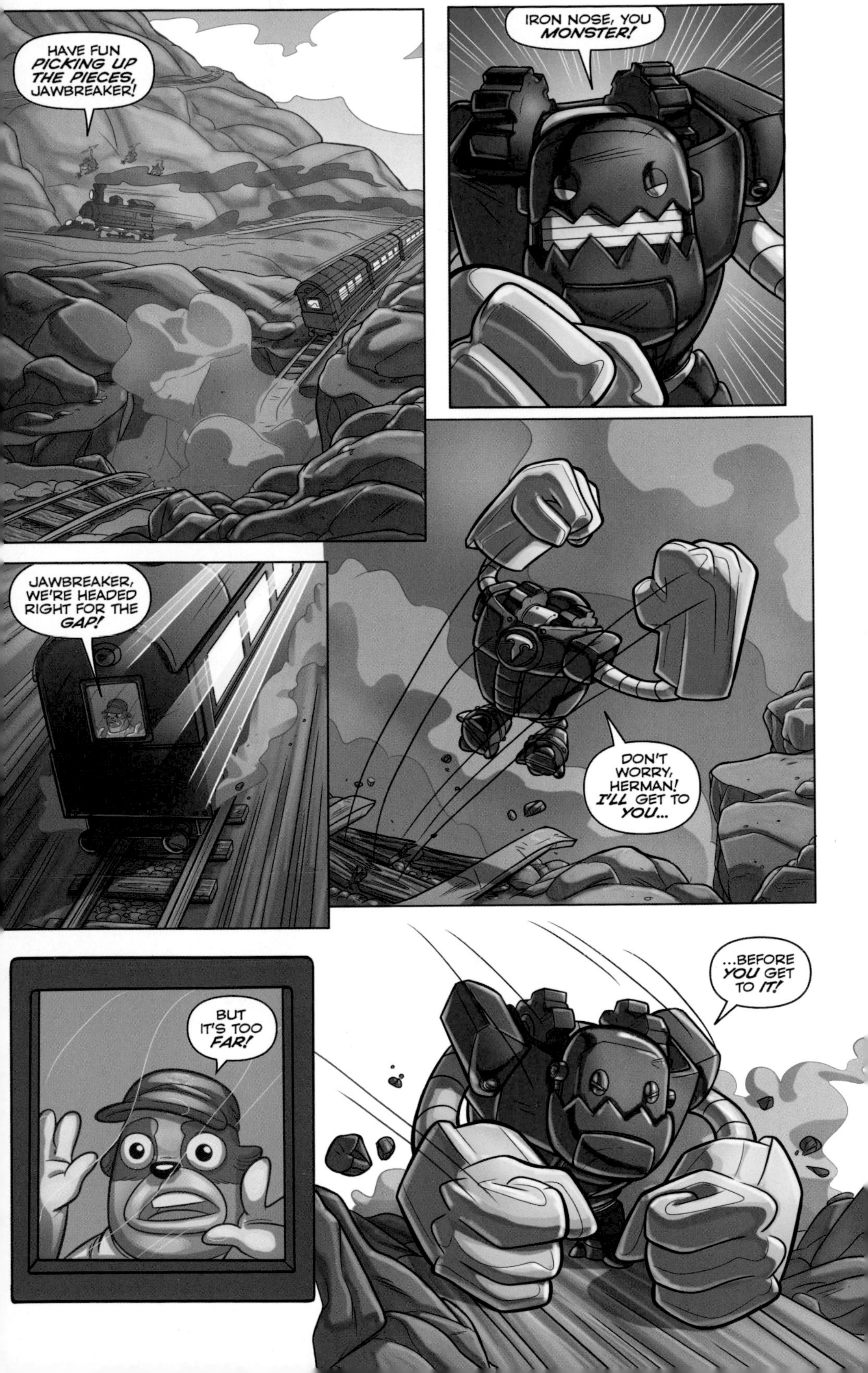
HAVE FUN PICKING UP THE PIECES, JAWBREAKER!
IRON NOSE, YOU MONSTER!
JAWBREAKER, WE'RE HEADED RIGHT FOR THE GAP!
DON'T WORRY, HERMAN! I'LL GET TO YOU...
BUT IT'S TOO FAR!
...BEFORE YOU GET TO IT!

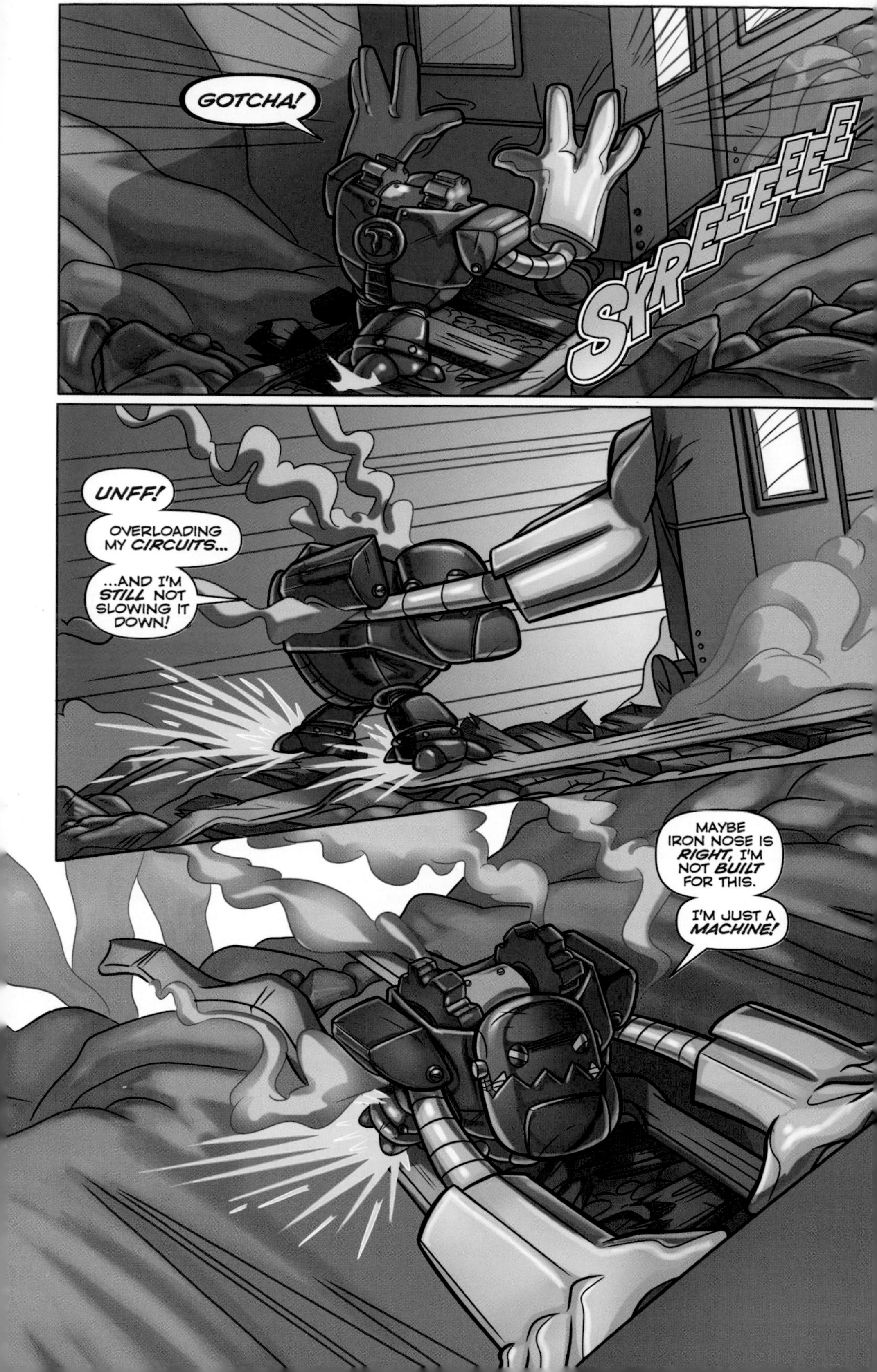
GOTCHA!
SKREEEEEEE
UNFF!
OVERLOADING MY CIRCUITS...
...AND I'M STILL NOT SLOWING IT DOWN!
MAYBE IRON NOSE IS RIGHT, I'M NOT BUILT FOR THIS.
I'M JUST A MACHINE!

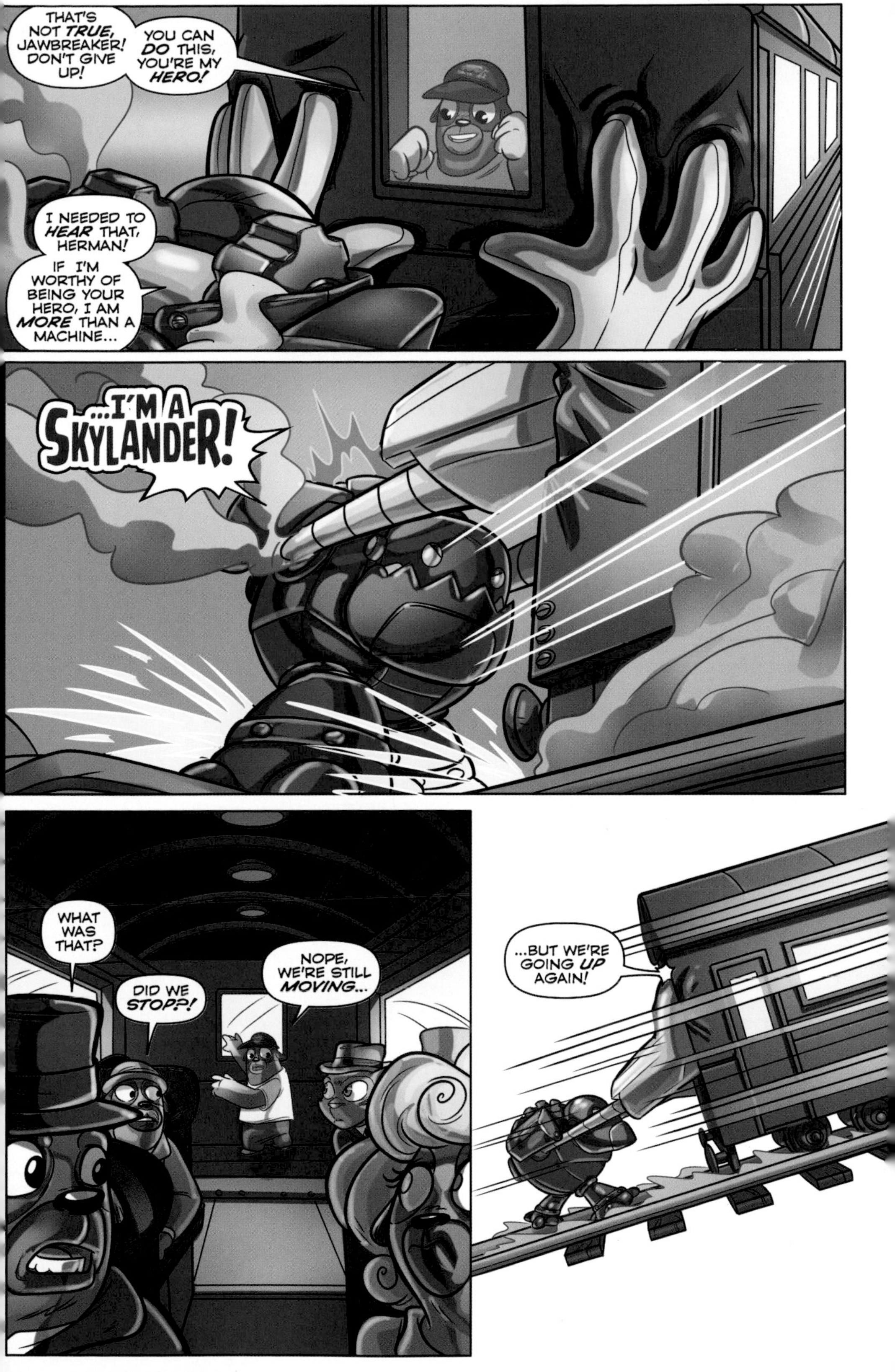
THAT'S NOT TRUE, JAWBREAKER! DON'T GIVE UP!
YOU CAN DO THIS, YOU'RE MY HERO!
I NEEDED TO HEAR THAT, HERMAN!
IF I'M WORTHY OF BEING YOUR HERO, I AM MORE THAN A MACHINE...
...I'M A SKYLANDER!
WHAT WAS THAT?
DID WE STOP?!
NOPE, WE'RE STILL MOVING...
...BUT WE'RE GOING UP AGAIN!

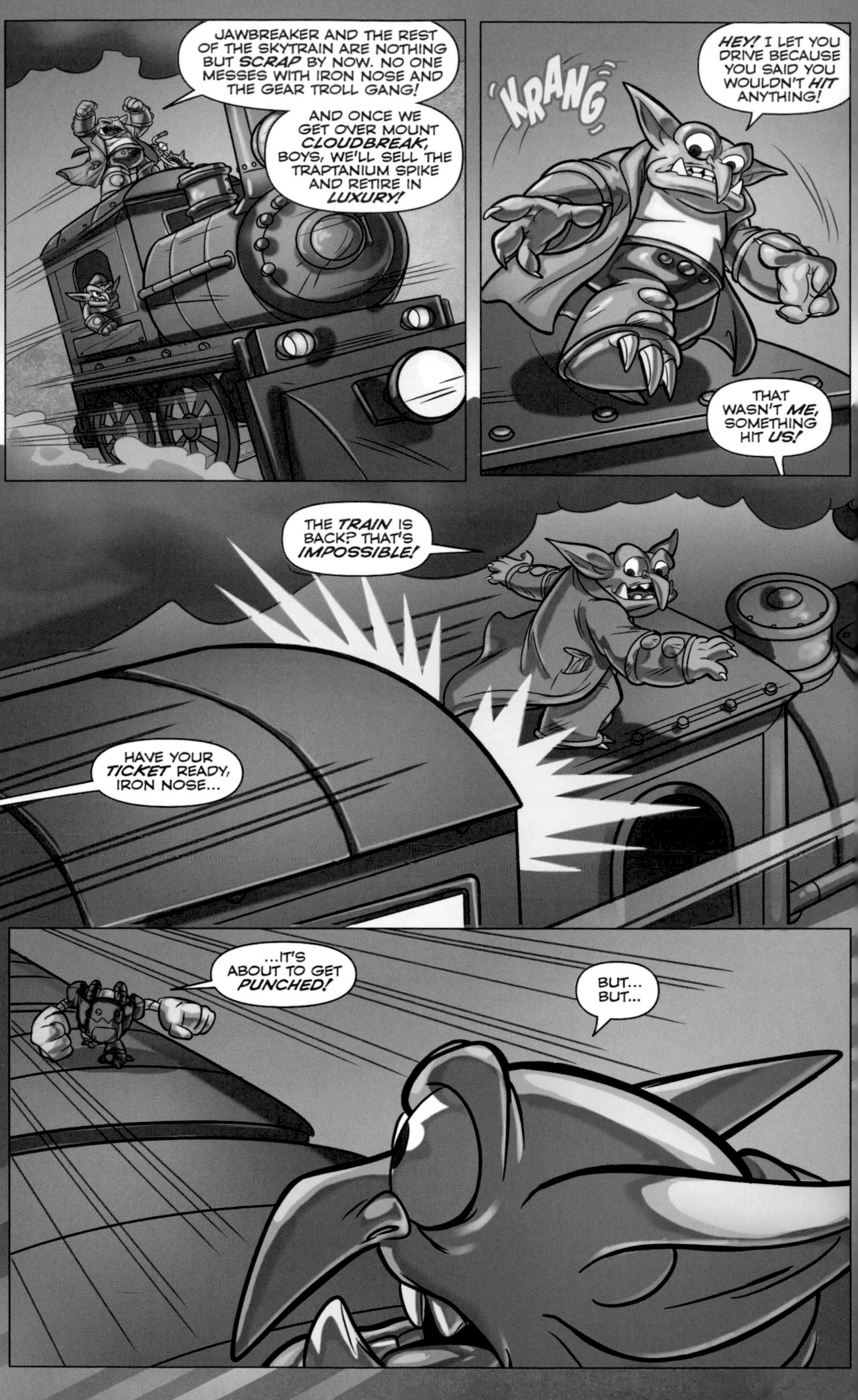
JAWBREAKER AND THE REST OF THE SKYTRAIN ARE NOTHING BUT SCRAP BY NOW. NO ONE MESSES WITH IRON NOSE AND THE GEAR TROLL GANG!
AND ONCE WE GET OVER MOUNT CLOUDBREAK, BOYS, WE'LL SELL THE TRAPTANIUM SPIKE AND RETIRE IN LUXURY!
KRANG
HEY! I LET YOU DRIVE BECAUSE YOU SAID YOU WOULDN'T HIT ANYTHING!
THAT WASN'T ME, SOMETHING HIT US!
THE TRAIN IS BACK? THAT'S IMPOSSIBLE!
HAVE YOUR TICKET READY, IRON NOSE...
...IT'S ABOUT TO GET PUNCHED!
BUT... BUT...

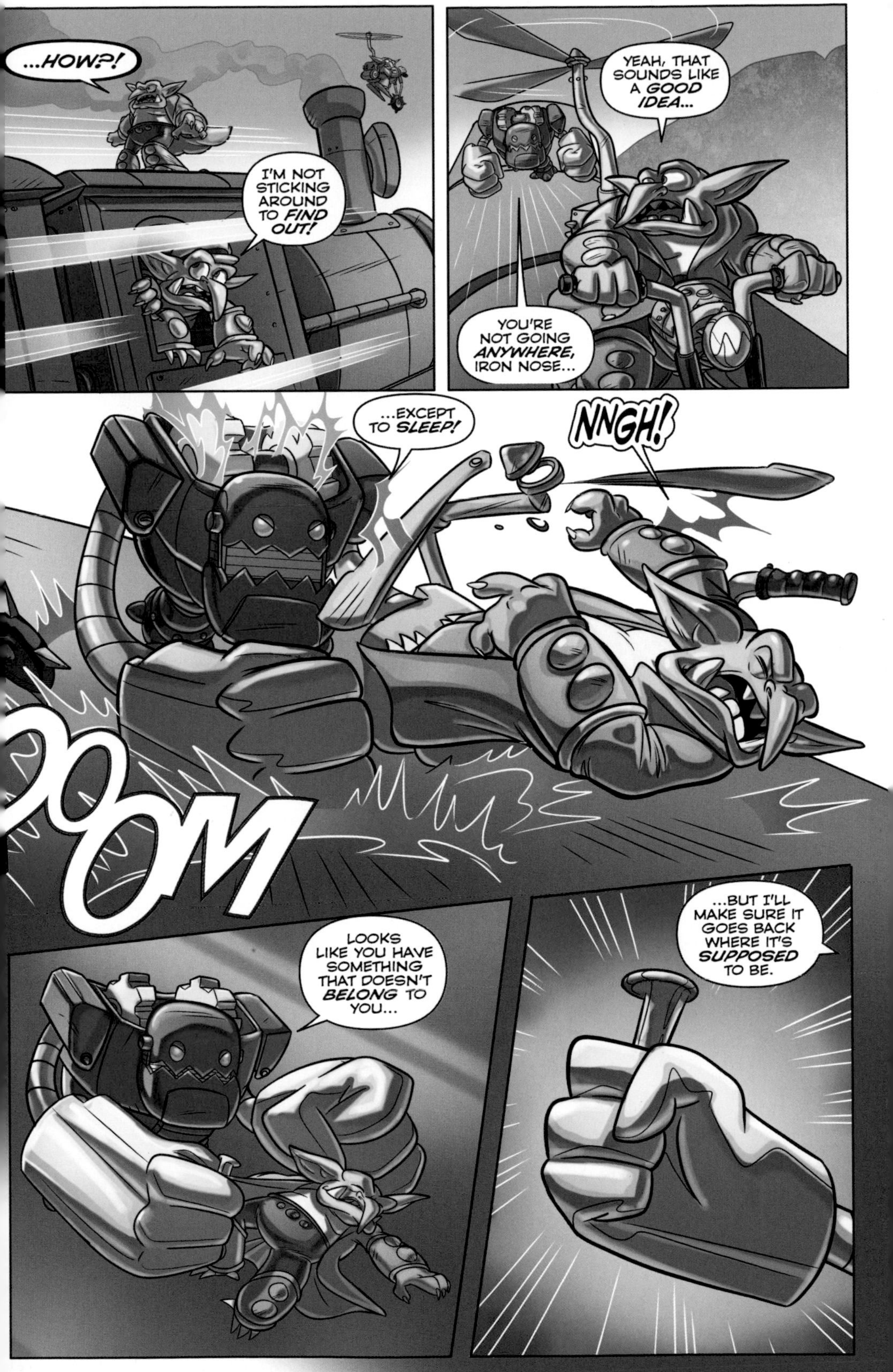
...HOW?!
I'M NOT STICKING AROUND TO FIND OUT!
YEAH, THAT SOUNDS LIKE A GOOD IDEA...
YOU'RE NOT GOING ANYWHERE, IRON NOSE...
...EXCEPT TO SLEEP!
NNGH!
OOOM
LOOKS LIKE YOU HAVE SOMETHING THAT DOESN'T BELONG TO YOU...
...BUT I'LL MAKE SURE IT GOES BACK WHERE IT'S SUPPOSED TO BE.

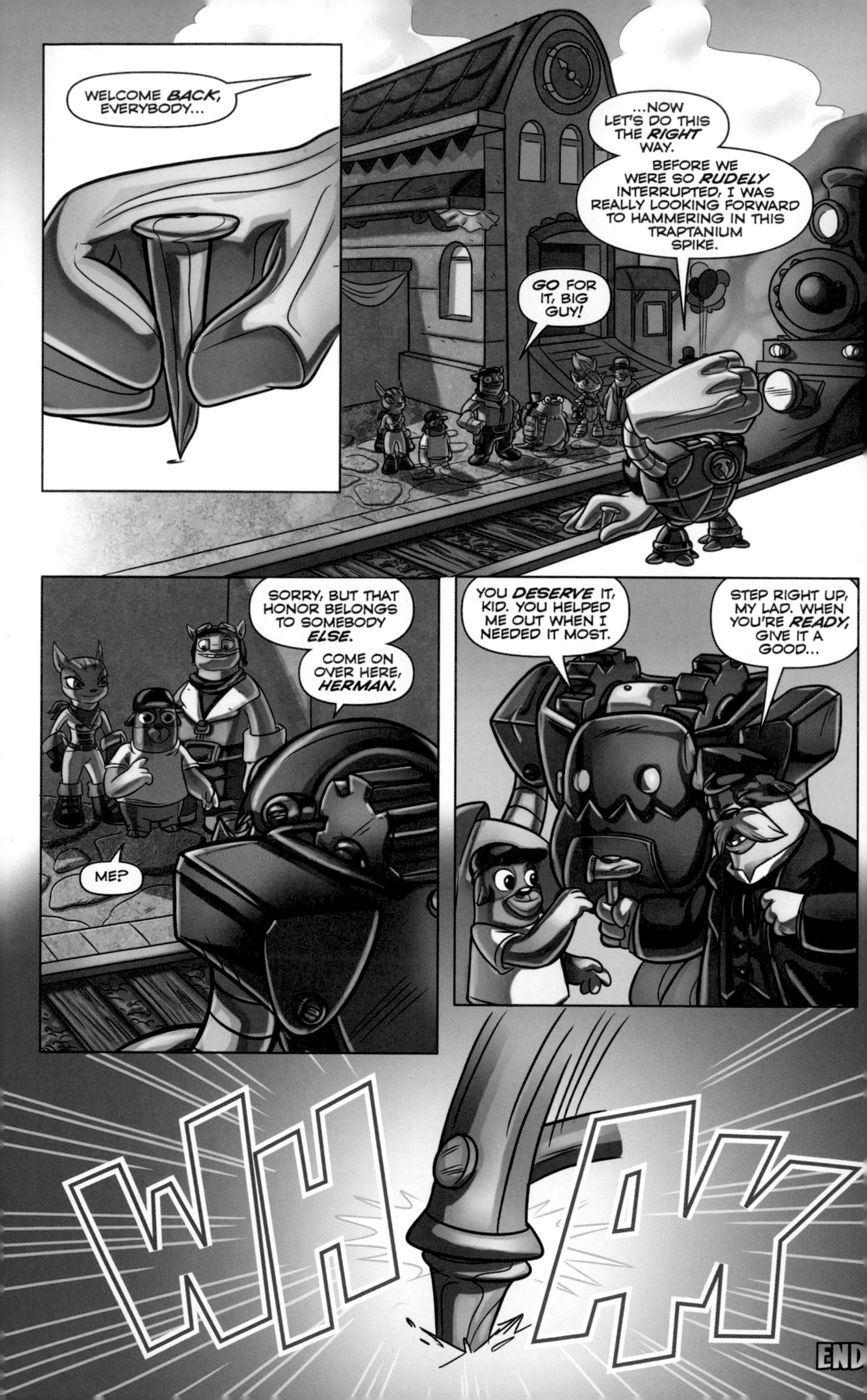

WELCOME BACK, EVERYBODY...
...NOW LET'S DO THIS THE RIGHT WAY.
BEFORE WE WERE SO RUDELY INTERRUPTED, I WAS REALLY LOOKING FORWARD TO HAMMERING IN THIS TRAPTANIUM SPIKE.
GO FOR IT, BIG GUY!
SORRY, BUT THAT HONOR BELONGS TO SOMEBODY ELSE.
COME ON OVER HERE, HERMAN.
ME?
YOU DESERVE IT, KID. YOU HELPED ME OUT WHEN I NEEDED IT MOST.
STEP RIGHT UP, MY LAD. WHEN YOU'RE READY, GIVE IT A GOOD...
WHAAK
END

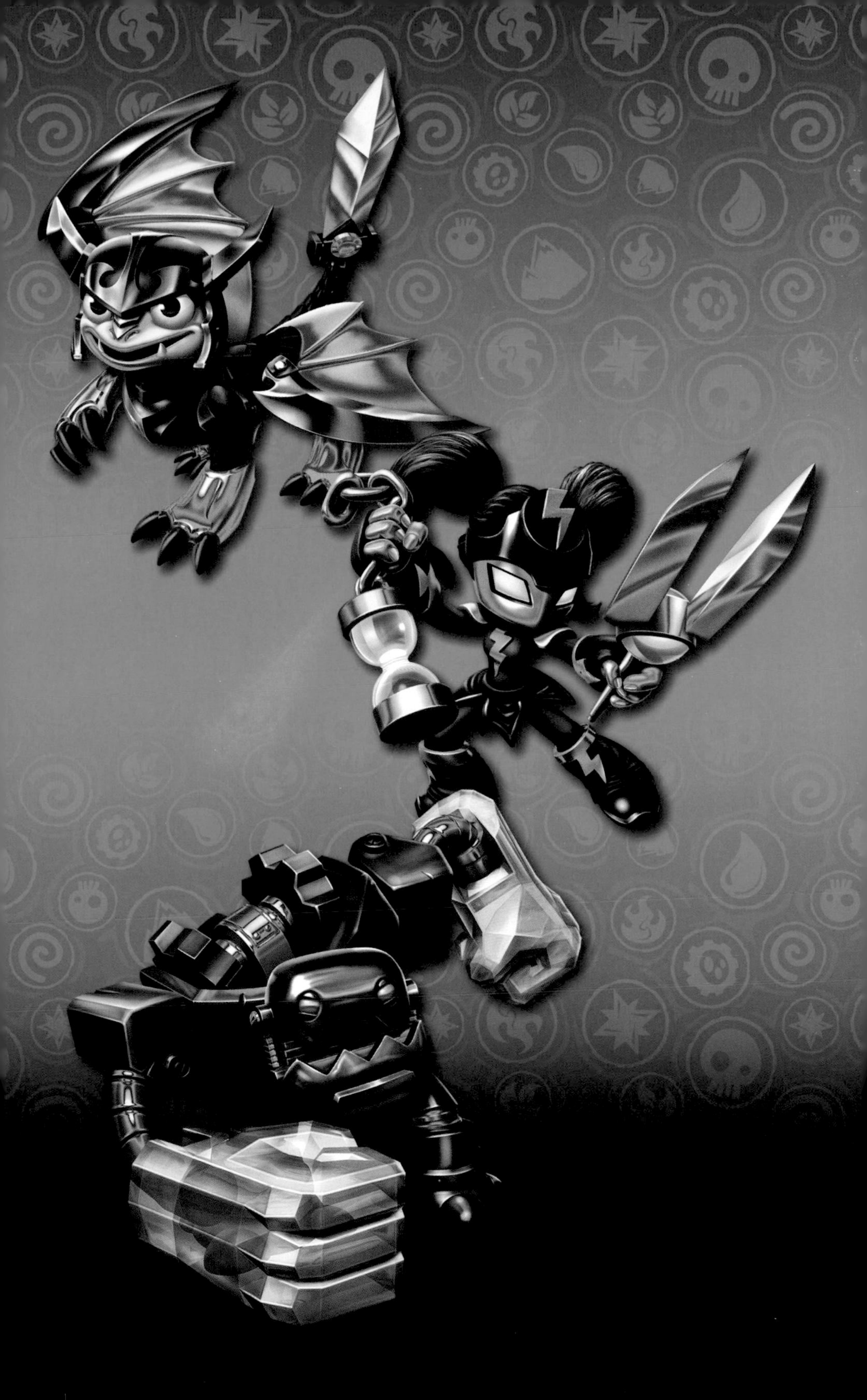

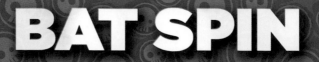

BAT SPIN

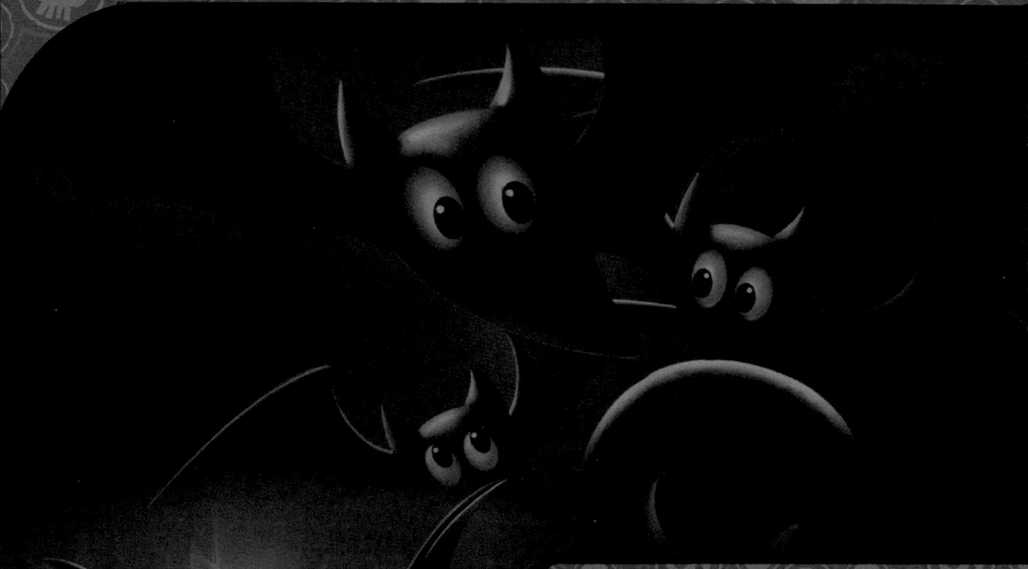

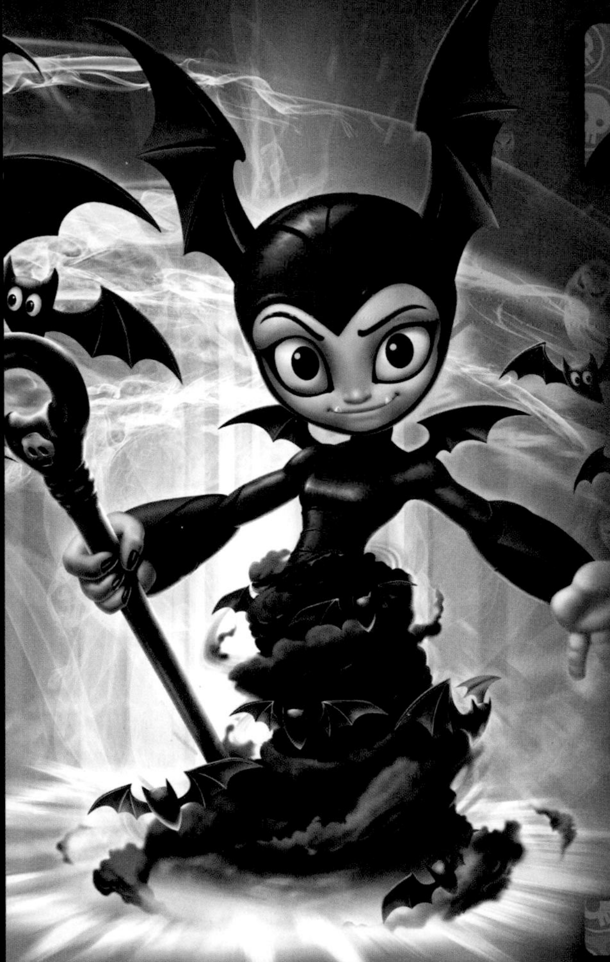

BIO

Bat Spin hailed from the underworld, where as a child she was separated from her people. After spending months searching for them, she eventually was welcomed by a colony of magical bats who raised her as one of their own. After many peaceful years living with the bats, the colony was invaded by an army of undead trolls, who were set on stealing their magic to build an ultimate sonar weapon. Bat Spin quickly took action and used powerful abilities that she had learned growing up with the bats and essentially becoming one of them. She heroically defeated the trolls and saved the colony. This caught the attention of Master Eon, who saw at once she would make a worthy Skylander.

BOUNCER

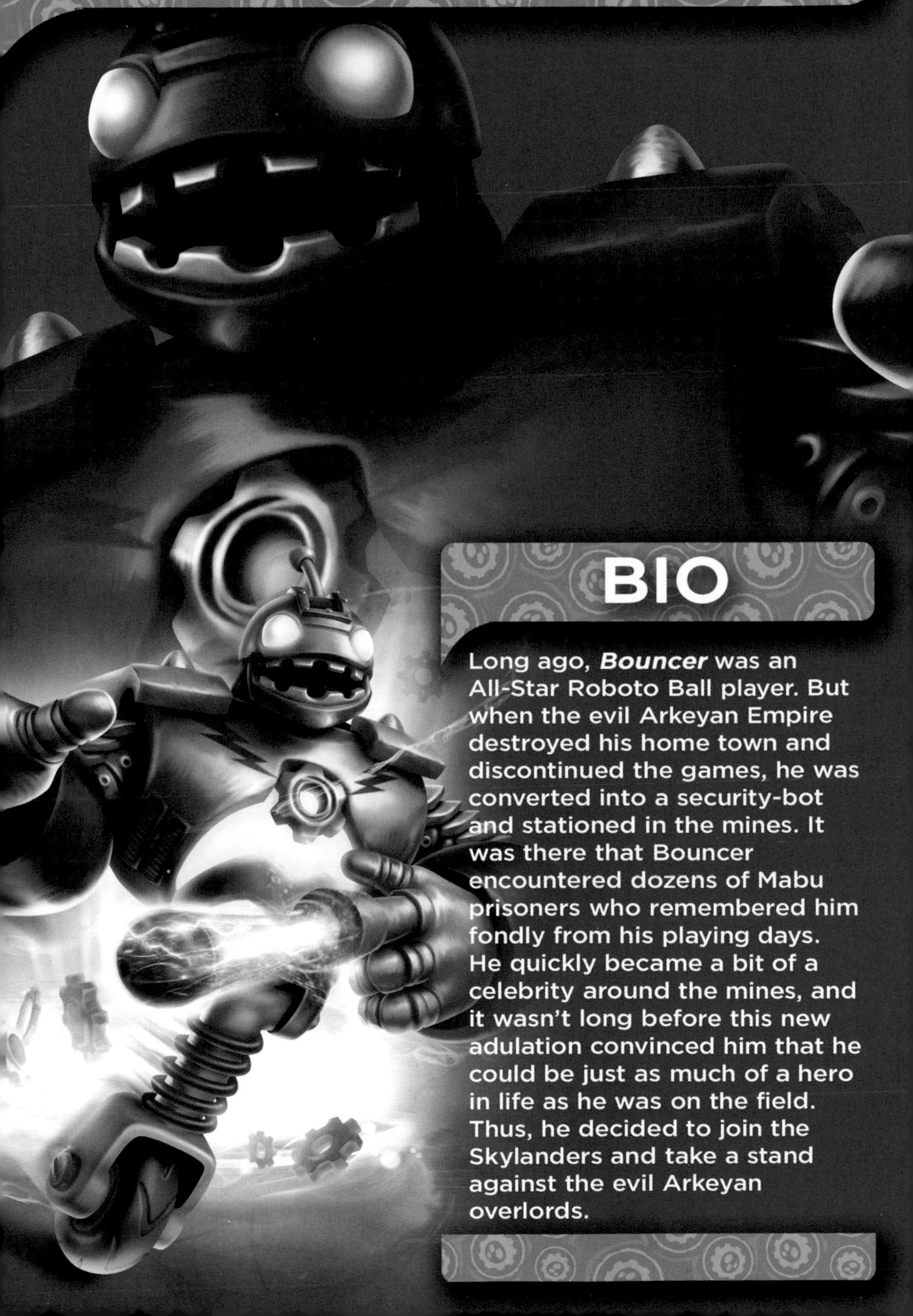

BIO

Long ago, ***Bouncer*** was an All-Star Roboto Ball player. But when the evil Arkeyan Empire destroyed his home town and discontinued the games, he was converted into a security-bot and stationed in the mines. It was there that Bouncer encountered dozens of Mabu prisoners who remembered him fondly from his playing days. He quickly became a bit of a celebrity around the mines, and it wasn't long before this new adulation convinced him that he could be just as much of a hero in life as he was on the field. Thus, he decided to join the Skylanders and take a stand against the evil Arkeyan overlords.

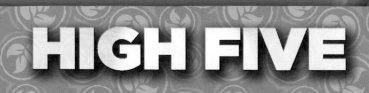

HIGH FIVE

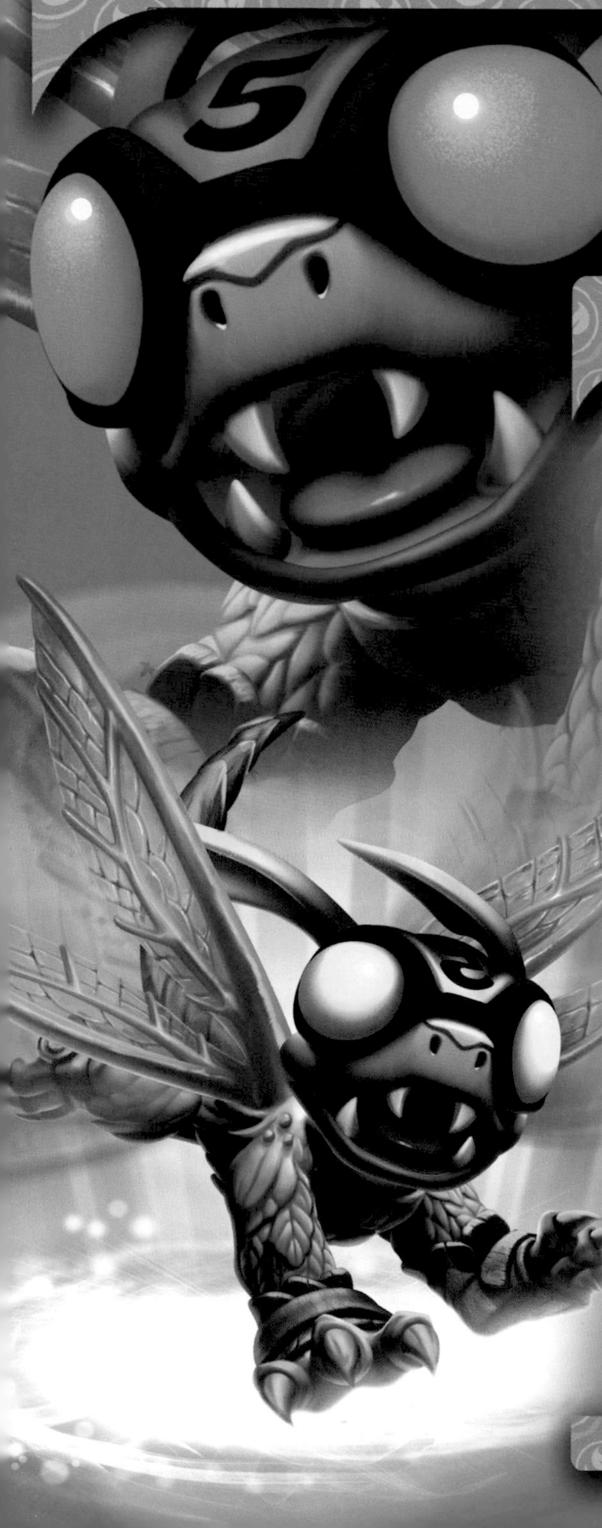

BIO

Growing up, ***High Five*** was one of the most skilled sky racers of all the dragonflies. But as the fifth son of the Royal High Flying Dragonflies, he was not allowed to enter any of the racing tournaments that took place each year because of his age. Instead he was forced to watch from the sidelines as his four older brothers competed for the coveted Trophy of Sparx, which legend has said holds magical properties. One year, during the biggest racing event of the season, High Five learned that the Troll Racing Team had stolen the valuable trophy and were going to use the race to cover their escape. He quickly took action, jumping into the race and using his amazing flying skills to weave and dodge his way to the front of the pack, where he caught up to the trolls and brought them down. For his actions, High Five was given the Trophy of Sparx. Even more importantly, he was made a Skylander, where he now helps protect Skylands from any evildoers!

NIGHT SHIFT

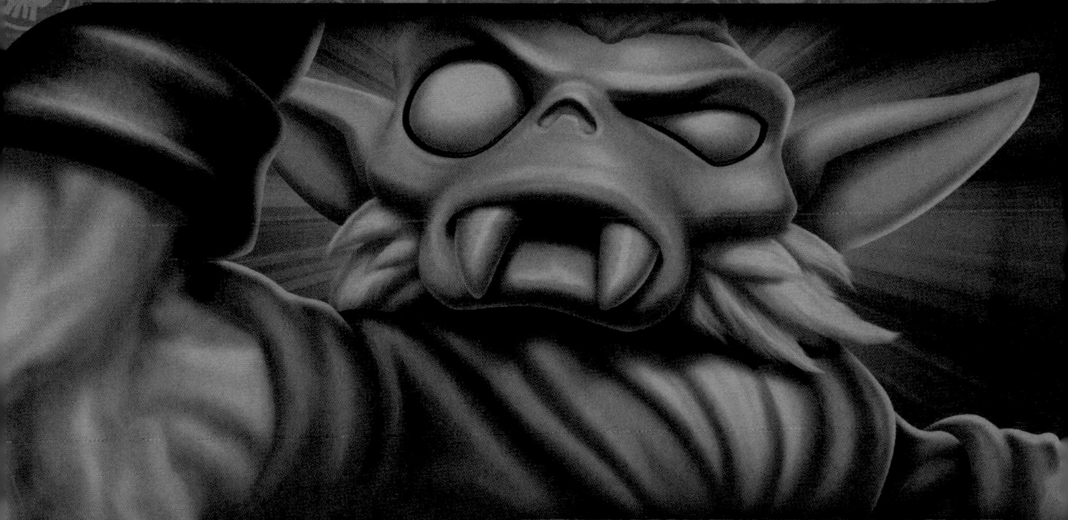

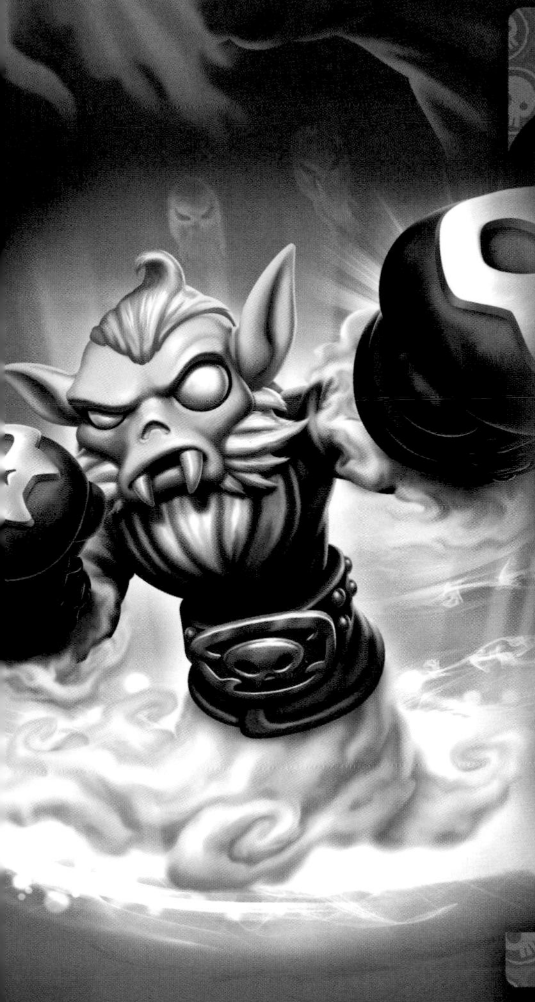

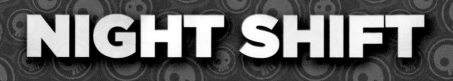

BIO

From high up in the gloomy Batcrypt Mountains, ***Night Shift*** was a full-fledged baron and heir to a great fortune. But one day he decided to leave it all behind to pursue his dream as a prizefighter. It wasn't long before Night Shift became the undefeated phantom-weight champion of Skylands, famous for his massive uppercut and for having once bitten an opponent in the ring. Unfortunately, a rule change made teleportation illegal and Night Shift was forced to give up his belt, officially ending his career as a boxer. Crestfallen over being disqualified from a sport he loved so dearly, his spirits picked up when he was sought out by Master Eon, who told him that his skill as a fighter could be put to great use as a member of the Skylanders.

BLADES

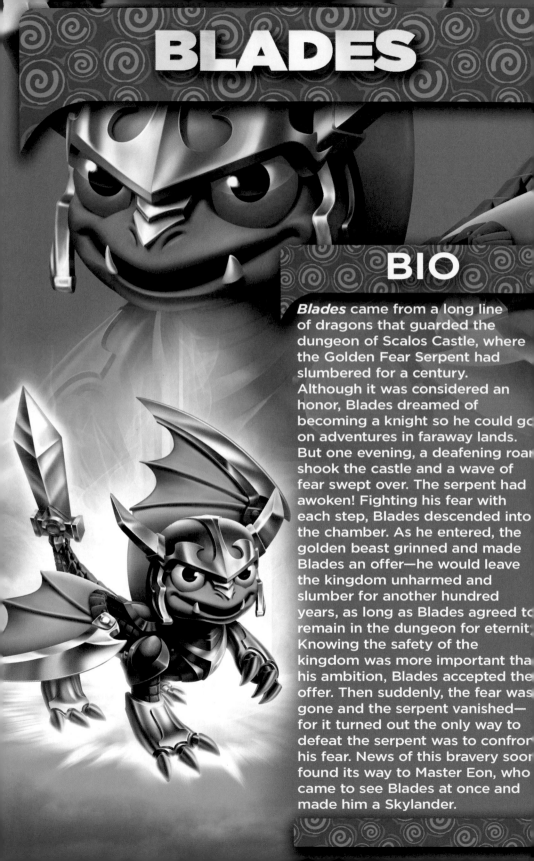

BIO

Blades came from a long line of dragons that guarded the dungeon of Scalos Castle, where the Golden Fear Serpent had slumbered for a century. Although it was considered an honor, Blades dreamed of becoming a knight so he could go on adventures in faraway lands. But one evening, a deafening roar shook the castle and a wave of fear swept over. The serpent had awoken! Fighting his fear with each step, Blades descended into the chamber. As he entered, the golden beast grinned and made Blades an offer—he would leave the kingdom unharmed and slumber for another hundred years, as long as Blades agreed to remain in the dungeon for eternity. Knowing the safety of the kingdom was more important than his ambition, Blades accepted the offer. Then suddenly, the fear was gone and the serpent vanished— for it turned out the only way to defeat the serpent was to confront his fear. News of this bravery soon found its way to Master Eon, who came to see Blades at once and made him a Skylander.

DÉJÀ VU

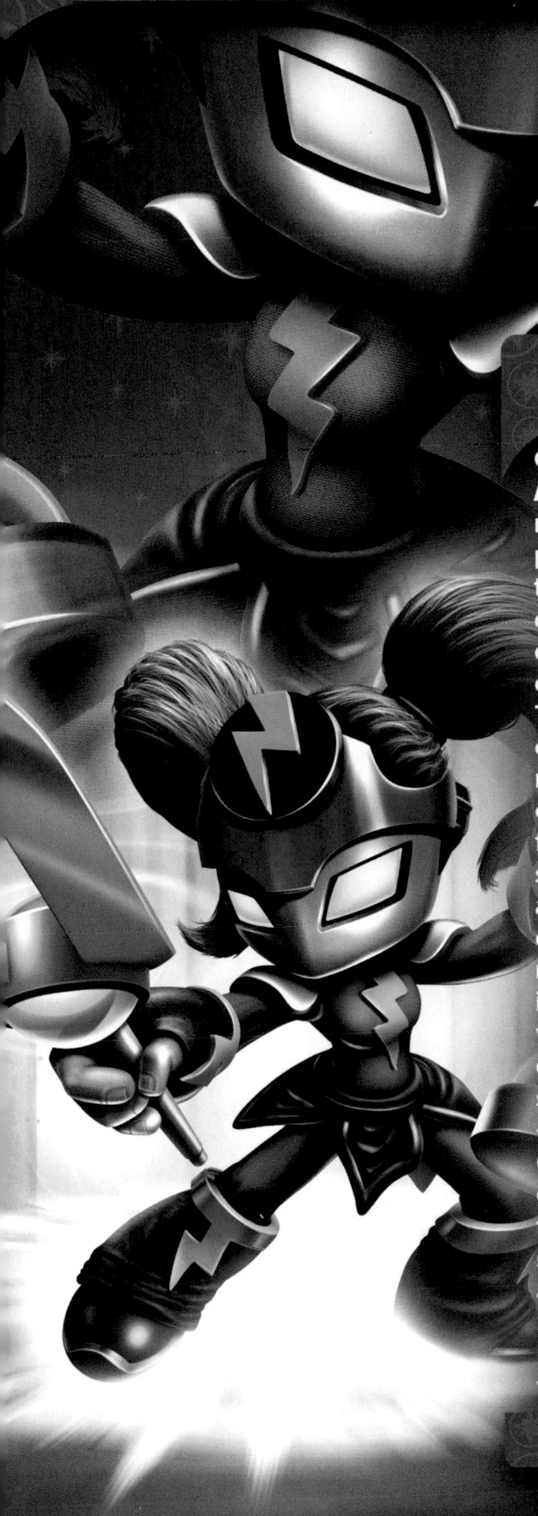

BIO

On a remote island in Skylands, *Déjà Vu* tirelessly worked on a machine that would make the perfect three-minute egg in half the time. After pouring over countless magic tomes, and even consulting the lost plans used to create the legendary Tower of Time, she finally completed construction of the huge machine. Unfortunately, a gang of evil giant sea slugs, searching for a way to acquire super speed, learned of her machine and set about to take it at all costs. Slow, but well armed, the massive slugs bore down on the island. But rather than allow her work be used for evil, Déjà Vu quickly jumped into action and set the clock's hands to thirteen —causing a time overload. Caught up in the blast, she was given an amazing power over time, which she then used to stop the evil slugs in their tracks and spin them home. Now as a Skylander, Déjà Vu uses her incredible powers to turn back the clock on evil!

TORCH

BIO

Torch's childhood was spent working with her grandfather as a dragon keeper, where she helped tend to a stable of dragons that protected her village. One year, an evil Snow Dragon unleashed a terrible blizzard that trapped her entire homeland inside a massive ice glacier! Torch was the only one to escape. Having always been fearless, she set out at once to rescue the villagers and her dragon from their chilly fate. Armed with her Firespout Flamethrower, she fought hard through the treacherous conditions and bravely defeated the Snow Dragon in an epic battle. After the village was free from its icy doom, Torch returned home to find her grandfather missing. The only token left behind was his lucky flaming horseshoe. Now as a member of the Skylanders, Torch wields her powerful flamethrower as well as her lucky horseshoe in hopes it will one day lead her to the grandfather she lost.

JAWBREAKER

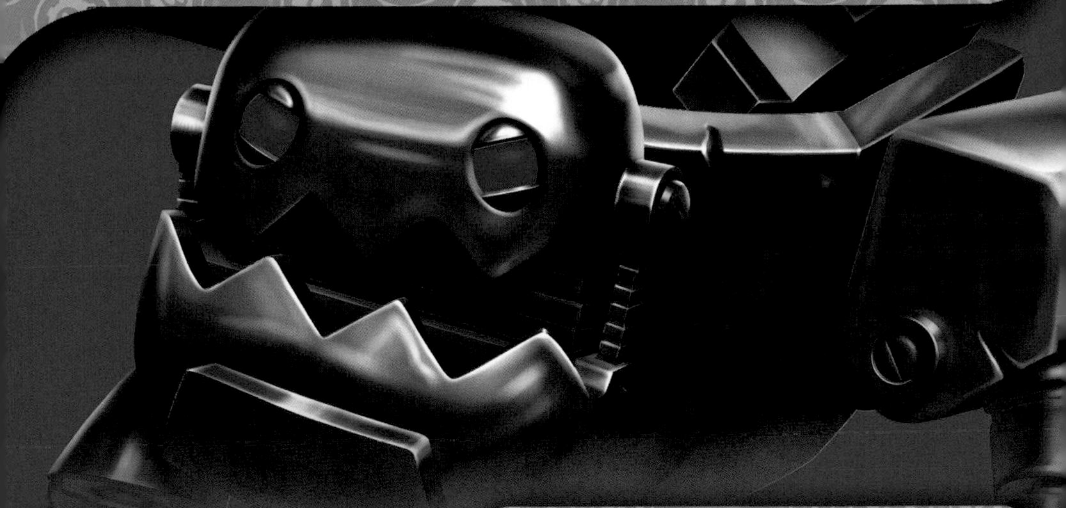

BIO

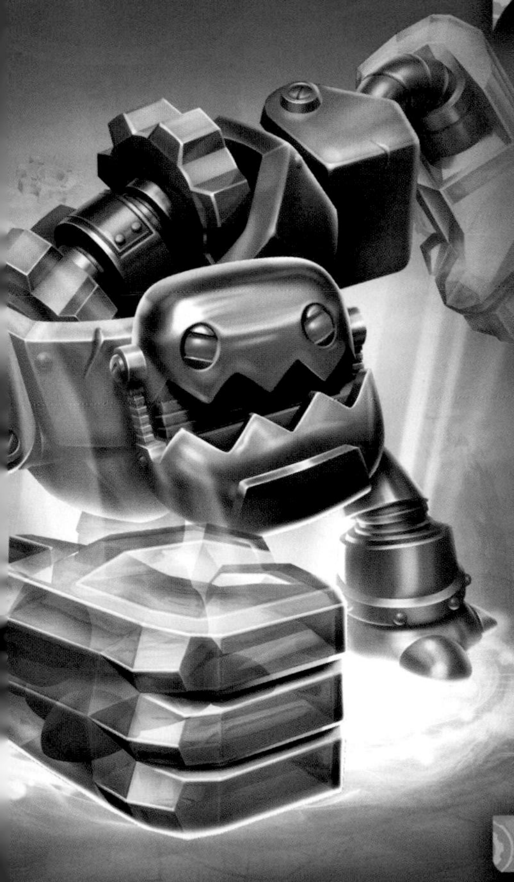

Jawbreaker hailed from a race of robots that operated and maintained a vast underground complex of enormous machines that powered the legendary Sky Train, which traveled between a thousand different islands daily. Like many of his fellow robots, Jawbreaker led an ordered existence—full of rules and regulations—which he followed happily. However, one day a huge army of Gear Trolls invaded the subterranean complex. Known for being major train enthusiasts, they were set on taking over the Sky Train for their own evil use. Jawbreaker quickly jumped into action and used his massive fists to beat the trolls into retreat. His quick action and ability to think for himself made him an individual. For this he was made part of the Trap Team, where he now uses his Traptanium-powered fists to deliver mighty blows to evil!

FROM THE WORLD OF SKYLANDERS TRAP TEAM™

SKYLANDERS

THE KAOS TRAP

THE GRAPHIC NOVEL ADVENTURES START HERE! SKYLANDERS™ THE KAOS TRAP

ISBN: 978-1-63140-141-1